SAVE THE
Last Dance

MANDI EIZENBAUM

Copyright © 2023 Mandi Eizenbaum
All rights reserved
First Edition

NEWMAN SPRINGS PUBLISHING
320 Broad Street
Red Bank, NJ 07701

First originally published by Newman Springs Publishing 2023

This book is a work of fiction. Any reference to historical events, real people, or real places are used fictitiously and are not to be construed as real. Other names, characters, places, locales, organizations, or events are products of the author's imagination, and any resemblance to actual events or places or persons, living or dead, is entirely coincidental. *Save the Last Dance* is a work of entertainment and should be read as nothing more.

ISBN 979-8-88763-966-6 (Paperback)
ISBN 979-8-88763-967-3 (Digital)

Printed in the United States of America

For the most loving, most dedicated, most giving mother in the world—mine.

"Our lives are fashioned by our choices. First, we make our choices. Then, our choices make us."
—Anne Frank

Sofia

Aware of her every movement, Sofia guardedly hid any sign of the headache that was relentlessly gripping her skull like a vise beneath her crown. She measured her steps with precision, as if she were still onstage, as the muscles in her back and legs cramped with every movement. She was relieved to be off the stage and out of the glaring lights. It seemed like everyone in the five boroughs and beyond had gathered there to see her that night, or at least, everyone who was an anyone. A flash of intense pride sparkled in her eyes and a soft exclamation of satisfaction caught between her painted red lips as she inwardly reveled in her own anticipated victory. She touched her temple gently and tossed her head toward the crowd of local fans and paparazzi that had gathered outside her dressing room. This was definitely her most shining moment.

It was Sofia's debut as principal dancer for the Tantsor Russian Ballet & Dance Academy. The school was mostly recognized by

Russian immigrants and artists, and Sofia knew her reputation was climbing among the renowned stars that preceded her there in Brighton Beach. She was lucky to have gotten a place in the troupe by way of her cousin Nathan's connections around the city, working her way up the ranks to soloist and now holding the envious position of principal dancer. Sofia was no stranger to the stage. She had undoubtedly become a quick rising attraction in theater world, a true prodigy of her art, and she was finally right where she had always pictured herself to be. At the age of twenty-five, Sofia had become one of the youngest soloists on the dance scene, and her years of effort and dedication were undoubtedly showing positive results for her. Her years of dreaming and planning were finally paying off. Tonight had been the premier of her lead role as Queen Nisia in *Le Roi Candaule*, and it was the moment she had been anticipating. If only her parents could have been there to see her.

She began her ballet studies in Ukraine, at the young age of seven, where she had been lucky to have trained in some of the best and well-founded schools in the country. Her parents had spared nothing to support Sofia's childhood dreams and caprices of becoming a prima ballerina. Like the time her father sold his most precious possession on the black market—a computer he had earned in a statewide competition from the Kryvyi Rih Institute of Economics and Technology—just so they could pay for her student fees at an eminent ballet academy in Lutsk. Her mother, a well-known and respected stage designer in Ukraine and the Soviet Union, with many connections within the theater community, had acquainted her with several choreographers and academy directors while shlepping her from one dance academy to another and sewing costumes for different troupes just to earn the extra money and privilege to do so. Sofia never thought twice about the cost to her parents in introducing her to the world of dance in all the biggest cities from Moscow to Kiev.

Even as a child, Sofia was praised for her early talents and grit, affirming her bright future on the dance stage. Her parents reminded her repeatedly to keep practicing and to be patient. "Draw not your bow till your arrow is fixed," her father used to say about her youthful impatience. Eventually, he told her, her time would come. Sofia never doubted she would make it to the top, but it was a definite struggle to maintain her composure. And while Sofia had had no say, and inevitably no control, over the choice to send her to live in New York, that one decision had definitely impacted her own future decisions and success.

Left to her own devices and leaving her secure life and her parents behind, Sofia had managed to adapt, climb, and practice her passion and her patience. Sofia's dreams had been uprooted, the bow and arrow quivering in her desperate hands, yet moving to New York to live with her uncle and aunt might have been an unforeseen blessing in disguise for her. Following in the pointe shoes of her Russian-born idols like Anna Pavlova and Irina Roizin, Sofia was given no other choice but to accept her move to New York, and in time, the move proved to be her greatest gift. She put years of hard work, sweat, and dedication into her one-and-only true love—the ballet. Now at the age of twenty-five and at the prime of her career, after seven long years of scraping her way into the limelight, she could finally reconcile with the choices her family had made for her. She had made it on her own merit. She was Queen Nisia in her first solo performance, after all. It had been a long and arduous climb, but Sofia never had any doubt she'd reach this summit. The reporters that showed up at the premier that night from *New York Newsday* and

New York Post were just the validation she needed that all her decisions, patience, and grit were finally paying off.

The aftershow celebration lasted way into the night. Aside from the throngs of neighbors from her Brighton Beach community, there were dancers and directors from rival academies, the usual paparazzi that followed red-carpet events of the theater world, and even some local celebrities that dotted the mob of artistic enthusiasts that had gathered at the trendy restaurant. Before the reviews were circulated in the entertainment newspapers, Sofia and the rest of the dance troupe were drunk with success, revelry, and vodka. Like a child waiting to hear her name announced as the winner of a school spelling bee, Sofia had been picturing this moment all her life. She had basked in the electric roar of the audience that night and had swelled with pride as the final lights lowered on the corps of dancers taking their final bows on the stage. Sofia Brenner felt more special and adored than ever before. Her heartbeat raced as the flashing cameras blinded her with dozens of electric white sparks. Squinting her eyes, she continued to ignore the pounding in her head and in her chest.

Becca Kaplan had watched the entire performance from the right side of the stage. It would have been unlucky to watch from the left. She swayed with every beat of the music, she gracefully lifted her arms every time Sofia swooshed across the stage, she elevated "en pointe" at just the precise moments. Becca had been preparing, just in case. She was only Sofia's understudy, biding her time in the darkened wings, but she reminded herself that she was, after all, the next in line after the newest soloist.

"Do you really think I…uh, I mean we…were good?" Sofia blushed and put on her best show of humility as the other dancers and theatergoers congratulated her.

"You were simply perfection. The show was spectacular." The compliments poured over Sofia as she sipped vodka after vodka. Becca stood statuesque and silent, supportive by her side. "Couldn't you just feel the love from the audience?" The permanent grin on Sofia's face was beginning to cramp, and she hugged her arms around her slim, strong torso. The word *proud* was an understatement for her raging emotions.

Nathan walked by, and Sofia felt Becca reflexively reach out and grab her arm. Becca's knees buckled, and her whole body stiffened as she filled her lungs with air and held her breath, her eyes glued to the scar just above Nathan's left eyebrow.

A wild smile crossed Nathan's face, crinkling his blue eyes and dimpling his cherry-tainted cheeks. "Great show tonight, Sofia. And the costumes were perfect, no? And you thought they would be too tacky? I told you that you could trust my judgment." The studio had entrusted Sofia with the task of commissioning the costumes, but it was Nathan who had procured the famously colorful and elaborate outfits from a "friend" of his at the Brighton Ballet Theater for her. Nathan winked a sparkling eye at his favorite cousin.

"Yes, everything was just perfect. Thank you, Nathan." Her words slurred with emotion and alcohol. Backing away from her older cousin, Sofia asked after her aunt and uncle.

"I took the folks home right after the show. They enjoy the ballet and watching you dance, but they said they're too old to hang out and go to parties with *molodi*, young people." Playfully, Nathan winked again, this time focusing his attention on Becca. Before walking away, he reached out to stroke Becca's cheek and sang out, "So I'll see you a little later? No?" It was really more a confirmation than a question. Becca turned her modest gaze downward, bobbed her head, and shuffled sheepishly from one foot to the other.

"Isn't this place great!" Sofia blurted, redirecting their attention back to the party. She was drowning in waves of triumph, victory, and self-importance. One by one, guests and strangers alike fought their way through the crowd to offer congratulatory words to Sofia and find themselves photographed with her for the tabloids that would surely be publicized the next day. Nathan faded into the crowd, and Sofia craned her neck to take in the jovial celebration.

As her eyes swept the room, contemplating the mob of adoring friends and neighbors that had followed them to the big city after-party, a bulky woman bumped into her from behind. It was Mrs. Mayerchik, a neighbor from their Brighton Beach condo block. Although the evening was balmy and warm, she wore a long wool coat with a fur collar and a huge animal-print hat that was twice the size of her head. "Oy, vey. There you are, dear. I almost gave up on finding you in here with this crowd. The show was fantastic, no? You should only have more *nachas* and good things coming from this!" Smothered in a syrupy Russian-laced accent, her praise was truly genuine, and her crimson-colored lips promised sincere praise. Her husband, a short man with a pinched face and gold-rimmed spectacles on his bulging nose, appeared at her side and nodded his agreement. He, too, was draped in a full-length black overcoat and an old-fashioned fedora hat.

"Hello, Sofia. I'm so happy for you tonight, and I am sure your parents would be proud of you also." Mr. Mayerchik had studied economics at the university in Kiev with Sofia's father and loved to bring up the past association every chance he got. The old couple squinted toward the entrance, offered loving bear hugs to Sofia, and said their goodbyes.

Sofia rolled her eyes at Becca and said, "God bless those two. A pair of *yentas*, but they have good hearts." Grabbing her by the hand, Sofia led Becca toward a group of reporters that had gathered by the bar. "Hello," she called out, her chin tilted upward toward the low ceiling. Without missing a beat, Sofia glided toward the bar and slurred, "Thank you for coming tonight. I am Sofia Brenner. Prima ballerina of the Tantsor Russian Ballet & Dance Academy. I hope you are all enjoying the party." She waved her hand like she was the queen of England greeting her loyal supporters.

Sofia was now weighing the consequences of the previous night's frivolity. Why did she have to drink so much? She could barely recall who she spoke with, what she was wearing, or how she managed to get home and into bed. Her head lay immobile on her pillow like a cement boulder sinking to the bottom of the Rockaway Inlet. Her eyes burned like fire when she tried to open them, and only then did she make out the black dress and gold stiletto heels she had thrown on the floor of her bedroom before falling into bed.

Scanning the room through heavy-lidded eyes, her sight landed on the red velvet box that sat open and empty on her bedside table. She grabbed at her earlobes and felt the diamond studs that Ben had given her yesterday morning. They were meant to be a peace offering for not joining her for the premier or for the party afterward. "These are like stars in the sky that will watch you and the performance for me," he had said. Clumsily removing them from her ears, she replaced the earrings in the velvet box. She was grateful for his romantic gesture; she knew he would have found a way to cancel his business meeting and attend the show if he could. She shoved the box into the drawer of her bedside table and tingled with cozy warmth.

Sofia's mind, still foggy and sloshing with vodka and excitement, began spinning with vague images of the night—the one (and only!) misstep in Act III and the huff she could hear from Boris in the wings, the restaurant's host shamelessly patting her behind as she walked into the party, the reporters all pressing to speak with her, the sea of strobing camera flashes that stalked her throughout the night. She savored the recollected praise for her performance and snapped to awakened attention to slowly roll out of bed.

The clock on her bedside table told her she probably missed breakfast. Her teeth felt furry, and her tongue was as dry as the sand at Coney Island. She had to pee, but the startling scraping of wood against linoleum steered her toward the kitchen instead of the bathroom. As she opened her bedroom door, she could smell the strong aromas of raw onions and chicken schmaltz that Tyotya Anika must have begun preparing for Shabbos dinner. Taking in a deep whiff of the familiar smells, Sofia called out, "Dyadya…Tyotya. Is that you two I hear in the kitchen?"

It was Friday, the busiest day for her uncle at his butcher shop. He never missed a day of work in the past twenty-seven years. It had taken him a grueling eight years in America, living in poverty and working to save enough money to buy the only kosher butcher shop in the neighborhood. The shop was Dyadya Sol's pride and joy—the one thing that anchored him to the American dream and his new home. By this time of day, especially on a Friday, they would normally both be at the market already. So what were they doing at home now?

Stumbling into the kitchen, Sofia saw her uncle and aunt frantically scrambling around like ants at a picnic, both half dressed in their pajamas, shoes, and coats. Anika was wildly opening and closing cabinet doors, hunting for something she couldn't find, coming away with nothing in her shaking hands but continuing nonetheless with her frantic search. Sol was holding open a black canvas overnight bag with a gold Prada plate shining on one side. He was at the kitchen table, stuffing the bag with men's clothing—a pair of jeans, red boxer shorts, a rolled ball of sweat socks, and a faded Pink Floyd T-shirt.

"Is everything okay? Don't you guys have to be at the shop? What's going on?" Sofia stifled a tired yawn. She brushed her hand through her red hair, shoving loose strands behind her ear. The crush of her skull begged for a glass of cold water and a couple of aspirins.

Her dazed aunt ignored her and continued with her frenzied search of the cabinets, but her frantic uncle looked up from his packing. His eyes were moist and distant, and he coughed into the air as if he needed to shake loose his words that were trapped in the back of his throat. "Hurry up and get dressed, Sofia. It's Nathan. He's had an accident."

Maya

I hear them swarming. I approach the structure where they nest in the dark eaves until the first workers show up, and my body recoils with disgust, while alarms flare like bombs bursting inside my head. I try to reconcile that they've lived here longer than we have, but I will never get used to their hovering, encroaching, threatening presence. I remember the first time I was tackled by one of these flying foxes. My mother had left early for work at the dairy shed that day and had forgotten to take her water canteen with her. I offered to bring it to her on my way to school, but nobody had warned me about these nocturnal creatures that remain active in the early morning hours. Just as I was sauntering by an open window of the tailor's shed, one flew out at me, pouncing on my skull and clawing at my scalp. I forgot about my mother at the dairy; I forgot about getting to school. I dropped the canteen and my schoolbooks in a muddy puddle and started screaming at the top of my heaving lungs. Arms flailing and feet tumbling over the cracked cement path, I ran all the way back to our cottage and jumped into the shower. In the cold dribble, I washed my hair at least twelve times. I scrubbed my scalp raw and vowed never to walk by the tailor's shed ever again.

Now walking down that same cracked cement path past the animated shed for the millionth time, I touch one hand to my swollen belly and the other to the bun of hair gathered at the nape of my neck, reassuring myself that all is safe and secure. The sun is barely breaking over the horizon, and the air is still saturated with wet dew. I picture those nocturnal creatures hanging upside down and hunkering to strike out of the dark. Suddenly, I feel the baby give me a little kick, as if it senses my unease. I rub at the stab with soothing circles and whisper words of comfort into the humid air. Swearing out loud, I shiver and explode with annoyance, "Those damned bats! Why can't anyone do something about them!"

Kibbutz Gan Notzah has been my home for almost three decades. It is surrounded by lush green mountains to the north (snowcapped in the winters!), the Kineret (or the Sea of Galilee) to the west, and the border of a militarized fence to the south. The Jezreel Valley, with all its beauty, bounty, and bewilderment, is a true source of pride and purpose for the state of Israel. Our *kibbutz*, or communal settlement, is rich with fertile soil—perfect for our abundant fields of almond trees and sunflowers—and just a small piece of Israel's contemporary history. The kibbutz movement comprises less than 2 percent of the country's population, but it is responsible for approximately 40 percent of the nation's agricultural production. At the same time, it is a huge chunk of the history that tells of the survival of many immigrants, in particular, that of my Russian descendants. I was born and raised here, brought up to revere our way of life on the kibbutz; despite its limitations and modern setbacks, we are encouraged by our parents and our teachers to take pride in our country, to work its land, and pass on our people's rich culture. I do my best. I really try.

I inhale a deep breath and cover my head with both hands as I speed past the tailor's shed. On my routine stop to catch my mother at the dairy shed before I have to show up for work in the kitchen, it is still early enough to know that the little pests are very likely still hanging in the shadows.

Admiring the rising sun as it pushes its way up over the valley and trying to overlook the hidden threat of the bats, I am not watching where I am going, and suddenly, I am startled out of my paranoid craze. Danny puts out his large dirt-stained hands and grabs me by the shoulders.

"Fancy meeting you out here. Is everything okay?" When I left our cottage just moments ago, he was just getting out of the shower.

"Everything's fine. I'm visiting Imma, and then I'm on my way to work. How'd you get out of the house so quickly?"

"I guess I'm just excited today. We're getting a new truck that will make our work twice as easy and fast. Those almonds don't stand a chance against this new contraption your dad finagled for us from the cheap bastards on the board of directors!" Danny lets out a loud snort, and his caramel-colored eyes sparkle in the dawn's light. His broad chest pumps full with pride.

They say opposites attract, and it must be true. My father, Noam Grinskind, is definitely my mother's opposite. Abba is an introverted intellectual, a graduate of the Kryvyi Rih State University of Economics and Technology in Ukraine. My father is gentle and kind like my mother, but he is less demonstrative of his softer side than his wife. Israelis are often referred to as *sabras*—the thorny fruit from the cactus—and he is the quintessential *sabra*; he can seem prickly and indifferent on the outside, but those who know him see his softer, sweeter inside. Even though he was born in Ukraine like Imma and had to leave, giving up his prestigious engineering job and ancestral homeland, he came and settled on Kibbutz Gan Notzah back in 1982. Proudly, stoically, my father works on the board of directors as treasurer of the kibbutz. So well-liked and capable is my father that he continues to be appointed to the position year after year since joining the collective. Abba never hesitates to recall his days as a youth in Ukraine, especially those years studying in the university and being swept up by a very popular socialist youth movement. It is from this group of young, pioneering zealots that he learned of the dream of a self-sufficient, independent, and free Jewish state. He never thought he would leave his family in Ukraine, and now he would never leave the kibbutz.

"That's right. I almost forgot. Well, good luck with that thing. And, oh—don't forget I'll be going to Haifa later today. I have class at two o'clock."

"I can't believe you are still going to dance classes in your condition. I hope you'll be back for dinner, no?"

"I'm fine, Danny. The doctor said—"

"The doctor said, the doctor said… I know what he said, but what about what your husband says?"

"Are we really going there again? I'm fine!" I feel the familiar frustration rise with the inflection of my words and the heat in my freckled cheeks. Kicking at a loose stone with the toe of my boot, I pose my final offer. "I'll meet you in the dining hall for dinner."

Before I can turn and carry on toward the dining hall, Danny softens and reaches out to cradle my belly in his hands. "Just take care of my little one in there. Don't overdo yourself, and call me when you're on your way back home." He leans over and covers the front of my snug apron with tiny wet kisses. Feeling a bit woozy, I pull away and force my chapped lips into a smile.

Danny's tall, bulky silhouette fades as I watch him walk toward the almond fields. I stand for a moment longer listening to the megabats' claws scraping along the wooden beams inside the tailor's shed to my left. I pray I make it through my four-hour breakfast shift in the communal kitchen.

Two months until my due date, and my body continues to beg for the ballet. The soothing sounds of the musical scores, the graceful motions of the dance—all I can think about is going to the studio and letting myself go. If my unborn baby's constant thrusting and kicking is any indication, I'll be giving birth to a dancer just like me. *Wouldn't that just be a kick in Danny's pants!* The thought of having two dancers in the family would certainly drive the man to insanity. I chuckle spitefully under my breath.

I peel about three hundred potatoes and prepare scrambled eggs for seven hundred hungry kibbutzniks before the opening of the dining hall at six o'clock sharp. Most people living on the kibbutz are at their respective jobs by seven each morning—our days communally beginning at sunrise and ending by dinnertime. It is my job to see that they are all fed and fueled for the hours of intense labor that define our existence. Kibbutz Gan Notzah has two major industries that support our collective revenue: sunflowers (for their seeds) and almonds. We are playfully regarded as "The Nut Farm." We are surrounded by sweet smells and colorful fields as these two industries continue to give us something to wake up to and sustain our meager reserves. We have nowhere near the wealth of some of our neighboring kibbutzim, but we are content and safe within our walls.

Slowly, the residents begin to saunter into the dining hall and sleepily await their breakfast. *Three more hours, but who's counting*, I think to myself.

Rivke, the head cook, waddles over to me and shakes her raised fist. "You are daydreaming again, Maya. Don't you know how dangerous it is to have your *kepee* always in the clouds?" Her heavy Russian accent and glistening sapphire eyes stab at me and burst the bubble that floats around my head. She's right, I know. I listen to the popping heat from the deep fryer behind me.

"Sorry, Rivke."

"No time for 'sorry' now. Get to work on those pots in the sink…please." She's feisty, opinionated, and impatient, but she's caring, wise, and helpful. I lower my stare and look back up at her through thick, blinking eyelashes. Her smooth, pale complexion and petite frame suggest she must have been quite beautiful in her youth, and I wonder why she doesn't have a husband and children of her own. She tugs at the edge of the bandana covering her reddish curls and turns her back. The sink full of the morning's pots and pans calls to me.

At eleven o'clock and not a minute too soon, I untie my stained apron and throw it in the hamper by the kitchen door. I have exactly three hours until my ballet class begins—just enough time to get to Haifa and grab a fruit smoothie with Irena. Danny doesn't like her—mostly because of his acute jealousy over my time spent with her and our shared love of ballet, both of which exclude him from a very significant part of my life. Even though I've known Danny since we shared a crib in daycare, even though we went off to the same army unit for our basic training, and even though we are now married and in the throes of starting our own family, Danny has unwilfully come to accept that my first priority will always be Irena and the ballet.

Imma brought me to Haifa for my first dance audition. She had been told about a new Russian academy that had just opened there, and she swore I had the talent to make a big star of myself on the stage. "Just look at your long body, your graceful poise, your spirit and energy."

Just as Imma had sensed early on, I fell in love with ballet from the minute she walked me into the academy for the first time. That was nearly eight years ago. Before army service, before marriage, before babies and motherhood. My life was all about the beauty and grace of the dance, the harmony of the musical scores, the intensity of the dancers… I inhaled it all then, and it remains the air I breathe today.

Imma paid for my lessons from her well-guarded, hidden savings. She had accumulated a small amount of savings by selling the jewelry she was able to sneak out of Russia before immigrating and moving onto the kibbutz. She would say that a woman always needed to be prepared with a means to support herself. Her exact words were, "a woman needs a *knipele* of her own…a Plan B for security and freedom." Even though I never understood exactly what she meant by that (didn't the kibbutz take care of us all?), I appreciated her foresight, generosity, and courage to be self-reliant.

And from my very first ballet lesson, it was Irena who befriended me at the academy and offered me her friendship and guidance. Irena was a real-life, heart-and-soul ballerina, and she gave color to my vague little world. Between my mother and Irena, I was given a chance at a whole new purpose, one for which I will forever owe them each my profoundest appreciation.

 I arrive in front of the Russian Ballet Conservatory of Haifa just in time to see Irena stepping out in her black leotard and stockings. She is wearing an oversized sweatshirt with "I♡NY" printed on the front. On her feet, she wears a pair of clumpy black military boots. Gan Notzah's beat-up delivery truck screeches to a halt in front of the academy, and I jump out of the passenger seat before it comes to a full stop. Turning to Itzik in the driver's seat, I thank him for the lift and remind him that I will be taking the four o'clock bus back to the kibbutz. Irena steps out into the midday sun and opens her arms, ready to embrace me. "There you are, my friend. I thought you'd never get here!"

Sofia

Pushing herself through a trudging mass of physical agony—sore quad muscles, cramping toes, and a splitting headache—Sofia accompanied her aunt and uncle to the hospital. They found their way to Nathan's room where he was sitting up in bed and whispering something to a nurse in hot-pink scrubs. A large white patch of gauze was taped across Nathan's narrow nose, and his bloodshot eyes rested half open on inflated purple balloons. His right hand was wrapped in a mountain of cotton, and his exposed torso was bound in a solid plaster cast. Nathan jerked to attention as we charged into the room.

"*Oy, mame-mina*! Look at you, my dear, sweet Nathan. How are you? What happened? What are they giving you?" Aunt Anika ranted through wet tears and guttural pants. She rushed over to Nathan's side, nearly knocking the nurse to the ground. She touched his cheek with delicate fingers, and then prodded and stroked every inch of his body with her other hand, assuring herself that he was all in one piece. Nathan winced when she brushed her hand along his ribcage. He blushed with embarrassment, but he didn't dare push his mother away as she showered him with more wet kisses on his dimpled cheeks.

Uncle Sol smirked at the nurse who had been awkwardly pushed out of the way. He shoved his bent body between his wife and the bed, interrupting his wife's bluster. "Are you okay, boychik? What can we do for you, my son?"

Sofia waited her turn to address her cousin and simply said, "You look like shit, and how'd you manage to get a private room, you rascal?"

Frowning and ignoring Sofia's off-the-cuff remarks, Nathan said, "I'm okay, guys. Just a bit banged up. I guess I was lucky. The car, on the other hand, has seen better days." Nathan tried to laugh at his own joke, but he quickly clasped his side and swallowed a desperate gulp of air. After ten more minutes of *kibitzing* with his family, recounting the details of the crash the night before and smiling through his obvious discomfort, Nathan was finally able to reassure his parents that he would be back on his feet in no time. He tried to wiggle the fingers of his bandaged hand and cringed. Smiling coquettishly at the nurse who had been silently keeping herself busy typing notes into her iPad, Nathan said, "Arlene, would you mind showing my parents to the vending machines? I'm sure they could use a little nosh." Nurse Arlene smiled back and put up her arm to steer the mother-father dynamic duo out of the room. Sofia let out an amused chuckle. No one could resist Nathan's charms, even when he's all banged up.

Sofia's stomach grumbled at hearing Nathan mention food. Between her ongoing euphoria over the performance the night before and the splitting headache that would not relent, she had forgotten that she hadn't eaten anything since yesterday's breakfast. She just needed a bag of salty pretzels and a diet coke to soak up the remaining alcohol in her stomach and tide her over until Shabbos dinner. Just as Sofia was about to leave with the others in search of an improvised lunch, Nathan called her back.

"Hey, Sofia, can you stay for a minute? There's something I need to talk to you about."

Sofia grumbled under her breath. She stopped short of the doorway, plastered on a sympathetic grin, and turned back into the room. "Yes, of course. Do you need something? Are you hungry too?"

"No, it's nothing like that." Nathan waited a beat to be sure his parents were out of earshot. When Sofia closed the door, he said, "There's something you need to know, cousin." His smile faded, and his swollen blue eyes shimmered with tears. Sofia didn't see this look from Nathan often, so she knew immediately that he meant business.

"Spit it out then. What's up?" Sofia's voice was low and quick. She had little patience for riddles and mysteries.

"I wasn't exactly alone in the car last night... Becca was in the car with me." Nathan touched the bridge of his nose, and Sofia could see his nervous fingers trembling.

Becca. Her soul sister. Her family away from her family. "What do you mean? Where's Becca now? What happened to her?"

"We left the party last night around one thirty, and I was driving Becca home. She was nervous that her parents were going to be upset with her about getting home so late. So she asked if she could use my phone to call home. We were on the Belt Parkway already. We were only fifteen minutes from her house!"

Sofia listened as Nathan dragged out the details of the accident. A foreboding pall strangled Sofia, like a headscarf tied too tight around her throbbing head. "Get to the point, Nathan. What exactly happened, and where is Becca now?"

"I'm getting to the point, cousin. Patience!" Nathan took a deep breath and bit down hard on his chapped lower lip. He shuddered with pain and reached for his side. Sofia couldn't tell which was more painful for him at that moment…the rehashing of the accident or his broken ribs. Nathan closed his eyes, squeezed out a trickle of tears, and continued to speak in whispers. "As I was saying, we were on the parkway, almost home, when I reached for the glovebox to get my phone. Somehow, my foot slipped from the gas pedal, and the next thing I heard was screeching rubber and the shatter of glass and metal. I'm so sorry." Nathan's words faded into the sterile air as he turned away from Sofia. "I'm so sorry," Nathan repeated. "I never meant to hurt her." He punched the mattress with his uninjured hand and let out a mournful growl.

Sofia staggered on her feet. She was either going to pass out cold or throw up all over herself. Her freckled face paling, she said, "I'm asking you again, Nathan. Where is Becca now?"

"The nurse was just telling me that she is still in the emergency room. They haven't found a room to officially admit her yet. She should be okay, though. She has a broken leg and a few bumps and bruises."

The first thought that crossed Sofia's mind that minute was if anyone had bothered to contact Becca's family. She asked Nathan, and he told her that he had given Becca's home phone number to the nurse who swore she would call as soon as she could. Sofia let out a deep, sorrowful pant. She ran out of the room hearing Nathan's useless pleas for forgiveness and went straight to the nurses' station to ask for Nurse Arlene. The nurse at the desk informed her that Arlene had indeed called Becca's parents and that her friend had just been admitted to a room on the fourth floor.

The next thought that crossed Sofia's scrambled mind as she waited for the elevator to take her down two floors to Becca was, *If she broke her leg, she could lose her scholarship. Or worse, maybe she could be dismissed from the troupe altogether.* Sofia swallowed hard and grabbed hold of the handrail along the wall of the whining elevator cab.

Sofia quickly found room 419 and flew though the open door. She felt like she had just stepped through a time-traveling portal: standing next to one of the two occupied beds were Mr. and Mrs. Kaplan, both dressed in stained rags and covered heads (Mrs. Kaplan donning a red handkerchief and Mr. Kaplan wearing a frayed tweed newsboy's cap), and their three younger children (Yossi, age fourteen; Dina and Deborah, twin girls, age seven). The whole *mishpachah* was there, crowding around poor, disheveled and bruised Becca. It was like stepping into a scene from prewar Soviet Union. Sofia coughed and stepped into the overcrowded room.

"Sofia, *bubeleh*, you are here! Do you see what happen to our *sheyne*, beautiful Rebecca? This what happens when you go out late in the night. This girl will give me heart attack one of these days!" Mrs. Kaplan's heavily accented words sputtered from her quivering lips. She wiped her nose with a yellowed hanky and turned a weeping eye back to her son. "Yossele, don't be so *foyl*, lazy. Bring a chair here for Sofia. Come sit, sit. Girls, bring some rugelach for Sofia. She's too skinny." The whole family was in instant motion to accommodate their daughter's best friend. It never ceased to amaze Sofia how, after decades of being in the United States, Becca's parents still clung so tightly to their old ways, never adapting their beliefs much or even fully grasping the English language. But after a lifetime of fear and having to hide their ancestral customs and religion in the old country, Sofia supposed they probably felt free and safe enough to live as they wished now in America. She leaned over to kiss Mrs. Kaplan on the cheek and took a seat next to the foot of the bed.

An ancient woman lying in a second bed let out a sudden loud snore. Her hair was silver and wiry and sprawled around her wrinkled face like a halo. Her intermittent wheezing and snuffling made the seven of us feel even more imposing. For sure, the Kaplans were going to be kicked out of the room any minute now.

"Hi, Sofia. I'm so glad to see you," Becca muttered. "My parents have been here all night, but we just got the room. How's Nathan? Have you seen him?" Becca smoothed her long, tangled hair with her hand and slid up straighter in the bed. Mr. Kaplan coughed and began pacing back and forth in the small space by the window.

Sofia held her breath as the color began to slowly return to her cheeks. It was clear that Becca was going to recover from her injuries. Sofia just hoped the injuries would not affect her dancing. "You have no idea how bad Nathan feels about this. I just saw him upstairs, and he is so sorry for everything. He sends his love, Becca." Sofia added that last sentence on her cousin's behalf. Becca's sallow pallor turned rosy, and a broad smile beamed across her bruised face. Mrs. Kaplan licked her meaty forefinger and smudged away a glob of sticky cookie crumbs from the corner of her daughter's raw lips.

Suddenly, a heavyset woman wearing hospital scrubs covered with Bart Simpson's cartoon images appeared in the open doorway of the cramped room, wheeling a portable computer monitor behind her. Knotty, pink dreadlocks cascaded down her back all the way to her inflated rear end. Armfuls of gold bracelets jangled as she moved. The large nurse whistled a bubbly tune through the gap in her front teeth and headed straight for the sleeping old lady. The Kaplans took a collective gasp, sucking all the remaining air from the room. The nurse stopped short, put up her dark chubby hand, and shot daggers at all of us with disdainful warning eyes. With a heavy Caribbean accent, she hissed, "No, sir, we cannot have so many—" Before she could finish her recrimination, Mrs. Kaplan stood up and blocked the tight space between the impinging nurse and her flustered husband.

"Stop your whistling, young lady," Mr. Kaplan snapped at her, completely out of character for the five-foot-six-inch passive man he was. He gently shoved his wife out of his way and stomped toward the *zaftik*, meaty, nurse. Everyone, including Becca's young siblings, turned to look at him, expecting a full-out war over his folkloric concept about whistling indoors and the bad luck that the act could bring down on them. Sofia was losing what was left of her patience and her compassion for the day as she silently witnessed Becca's battered body and the comical interaction between the Island Queen and the Ancient Troll.

Sofia wanted to diffuse the tension that was filling the room. She wondered if the air-conditioning was working as the small space filled with heated unease. Distracting everyone from the scene that was surely about to play out, she raised a finger in front of her lips and pointed to the sleeping old woman in the next bed. Whispering, she asked, "Nurse, are you here to check on Becca? Is she okay? When can she go home?" Sofia fanned her hand in front of her face.

The nurse tsked through her big gapped teeth and ignored the Kaplan family. Turning her full attention toward Sofia and checking the chart hanging from the mobile monitor, she assured Sofia that Becca would be going home just as soon as they complete a few more tests to rule out a possible concussion.

Mr. Kaplan harrumphed. "Feh, more tests."

Mrs. Kaplan put a hand to her chest and said, "Oy, *gevalt*. Does the doctor really think she has a contusion?"

"Not a contusion, Mrs. Kaplan, a concussion." Sofia put an arm around the older woman's slumped shoulders while the nurse explained about the head injuries that Becca had suffered.

"The paramedics' report says she hit her head pretty hard against the windshield. The doctor just wants to be sure that the bump on her head is nothing more serious to worry about." Becca raised a black-and-blue arm to her forehead and rubbed it with the tips of her shaking fingers.

"My head feels fine. I just have a little headache. It's my leg I'm more concerned with," Becca advised, staring at Sofia.

"Consider yourself lucky, Rebecca. You're young, and the x-rays of your leg show that the bone only suffered one clean break. The doctor will set it, and uncomfortable as the cast will be for a while, you should be walking again on your own in a few months."

Yeah, I'm real lucky, thought Becca. A heavy tear escaped from the corner of her eye and rolled down to her chin.

Sofia could read Becca's thoughts and couldn't bear the sadness she saw sweep across her heart-shaped face. What would Becca do if she couldn't dance anymore? It was an option Sofia had never had to face, and the idea of Becca losing out on her dream was more than she could bare. Suddenly, her chest heaved; she couldn't breathe. She clutched her hand to her throat and turned toward the open door.

"You're going to be fine, Becca. I'm sure of it," Sofia managed to choke out.

Taking advantage of the nurse's earlier admonition about the number of people in the room, Sofia hastily offered to take her leave. "I'm going to go back down to check on Nathan and then take my aunt and uncle home," she explained. "*Gut Shabbos* to you all, and I really hope you feel better soon, my dear Becca. You know I'm here for you if you need anything at all."

Mr. Kaplan clucked his tongue and pinched his lips together in a thin line. Mrs. Kaplan waddled over toward Sofia and gently pushed her past the nurse and the mobile monitor. Tripping on the foot of the old woman's bed, she let out a low grumble, "I no know what we will do, Sofia. Of course, we want best for our little Rebecca, but we also worry about hospital bill." Mrs. Kaplan kissed Sofia lightly on both cheeks and squeezed her with her big arms. "Tell Nathan we send *beste vauntshen*, our best wishes, and that he should feel good soon. Now go home with your dyadya and tyotya. Tell them *Gut Shabbos* from all of us, and please, eat before you disappear!"

4

Maya

I can't get out of bed. The stitches across my belly are still raw, and my muscles are stiffening with every second I lie here, which I have been doing for at least twenty-three hours every day since the surgery. Aaron keeps me from resting at all, and I am trapped between my own inadequacies as a new mother and his wailing cries for attention.

My time and my destiny have finally come to fruition. After two previous miscarriages and three years of trying to start our family, I should be over the top ecstatic. Yet all I feel now is weakness and a big empty hole in my stomach. I think I understand the truth of motherhood and the irony of calling giving birth "labor."

Is this what it all boils down to? Are there any other choices?

Living my whole life on our tiny kibbutz, an aging and disintegrating idea of a collective community, I should know all about labor. Kibbutz Gan Notzah, my own birthplace and my family's home for almost thirty years, is a tricky source of beauty, pride, and danger.

I am proud to play my small role in keeping Gan Notzah running smoothly and lucratively. In a time when our antiquated existence is losing its appeal with the vast majority of the outside world, I still appreciate the sense of community and self-reliance and the protection that our small group offers. Yet, really? Is this it for me?

After graduating from high school and completing my mandatory military service in the Israeli Defense Forces, I unquestioningly returned to my life and my family at the kibbutz. As was expected, Danny and I ultimately got married as that was the next step for me to take on Kibbutz Gan Notzah.

Finish high school. Complete mandatory military service. Find a supportive job on the kibbutz. Start a family. Period.

End of story?

Danny and I have been inseparable since our first days as children in daycare. Everyone always suspected we would eventually get married. We are made for each other, really. It is Danny's warmth and companionship I seek when I'm scared. Or happy. Or sad. He is kind, patient, and generous. The only things we don't share are my passion for dance and Danny's passion for working in the fields.

Danny is a disaster on the dance floor. As a loyal gesture and show of his love, however, he had secretly arranged for my friend, Gali, to give him a few dance lessons before our wedding day. Her tutorials wound up being all for naught. To this day, Danny still has two left feet and a nagging aversion to anything related to dancing.

Anyway, my dancing dreams may have been squashed now with the miraculous birth of our son, Aaron. The doctor had said I could continue with light dance and exercise since I had been doing it for so many years, but I was advised not to do any heavy work until after the baby was born. After all, I had miscarried twice before, and this pregnancy could have proven to be just as difficult, if not altogether dangerous, for me and the baby. I suppose there is some validity to the doctor's warning. As it turns out, the third time is a charm, as they say, and Aaron is now growing louder, stronger, and needier by the day. I had made it through another difficult and dangerous challenge, but now my tired body twitches with longing and cramps with desperation to get back into the dance studio. I cringe from the petty selfishness that has overtaken me.

A sudden knock on my bedroom door jolts me out of my sluggish trance. "I know you're resting, Maya, but you have a visitor," Danny announces, pushing the door open only a crack and sticking his head into our bedroom turned nursery.

I immediately assume it is my mother. She has been checking up on me—lovingly and annoyingly—every day after work. Shula, my mother, has always been a mystery to us. Naturally gregarious and friendly, all we ever learned about her past is this: she came to Gan Notzah on her own, leaving the rest of her family behind in a small town in Ukraine. Unlike her parents who were too old to change their traditional way of life, my mother bravely adopted the idea of abandoning the Soviet regime and moving to a collective life on a Jewish kibbutz. She met and fell in love with my father, Noam Grinskind, a handsome, serious young man with kind eyes, and the treasurer of the kibbutz. Less than a year after they met, they were wed in the rec center, and since then, they have not left each other's side for longer than a single workday. They honeymooned for a week in the southern city of Eilat, and to hear my mother talk about it, anyone would think her life truly began at that point. Nothing before that mattered or needed further discussion.

"Tell Imma I'm fine and that I am resting in bed," I say weakly. As an afterthought, I lean over the edge of my bed and peer into the cradle where Aaron lays sleeping. "Aaron is fine too. He hasn't woken up since you last fed him."

Danny whispers at the door, "It isn't your mother who is here." Before he could finish explaining, Irena bursts past him into my bedroom carrying a large bouquet of yellow roses. "You didn't think I wouldn't come to see you, did you, my sister?" she asks with an assured singsong inflection in her voice, no concern for waking the baby from his slumber. "Just because you haven't been able to come to Haifa doesn't mean I would forget all about you." Irena blows me a kiss and tosses the roses back to Danny, who is standing in the doorway, his mouth hanging wide open with contemptuous shock. I straighten up against my pillow and run my hand over my matted hair.

Watching Irena slink around my room, touching every knick-knack and wrinkling her nose in judgment, my attention is drawn to the silver picture frame on my dresser. It holds a blurry photo of Irena and me after our first dance recital together, both of us in matching pink tutus and satin ballet slippers. Although Irena is a few years younger than me, her worldliness and gumption has always kept our friendship in balance. I remember how Irena used to tell everyone that it was no coincidence that she shared the same heritage and the same name as her idol, Irina Roizin, the founder of the famous Russian International School of Dance in New York City. She is so proud, and she believes in fate; it is her destiny to become an international star as a prima ballerina, just like Roizin did. Irena makes everything sound so simple, so right. I envy her confidence, her stamina, her freedom. She is my inspiration.

Now in my stuffy bedroom, all dusty and smelling of dirty diapers, Irena is still wearing her pink leotard and stockings. Her hair is tied up in a neat, tight bun. She must have come straight from the studio in Haifa. A bubble of jealousy squeezes up from my chest, but I push it back down my throat. Irena settles her petite frame on the foot of my bed, and I whine, "Please don't look at me. I must be a mess. Let's talk about you."

In contrast to Irena's self-assured, impeccable air, I crumble, sinking deeper into my messy bedsheets. Dark half-moons sit under my dull blue eyes, and red blotches cast shadows over my pale, freckled cheeks. My strawberry-blond hair hangs limp over my shoulders in greasy strands. It's a good thing she can't see my bloated stomach and swollen chest bumps hiding under my sheets. I twist my swollen legs and pull my blanket up to my chin.

"I don't care what you look like, my dear. After all, you just had a baby! A baby! Imagine that! Our baby has a baby!" Coughing into her manicured little hand, she adds, "Although I do believe we are going to have to take you to the salon as soon as you can get out of that bed. So before we talk about me, tell me. How are you and baby-Aaron doing?" She pats my foot over the coverlet with one hand and swipes her nose with the other.

"We're doing well. And the roses are beautiful. Thanks for bringing them." I point to the closed door where Danny is no longer standing and paste a smile on my face. No need to get into the details of my uncontrollable flatulence and leaking breasts. I cringe and turn to the cradle next to my bed and put a finger in front of my cracked lips. "He's sleeping now, finally, and I hope we don't wake him up."

Irena and I have been attending dance classes together at the Russian Ballet Conservatory of Haifa for almost seven years. Irena, however, has finally gone on to claim growing fame and stardom with the troupe, while I continue to take the occasional lesson or teach some of the younger children's classes whenever Ilan is desperate for instructors, and I can get off the kibbutz. We have spent hours in the studio together, dancing and choreographing dozens of ballet entrées—and dreaming of becoming prima ballerinas together.

This is the first time my friend has come here to the kibbutz, and it is a bit odd to see her here today with the farm silhouetting the space from the window behind her. She is an anachronism here, as out of place as finding a diamond in a plate of *babaganoush*. I brush another strand of fallen hair from my forehead and roll my tongue over my parched lips.

"Now let's hear about you. How's everything going?"

"Everything's just great…and Ilan is good too. When I mentioned that I was coming here to see you today, he asked me to bring you his regards. Oh, and I almost forgot…" Irena's face bursts with red flame, and her voice rises a full octave. "The Performing Arts Center in Tel Aviv is presenting *Concerto DSCH* next month, and they asked me and Ilan to dance the leading roles! Can you believe it, Maya? Dancing in a Ratmansky ballet…in Tel Aviv!"

I don't know if I am feeling more emotional by the news of the performance or by Irena's gushing excitement. I want to share in her joy. It had always been our shared dream to become professional ballerinas and dance in all of those world-renowned Russian ballets, but today, I just can't seem to pull it together. All I know is that new flames of envy are licking at me, and my body is burning from the tip of my throbbing head down to my calloused toes.

Standing up from the foot of the bed, Irena begins wandering around the room again, and I wrestle under my sweaty sheets to break free from the self-absorbed jealousy that blisters inside me, inside my new, misshaped, foreign body. It is unnerving to share passionate talk about dance again, yet I try to appear happy for my dear friend. As hard as I try to refocus myself, I can't shake the self-pity and resentment that jumble around in my head. While Irena blathers on endlessly about the plans and details of the performance in Tel Aviv, I find myself drifting farther away, my mind separating from my body and floating above my bed where I had dreamt countless dreams of the day I could be where Irena is right now.

It's not fair, I dare think to myself.

Shortly after Irena leaves, Danny convinces me to accompany him to dinner. Imma has come by again and offers to stay with baby Aaron while Danny and I relax in the dining hall. Her kind gesture is coated with pity, but truthfully, I am desperate to get out of bed, out of my ragged nightgown, and out into the fresh air, so I agree to give it a go. On our way there, Danny comments on Irena's surprise visit. As much as he clearly does not like her, his face wears a hopeful expression—one that says he hopes the visit will snap me out of my recent melancholy. We make our way slowly, hand in hand, along the cobblestone path from our cottage, but the short stroll and the cool autumn breeze does little to boost my spirits, and my stomach continues to spasm with cramps. Irena's visit has left me more tired and weak and confused, and I am still silently and selfishly fuming about her success and my misfortune.

If only I hadn't gotten pregnant…*if only*…

I know Danny has been concerned about my ever-changing moods, so I stop to reach up and kiss the dimple on his stubbly chin.

As we reach the dining hall entrance, and I sniff the familiar aromas of freshly baked pita and earthy vegetable salads, Danny bends down and whispers, "I love you, Maya." His hot breath and bristly jaw scrape against my skin, and goosebumps quickly erupt up and down my arms.

I want to explain to him what is bothering me, but I'm not even sure myself what is going on in my head. I keep going from one extreme to another, like a seesaw bobbing up and down. As much as I love him, a deep passion for the theater keeps kicking up and knocking me right off my feet. It's a passion that Irena's visit has fueled, vibrant and wild. One minute I'm happy and content and full of giggles; all I want to do is hold onto Danny and Aaron, my two boys, and never let them go. Then the next minute, something snaps, and I don't have the patience for Danny's mushy fondling or even (dare I admit it!) the sight of my newborn son. Some days, holding Aaron in my arms is like holding a grenade in the palm of my hand, and Danny is as annoying as those menacing megabats.

I'm not *exactly* sad, but one thing is certain…the pregnancy has unleashed a gush of unseemly consequences and uncontrollable emotions—the rollercoaster of fear, self-pity, and unsureness is driving me crazier than anything else. I cry, holler, and complain about every little mishap, every comment people around me make, every time Aaron coos in his cradle. I hardly laugh anymore. I don't know if I'm cut out to be a mother.

Am I losing my mind?

My appetite is hardly satisfied with our hasty dinner of roasted chicken, rice pilaf, and broccoli spears, and I can't take a single bite without feeling queasy. I beg Danny to skip dessert and take me home.

Luckily, it is soon after that one (and only) visit from Irena that I begin getting around on my own two feet again. At first, I wobble around slowly, dragging my feet beneath me. My stitches still tingle, but for the most part, if I don't look at them, I don't notice them. Little by little, my stamina and my state of mind rebound, and my body grows steady and strong again. All I need is to occasionally break out of the confined walls of my bedroom and clear my head, to breathe different air, see different people, become creative and productive again. Take a few more pills.

One afternoon, after about a month of lying in bed, skipping meals, and popping more pills than I could keep track of, I have a spontaneous thought. I watch my mother saunter up the path leading to our cottage from the milking shed. A heavy backpack swings from her shoulder. I grin at her and wait for her to get a little closer before yelling out my greeting.

"Hi, Imma. You always have such perfect timing. I was just thinking…" I gulp down a mouthful of air and blow it back out through my nose. "Do you think we could go for a ride somewhere? Just me and you? Maybe if we hurry, we can take a ride out to Haifa."

My mother smiles and snaps her fingers as if she were hearing a favorite song playing in her head. "Actually, that sounds like a great idea, Maya. A drive to Haifa would be a welcome break from my work and all the cows." She laughs, as if she is the one who needs the diversion and not me. "I just passed Hani outside the nursery. Let's see if we can catch up to her before she goes home for the day. We can leave Aaron with her for a while, and I'm sure she wouldn't mind watching him." Imma joins me on our front porch and sneaks a peek at Aaron in his cradle. Without saying another word, she lifts him up, hugs him tightly against her dirty bib, and leads me down toward the nursery.

With Aaron safely tucked in at the nursery and Imma behind the wheel of an old Honda from the car pool, I strap the seat belt across my lap and adjust it so it doesn't rub against my stitches. Excitement bubbles up from deep in my chest, like puffs of steam escaping from a pot of boiling water. I remember our ride to Haifa together for my first dance audition. Grinning from the memory, I take two pills from the vial in my pocket and swallow them down, dry and hard. Imma turns the car onto the dirt road that leads away from Gan Notzah, leaving a plume of dust in our wake. She turns to me with a gentle, understanding smile and reaches across the seat to touch my arm.

"This is such a great idea, Maya. Let's choose to be happy now…before we lose any more chances."

5

Sofia

The Jewish holiday season was coming to an end, and Sofia was finally able to regroup and get back into her routine again. Between Rosh Hashanah and Simchat Torah, she had spent most of September, October, and November commuting back and forth for each holiday from her new apartment in Brooklyn and her familial home back in Brighton. She attended services in her family's *shul*, heard the blasts of the shofar, atoned with her community, had several meals in their communal *sukkahs*, and danced with the Torah to celebrate its renewed commencement. Walking home from the laundromat that morning, dragging her wheeled shopping cart filled with her fresh wash, Sofia couldn't recall the last time she had done any of the menial household chores she had to worry about and were piling up on her to-do list. Things like doing the laundry, cooking meals, paying bills, or running the vacuum cleaner were all tasks that, in the past, had taken place around her but never involved her. This morning, she took her time strolling through her new environment, admiring her unfamiliar surroundings, and taking in the slower pace of the crowds, the colorful outfits of the neighborhood inhabitants, and the pungent aromas of Indian spices that clung to the chilly air. She was farther away from the dance academy (a fifteen-minute bus ride on a good day), but the escape from her family and community made her feel free and liberated. It even gave her a chance to break away from her commitments to Boris, the studio, and her strict schedule of practice.

But it was this time of year that usually made Sofia especially melancholy and thoughtful of her days back in Ukraine. This year, living on her own, was no different, and Sofia carried the weight of those memories with her. As she walked past the Carvel ice cream shop lugging the cart of laundry behind her, Sofia replayed some of her holiday memories with her parents in Lutsk. They did not have an extravagant life, but they were together, the three of them, safe and comfortable. Until that one day when everything changed.

"My *sheynele*, I have news for you." With red-rimmed eyes and tears threatening to spill down her cheeks, Sofia's mother spoke in a gravely, ambiguous monotone, "Your father has been…drafted…yes, that's it. He's been drafted…by the government…to work on a new project." Her mother's words were clipped, measured. Then she inhaled deeply, and her lips curved up into a smile. "You know, he is one of the best engineers in the country, no? Well, they have asked him to join a group of scientists working in Moscow, and he will be gone for a while."

"What does that mean, a while? And who are they? When is Papa coming home?"

Her mother swiped at the tears streaming freely down her face. She choked on her next words, barely making clear sense. She knew Sofia was precocious and wise for her sixteen years, so she chose her next words carefully. "Well, that's the thing, dear Sofia. We don't know when he will…" Her voice faded, and that was the last time Papa or his government project was mentioned. In just a few short weeks, the details were somehow all sorted out, and Sofia was put on a plane by herself to join her uncle and aunt in "Little Odessa," aka Brighton Beach, New York.

A dog barked, and a baby wailed, the sounds jarring Sofia back to the sidewalk in Brooklyn. Almost ten years had passed since those last days back in Ukraine with her parents; the sad and defeated images of her parents still rattled her until her insides twisted up in knots, and the uncertainty of father's disappearance remained deep in a hidden pocket of anger and resentment in her core. She tried to shake the thoughts of her parents out of her head, and her stomach gurgled. The wheel of her shopping cart rolled into her heel. *"Ach! Damn it!"* she cursed out loud. Wiggling her foot, she limped into the ice cream shop with her laundry, contemplating whether she should get a soft-serve cone or a flying saucer cookie sandwich.

Nathan's and Becca's car accident had changed Sofia's life in more ways than one. Nathan had lost his job at the pharmacy, and his broken ribs needed more medical attention than he expected. At least, according to Aunt Anika, whose inflated attentions on her one-and-only son caused him to move back home where she could keep constant vigil over his recovery. This, of course, meant that he was to reclaim his old childhood room—the room that had been Sofia's since her arrival there seven years ago. Her relatives would never think of putting her out, but Sofia had found herself relegated to sleeping on the lumpy old sofa in the living room. Her clothes and personal belongings were shoved into suitcases and stored in the hall closet, and her life became small and confined; she had become nothing more than a trespasser. Nathan apologized for the situation every waking moment, but his kvetching did little to appease Sofia and began to annoy her to no end. She was going to explode if she heard the words "I'm sorry" one more time. The time had come for her to get out and find her own place.

Nathan's heavy sense of culpability led him to call on some old connections around the city, though, and while Sofia spent the next four months after the accident traveling around the country with the troupe, performing shows in Chicago, San Francisco, and Miami, he was able to secure a decent, rent-controlled apartment in the Bay Ridge neighborhood in Brooklyn for her. Nathan's contrite guilt about the car accident had led to something positive, and Sofia was able to take advantage of his misfortune. Perfectly situated just far enough from her suffocating community in Brighton Beach and the Tantsor Russian Ballet & Dance Academy and studios to offer her some personal space, her new home in Bay Ridge was like a sudden blessing in disguise, and Sofia could not deny her cousin still had a magic touch to turn bad luck into good, even from the confines of his recuperation.

Although she sometimes missed her family and the camaraderie of her old neighborhood, Sofia quickly adjusted to the peculiar nuances and differences of her new environment. She enjoyed the newfound freedom and independence of living on her own and managing her own affairs. She was no longer under the constant surveillance of nosy neighbors or unnerved by the constant bustle and ruckus of Brighton Beach. Her new apartment was conveniently situated just fifty feet from the subway and around the corner from a host of practical ethnic business establishments; a quick five-minute walk down the street found Sofia surrounded by a Duane Reed drugstore, an eclectic coffee shop, a Korean-owned supermarket, a flower shop, and a Hallel meat market. But when she was in the comfort of her two-room apartment, she reveled in the calm silence and privacy that her own space now afforded her.

Around the same time Sofia moved out of her aunt and uncle's apartment, Becca was able to abandon her crutches and begin walking on her own again. However, the cast had left her leg thin and weak, and she still sauntered about with cautious hesitation and a slight limp in her step. In the two months she spent convalescing, Becca had been suspended from her position as Sofia's understudy and was pushed down the ladder of the corps de ballet's main troupe—a group that was growing by the day and now included nineteen other secondary dancers besides Becca. *At least she didn't lose her scholarship*, Sofia braved.

Ice cream cone in hand and zigzagging her way back to her apartment, Sofia was careful not to step over the sidewalk grates (it was certain bad luck to step over them!). She licked the soft ice cream dibbling between her fingers and awkwardly dragged her shopping cart full of laundry behind her. Glancing up into the shade of a thick oak tree, Sofia urgently remembered the most important chore she had set for herself that day.

She had waited through the holidays to talk with Boris, but she couldn't put it off any longer. For Becca's sake—and for her own sake—Sofia needed to confront her director with the speech she had been rehearsing in her mind for weeks. After dumping the cart of laundry on the sofa, Sofia made her way back out to the bus stop.

When she finally arrived at the academy, she took a deep breath and headed straight for Boris's private studio. She found him there practicing a challenging movement from *Don Quixote* and entered the studio on her tiptoes.

"Hey, what are you doing here today, Sofia? Didn't you say you needed to take the day off to do some 'personal stuff'?" Boris was a flawless dance master and an even more astute director. He was an intimidating force to be reckoned with, but he'd have to understand.

"Hi, Boris. I, uh, actually, uh, need to talk to you. Um, I hate to interrupt your practice, but it's important." A soft whisper floated into her ear: *Pull yourself together, Sofia. This isn't that difficult. Just stay positive and in control.*

Boris wiped the sweat on his neck with a towel and glided over to the stereo to lower the volume of the music. "Sure, what's up?"

"Well, it's Becca."

"Yeah, wow. I can't believe her bad luck with that accident. Not to mention her slight demotion in the troupe."

"Yeah, well, that's just what I wanted to talk to you about, Boris. It's been a few months, and I am sure she's ready to come back to the studio and resume her role as my understudy. Traveling without her these past months was hard enough for me, and I can't imagine how desperate she is to get back to her role. So I was uh, wondering if, uh, you would consider reinstating her as my backup." As erratic and unsure as her words sounded falling from her lips, they were finally, hopelessly, out of her mouth. She considered the consequence of the accident again. She needed Becca. The alternative was unthinkable.

"We agreed in the end that Nina Cassel was going to be your understudy, no?"

"Well, I was thinking it over, and, well…" Sofia didn't want to remind Boris of Nina Cassel's first audition at the Tantsor Russian Ballet & Dance Academy. Her performance was nearly perfect. That was nearly a year ago, and the memory of Nina's arrival still always managed to send Sofia's head to pounding and her *kishkes* to recoil with waves of jealous nausea. Nina could easily become her biggest nemesis, but not if Sofia could help it. Nina was a sly fox, but Sofia had a few tricks of her own up her sleeve. No, Becca would just have to be reinstated as her understudy!

Staring at Boris, Sofia cringed and hopped from foot to foot, refocusing her tiresome energy on the latest commotion that Becca was creating for her, as if she had nothing else to worry about. She sucked in some air and tried again. "It's just that Becca has worked so hard to get that position, and I hate to see her opportunity taken away just because of this temporary setback. I mean, Nina is a good dancer and all, but Becca has been backing me up for years. I really think she's a better fit for the role than Nina. And God only knows what she would do if she lost her scholarship here." She added that last bit for a subtle dash of concerned pity. She stared at her reflection in the mirrored wall, hoping her rehearsed words sounded as sincere as she had planned. Fluttering her eyelashes and staring down at her pointed toes, Sofia waited for Boris to respond. At that moment, she would agree to work with a circus monkey as long as it wasn't Nina.

It was four years earlier when she first saw Becca walk into the academy. She and Boris were in the middle of practicing a scene from their upcoming performance in *Sleeping Beauty*. It was a difficult adagio that they had been working on for weeks together. At that point, it had been four long, committed years at the Tantsor Russian Ballet & Dance Academy, and at the age of twenty-one, she had finally aced the audition that had won her that role as Boris's duet partner.

In the middle of their third attempt at a particularly problematic lift, Becca walked into the studio wearing a faded black leotard, black leg warmers, and a pair of worn ballet slippers that had been bound to her feet with white tape. She looked like a wretched mess, but she presented herself with the chutzpah of a poised, self-possessed career politician. In her tall, slender stance, she wore the signs of a dancer committed to hard work and the genuine love of the art. She showed no indications of prestige or elitism, and Sofia was instantly attracted to the intriguing, appealing yet out-of-place stranger. Becca watched the pair for a long while with an expression that popped from her intense gray eyes above high, freckled cheekbones like she was watching the real-time splitting of the Red Sea. Although scruffy and rough around the edges, Sofia immediately took a liking to the girl who would eventually audition for the academy, win a scholarship, and become the next young member of the academy's corps de ballet. Since then, Becca showed the grit, devotion, and aspiration of a starving artist with nothing but the passion for dance on her mind. She wanted nothing more than to work her way up the ladder of success.

Back in the moment again, waiting for a reaction from Boris, Sofia stuttered and attempted one more final plea. "As artistic director of the academy, Boris, I'm asking you to give Becca another chance. She needs our support." Sofia didn't mention Nina again.

Boris remained silent and pensive. Sofia could see the wheels turning behind his tired eyes and a thoughtful scowl pulling on his lips. The hush that settled between them seemed to go on for an eternity. Don Quixote's "To Dream the Impossible Dream" droned through the overhead speakers, but the music did little to equalize their uneasy silence. Suddenly, Boris scratched his clean-shaven jaw and flicked his towel at Sofia's shoulder. Turning the volume of the stereo back up, he exhaled and said, "Have Becca see me tomorrow morning, and we'll see what we can do."

With her mission accomplished with Boris, Sofia headed to the bus stop that would take her to Becca's home. She needed to see her and tell her about her chat with Boris. Then she would visit Nathan and pick up the money for her next rent check. As the first sights of the traditional peddlers under the darkened, crowded elevated train tracks came into view and the mixed aromas of familiar Russian foods struck her, Sofia felt a warm shiver run up her spine. She had a sudden craving and put her hand on her rumbling belly. Sofia rounded a corner and bought a *khachapuri* at Berikoni's Bakery. She ate ravenously as she walked the few blocks toward her uncle's meat market, where she stopped to schmooze with her Uncle Sol for a while. Between the ice cream earlier that morning and the cheesy khachapuri she was now scarfing down, Sofia figured she would have to add an extra two hours to her exercise workout tomorrow. She would never allow herself to go over the weight max set by her own demanding parameters and those of the equally neurotic directors and choreographers at the academy, not even for her favorite indulgences like ice cream and khachapuri. Sofia bought a bottle of vodka from the liquor store next door and continued to make her way to Becca's home. She was excited to see her friend and deliver the optimistic message from Boris. If Sofia was completely honest, she needed Becca to regain her position in the troupe as much as her friend needed it.

It was Becca who answered the door when Sofia arrived at the boxy, overcrowded apartment complex. Even with a cane in hand, Becca's swagger seemed stronger and more sure-footed than it did just the week before when Sofia had watched her attempt a rehearsal at the studio. Still, Sofia delivered the news with mixed feelings of apprehension and hopefulness and promised to meet Becca at the academy for moral support at nine o'clock the following morning. "What would I do without you, Sofia? You have given me back my hope and courage and…my life!"

"Let's not get so dramatic, Becca. We do what we have to do, and we help one another whenever and however we can," Sofia answered with a smug smirk. "Rest up for now, and we'll see you at the studio tomorrow morning."

Sofia reached her family's apartment block as the sun was setting in the distance. The sky was a pastel shade of orange and pink, and Sofia sparked with an air of accomplishment. It was the end of a good day. She entered her family's home without even knocking and found Nathan sprawled out on the sofa. Uncle Sol had not returned from the shop yet, and Aunt Anika had just stepped out to buy some sour cream for their dinner. She was disappointed she missed seeing her favorite aunt; Anika was usually home tending to Nathan and taking in sewing jobs from neighbors to help pay for Nathan's recent hospital stay. Sofia sat with Nathan in the empty living room that had been her crowded bedroom just a few months earlier.

"Those flowers are beautiful," she commented to Nathan, pointing at the bouquet sitting on the coffee table. "Sunflowers are Tyotya Anika's favorites, no?" She was feeling out of place, missing her family, and fishing for anything to say just to fill the uncomfortable space. For some reason she couldn't comprehend, Sofia felt awkward and deserted as she gazed around the apartment that had been her home for the past seven years.

"Yes, they are. Why don't you take some of them home with you." Sofia had just made a simple observation about the flowers; she didn't want them. Nonetheless, Nathan's response socked her in the stomach. With this gesture of accustomed hospitality, Sofia was acutely aware that she was being treated as an outsider in her family's home, a guest who only warranted the respect of an arbitrary visitor. Nathan, staring at his cousin's grim expression, clenched his jaw, hit his forehead with the palm of his hand like he had just remembered something important, and went into the kitchen to put on a pot of water for tea. "Make yourself at home, Sofia. I'll make us some tea."

Once again searching for conversation, Sofia yelled out, "I can't believe it's almost Hanukkah. Time is rolling by so fast." Nathan reappeared with two mugs and placed them on the coffee table.

"I know. I've been cooped up in this apartment for so long, I have to keep checking out the window to keep up with things. When Motty stopped driving by with the ice cream truck, I knew summer had come to an end. Now the days are shorter, darker, and I wait for Zelda each evening to bring over her Hanukkah *ponchik* for us."

Sofia fondly remembered the oily donuts filled with apple filling and sprinkled with white powdered sugar that their kindly neighbor baked from scratch every year for the Hanukkah holiday season. Nathan plopped down on the sofa next to Sofia. Letting out a hefty sigh, Nathan groaned, "Sofia, I'm going to go *meshuga* if I don't get a job soon!"

Sofia nearly spit a mouthful of hot tea at him. "I can't believe you still haven't found work, Nathan. What have you been doing all this time, sitting on your big, fat *tukhes* and milking your injuries for more attention? Shame on you, Nathan!" This was one of Sofia's most annoying pet peeves—people who sat around wallowing in self-pity, waiting for the Messiach to come and deliver them out of their misery. Her own father's words rang in her ears: "Success and rest don't sleep together." And her mother would always back that up with "Choices aren't always easy, but they are given to us free of charge." Raising her voice an octave or three, Sofia scolded Nathan like a child who just failed an algebra test because he skipped his class. "Come on, Nathan. This is not like you to sit around like an *alterkaker*!"

"Don't yell at me like that, Sofia. You know I would rather be working than sitting around here all day. I feel bad enough already. All I do is take up space and create extra expenses, and I have nothing else to give. I can't even fix the car after I wrecked it." Nathan dropped his chin and covered his wet eyes with his hand. Mumbling, he said, "Mendel is letting me come in to the pharmacy every morning to continue training with him, but he can only afford to pay me for working three days a week. It's not enough, but it's the best I can do right now. I give most of it to the Kaplans to help pay for Becca's hospital costs." He choked back a lump of tears and pointed a crooked finger at Sofia. Raising his voice, he went on. "And I'll remind you that we all make mistakes we regret later, dear cousin."

He was rambling and pushing the limits of Sofia's contrived compassion. Sofia didn't need to be convinced of how badly he felt about the accident and the consequences of that night, nor did she need for him to bring up past mistakes of her own; his self-reproach and worthless apologies were not going to change anything now. Sofia burped and could taste the sweet tea bubble up from the back of her throat and coat her tongue. "What nerve you have, Nathan!

You won't get any pity from me!" Sucking in her cheeks as if she had just bit into a sour lemon, Sofia lowered her eyes and said, "Look, cousin, the way I see it is like this. We may not be able to control accidents or random situations, but we can make choices about how we handle the consequences. Our choices are not always easy, but we are free to make them." She contemplated the truth of her last statement and waited a moment to let her words sink in before continuing. "You need to get up and think about how you can get out of this rut, Nathan. A life without choices is no life at all, and the choice right now is in your hands. My father used to tell me that 'success and rest don't sleep together.' He was right, you know. Jeez, Nathan, come on! You know I love you, but all of your heartfelt apologies and a five-dollar bill wouldn't even buy you a cup of coffee in this city! Now seriously, you need to get off this couch, be strong, find courage, and make the decision to keep moving on…like the Nathan I used to know!" She closed her eyes and tried to squeeze down the pain that threatened to stream down her face in hot, heavy tears. When did she start sounding like her father? Without looking at her cousin, she carried her lukewarm tea into the kitchen and snatched up the yellow envelope sitting next to the vase of sunflowers on the table.

6

Maya

We agree to have the religious ceremony of Aaron's *brit milah* on the eighth day after his birth, as prescribed by Jewish law, but I have insisted—a bit unconventionally—that we hold off on an actual party at that time. Danny fumed over the idea of postponing the celebration he had been waiting for all his life; but reluctantly, he finally gave in, considering I didn't give him much choice with my foul mood and lack of strength after the birth. As it turns out, it is Imma who steps in and keeps it all together for us by playing marriage moderator and party planner. So here we are, a full two months later, all gathered to rejoice in the happy occasion.

The sun blazes high in the clear blue sky, but the autumn winds blow evenly through the mountains and trap gentle gusts of air to challenge the sun's heat. In the open courtyard behind the babies' cottage next to the nursery, Gali helps me set the picnic tables with blue linen tablecloths and sunflower centerpieces. Nestled in each of the bright floral bouquets is a brown stuffed bear wearing a kibbutznik's cap imprinted with a blue-and-white Israeli flag. Colorful balloons are tied to tree branches and palm trunks all around the courtyard. I inhale a deep breath of air and position my feet into first position.

Rivke waddles toward us, a huge white cake balancing precariously in front of her large bosom. She whistles an old Russian tune as she approaches, and my brother, David, rushes to grab the cake from her flour-dusted, pudgy hands.

"Here, let me take that from you, Rivke."

"Always so kind, David. How is it you are not married yet?"

My brother has been asked that question since he turned eighteen. He inherited the very best of both our parents: Imma's dedication, pride, and positive energy and Abba's rational intelligence and charisma. Every gossiping member of our kibbutz (that is, everyone over the age of ten) has been placing bets on his eventual nuptials. My money has always been on Gali as my sister-in-law.

Rivke hands the cake to David and turns to me with a wide, yellow-toothed smile. "Shalom, Maya." She hugs each of us in turn with her thick arms. A chorus of "good afternoon" and laughter breaks out, and Aaron coos happily from his stroller. Danny struts around between the tables like a proud peacock shaking its tail feathers.

Every Monday, Wednesday, and Sunday, I teach a group of kids the basics of ballet and jazz. I still wonder, if I had not gotten pregnant with Aaron and I was still dancing in Haifa, would I have been chosen to perform in Tel Aviv with Ilan? Would I have been able to become a prima ballerina like I had always dreamed? Well, it really doesn't matter anymore. All the what-ifs and who-knows-whats are completely irrelevant. I am a mother and a wife now. I work the breakfast shift in the communal kitchen while Aaron spends most of the day at the nursery and Danny is in the almond fields. My days are full and relatively uncomplicated. My fantasies of dancing and performing are now a knot of distant memories. Work and family consume my every moment and every waking concern. I am not up for the challenge of hopes and dreams anymore.

When I least expect it, however, those outdated desires sprout up and stir, clinging to my heart where no one else can see them. I can be washing Aaron's diapers, preparing Danny's lunch box, or counting out musical beats in the kibbutz studio. Visions of flying across the stage with the incomparable Mikhail Baryshnikov still haunt me; they run through my veins like the blood pumping from my heart. Some things are hard to shake, but I keep the photos and posters of my childhood idol packed away in a box at my parents' house, buried but not forgotten. For now, I live silently and vicariously through my young son and the growing successes of the dancing duo of Irena and Ilan.

David hurries to put the cake in the small nursery fridge, and I pop two pills on my dry tongue. Danny and Gali begin setting out the plastic water pools for the babies. I squint up at the afternoon sun. "Have you seen my parents, Rivke?" I ask. "They told me they would be here to help with the party."

"I'll go down and check by the stables."

"Or maybe they are at Abba's office," I suggest as Rivke trudges back up the cobblestone path.

The late afternoon sun is still blazing hot, and I can see ripples of heat stretch over the playground. A soft wind blows the scent of almond and citrus through the air. Two of Danny's childhood friends appear; they are carrying a large red cooler between them. As they get closer, I hear their laughter and grunts. I show them where they can leave the box of iced drinks and point in the direction to where Danny and Gali are now stoking the barbeque flames. Smoke smothers their faces, and David wipes the back of Gali's neck with a blue napkin. The boys grab cans of Maccabi beer from the cooler and bring one of them to Danny. Gali joins me under the shade of a bougainvillea tree.

"I can't believe how big Aaron is getting already," Gali purrs.

"I know. Time sure flies quickly."

"And where did he get those gorgeous little dimples, huh, little *motek*, sweetie pie?" Gali teases with that baby-talk chortle that annoys me to no end. She leans into Aaron's stroller and tickles him under his chin.

I rock the stroller back and forth as Gali pulls his chubby fist out of his mouth. "I think he's going to be a handful with the ladies when he grows up," she jokes. I laugh.

Suddenly, Hani runs over from the nursery and thunders toward us like she has just seen a monster. Her face is white, and her hands are clenched in tight fists by her sides. She is shouting, but no words are forming from her hysterical screams. "What is it, Hani? Calm down and talk."

David throws down the spatula and rushes over. We all stand, huddled and waiting for an explanation for Hani's outburst, while the cassette deck plays a loop of children's nursery tunes. The words finally explode from her quivering lips.

"It's Kobi… He's been in an accident!"

My brother Yaakov is our youngest sibling, and Imma has spoiled him ever since I can remember. But when Kobi, as he is affectionately called, decided to make a career of the army, Imma couldn't find the humor in his whims any longer. The thought of her baby consciously putting himself in unnecessary danger every day… Well, the idea was just ludicrous to her, and she couldn't find a way to get behind any of his arguments about it. Kobi was the last of us to serve, and Imma and Abba had bided their time, both patiently and supportively, waiting to be able to relax with the knowledge that the worst of their worries had come to an end, and their three children had completed their civic duty with pride and success. Kobi's choice to prolong his service with the threat and constant worry of danger was not in their plans, though, and they didn't take his announcement lightly.

Kobi's decision to continue serving his unit in the Israeli army detonated like a bomb in our house. Imma cried for weeks on end. She mostly remained locked in her bedroom when she wasn't working at the dairy. Abba, when not in his office, spent hours listening to the radio and reading the local newspapers. He would pace the floor and rub his hands together as if conjuring a magic trick, trying to come up with a way to convince Kobi that the situation in Israel was far too dangerous for his choice of career. "What's wrong with staying here and working on the kibbutz?" Abba begged. "Serve your country, but do it the smart way…not the hard way!"

Kobi argued that being a farmer was not a choice for him. As difficult as the decision was for him to make, he unequivocally wanted to continue his military training and become an officer. "Abba, I know things here in Israel are tough, but that doesn't mean my decision is wrong or unwise. When you and Imma had to make the decision to leave your families in Russia, didn't you both feel like you were making the right choices for yourselves? Being smart or right is not always easy, Abba, but taking the easy way out is not always smart or safe either. Please try to understand, I have to make this choice on my own."

His decision nearly shattered our family. Imma took it the hardest, I think, and would just cry and hide in her bedroom with perpetual headaches. I agreed with Kobi, though, confident in my little brother's intense will and promise. However, I knew it was best to keep my opinions silently to myself and my mouth sealed shut. David, on the other hand, openly voiced his opinion on the matter and took sides with our parents. He swore his allegiance to the land and to Israel, but he insisted it was better to do it by cultivating and strengthening the land through a strong economy and independent industry. David is so much like Abba.

I can hear my baby brother's fight in my ears now, and I could see his determined eyes in my mind. He is so eager, so hopeful, so full of possibility.

In the shade of the bougainvillea trees, my knees lock, and I don't notice my fingers fussing with the hem of my blouse. I want to do something, but I can't. Danny shakes his head in disbelief and shields his wet eyes with his charcoal-covered hand. He looks at me, and his eyes tell me to go with David. The party guests stand in shocked silence, their eyes dulled with the possible consequences of the news. Everyone in Israel is acutely sensitive to random "accidents."

David and I sprint to my parent's cottage. When we get there, we find them stuffing Kobi's army duffle bag with his toiletry kit and rolls of socks. Imma bumps into Abba, and he nearly topples over the small table beside the sofa. Both of their faces are red and wrinkled, like rotting apples, and they are grappling for air. Imma rubs at her temples and clicks her tongue. Abba swears and massages his shin where it hit the table. The cottage is airless, soundless, claustrophobic; despite this, however, a cold shiver runs up my spine and chills me to my very core.

A car screeches to a halt outside the front door. Shmulik is skidding over the cobblestone path in a dusty old Toyota, breaking all the rules of transport on the kibbutz. My parents, David, and I all squeeze into the car as Shmulik winks kindly at Abba. "I'll get you there in ten minutes, Noam. Don't worry. Everything will be okay."

We only release a collective breath when we arrive at the hospital and are immediately introduced to the attending doctor. He assures us that while Kobi's injuries are serious and have caused a slight loss of blood, my baby brother would recover with time and some physical therapy. The bullet that entered the open passenger window of his jeep had only grazed his shoulder, but the impact of the crash had caused three broken ribs and a broken wrist. The wait until we are allowed to see him seems interminable, but thankfully, he is safe, conscious, and in good spirits by the time we are allowed in to see him. David teases him about his dreadful driving skills, but Kobi's smile and twinkling eyes beam with self-possessed composure. I watch Imma exhale wet, strangled breaths and crumple into a chair. Abba, in his usual attempt to stay calm and rational, paces nervously back and forth by the window. David and I continue to take turns every fifteen minutes, requesting more information from the nurses who know nothing more than what the doctor had already told us. So much for Aaron's bris.

When we return to the kibbutz from the hospital, I rush back to what's left of Aaron's party. All of the guests have gone home by now, and only Gali sticks around to help clean up the last of the mess. David makes sure Abba and Imma get back to their cottage. Aaron, exhausted from the day's activities, is asleep in his stroller, and I gently rub my thumb over his dimpled chubby cheek. A thick, smothering cloud of self-hate pounds down on me like a sudden dust storm. I failed him again. What kind of mother am I? What mother is not present for moments like this?

Danny tells me about Hadar's clown act we missed and the hundreds of well-wishes that had been showered on our family. A knife twists in my chest and stabs me in my lungs as I try to take jagged, deep breaths in and out. My eyes well up with tears, and my brain fogs with more guilt and self-reproach. I missed my son's bris celebration, and time would never give that moment back to me.

Choices and consequences.

Courage, I tell myself.

I sniffle, turn my bloodshot guilty glare away from Danny, and scan the now-empty playground. He sees me pull away and suddenly stops talking. He runs a large, rough hand over my shoulder and pulls me into his wide chest. He begins humming one of our favorite tunes in my ear, "*Yihiyeh Tov.*" I let Danny lull me with the soft, assuring tune that promises all will be good. Finally, my eyelids grow heavy as Danny leads me toward our cottage. Safe at home, I lay Aaron in his crib and fall into my own bed. I reach out for my husband and listen for the soft, happy coos of both my boys. "All will be good," Danny repeats in my ear.

Dreams may evaporate in tomorrow's morning light, but for tonight, I dream of hope and courage. It is what gives us life, after all, and we can hold onto that as long as we want.

Sofia

It was a new year, and the Tantsor dance troupe was newly cast to perform *Swan Lake* next winter at the old Montefiori Tobacco Factory, the newest and trendiest renovated playhouse in the Dumbo district of Brooklyn under the Manhattan Bridge overpass. The industrial-looking neighborhood, with its bulky brick buildings, high-techy professionals, cobblestoned streets lined with art galleries, and fancy little boutiques, was making her both giddy with excitement and nauseous with anxiety. She was going to present both swan roles in the ballet and an additional solo performance of *The Dying Swan*. Sofia beamed with robust strength. *Imagine me, performing The Dying Swan… the famous Anna Pavlova's most incomparable ballet solo!*

Sofia Brenner would be performing the most noteworthy role of her career in the footsteps of her unparalleled idol. If all went according to her plans, the entire world would witness her prominence and brilliance as a prima ballerina, and her lifelong dream would be fulfilled.

After the hectic holiday season had come to its end, Sofia's calendar filled with nothing but unending hours of grueling dance practices and mental exercises in focus and concentration. Consumed only with the show that was slated to open in eight months, Sofia spent a minimum of ten hours each day rehearsing in the studio, sweating and agonizing to perfect her routines. By six o'clock every morning, including weekends, her workouts and practices with Boris began relentlessly until at least four in the afternoon, sometimes even later. Her meals consisted of nothing more than bags of microwave popcorn and cans of Diet Coke. While Sofia and Boris were not prancing and twirling across the studio as a duet, they were directing Becca and Andrew from the sidelines—Boris banging out the measured beats of the music with a long broom handle on the hardwood floor and Sofia encouraging Becca through each move and graceful gesture. Becca had once again secured the spot of Sofia's understudy, and Andrew was Boris's young stand-in. Andrew Turner was a sure decision for the position of understudy for Boris, and Sofia didn't dare question Becca's ambiguous placement. Her leg was still wobbly and thin, but she managed to procure the difficult feats of balance, lifting, and spinning. The pair of backups was working out to be an exceptional team, which gave Sofia an extra burst of reserved confidence. Her spirits recharged and intact, Sofia ignored the resentful and envious stares of Nina and the rest of the troupe.

After three months of a nonstop, punishing schedule, Sofia needed a break. She had lost six pounds (she was always able to maintain her weight at exactly 103 pounds, even during those times when she ate her way through endless family and holiday meals), and her beautiful feet blistered and bled through the cotton stuffed into her pointe shoes. Even as the winter turned brutally cold that year, Sofia was constantly layered in sweat and convulsing with muscle cramps.

One night was all she needed. Or so she convinced herself. One night away from the demands and frenzy of the studio, and she would be refreshed and ready to carry on. With Boris's approval and the next two days free, Sofia decided it was time to call Ben.

"Hi, sweetheart. It's great to hear from you. Where have you been?"

While Sofia had been traveling with the troupe for most of the summer and fall, the Jewish holidays with her family had taken up the bulk of her time after that. She had barely spent any time at home, and her dance schedule and the new show kept her in the studio most of her days and evenings. She hadn't had the energy to even pick up the phone and call him, let alone make time for a social date. But Sofia knew Ben wouldn't turn her down, and except for that one time nearly a year ago because of a business meeting that could not be changed, he was always loyally available when she did call on him. With his rugged good looks and overflowing Southern charm and breeding, Ben had moved to New York from Louisiana in his midtwenties as a newly hired, up-and-coming hi-tech entrepreneur—a perfect specimen of the swaggering, confident, smooth generation that was inundating northern Brooklyn at the time. Ben was an admirer of the arts—literature, music, dance—and as inadequate as his personal expertise was in any particular form (Ben was quick to remind anyone who would listen that he had spent his youth perfecting his "art" in athletics as a two-time state champion running high school track), he was still captivated by the abundance and inspiration of art and theater in the city. He met Sofia, ostensibly, while browsing through a cramped bookshop soon after arriving in New York City, and from the very moment he laid eyes on Sofia, he could not deny his attraction to her, on so many different levels.

"I've been at the studio day and night. Practicing and rehearsing like a lunatic. We have a new show opening in Dumbo at the end of the year, but it's going to be a tough performance. Anyway, I was wondering… If you aren't busy, maybe we could get together and hang out tonight."

"Sounds like a plan. Let me take care of a few things here, and I'll call you back with a specific time. It has been a while since we… Well, you know."

Sofia had met Ben in an independent bookstore in lower Manhattan two years earlier. She was looking for a novel that her aunt suggested she would like by her favorite author, the Russian Nobel Prize winner Boris Pasternak, when she was sideswiped by a man bolting carelessly from around the culture and arts section. Ben had just moved to Brooklyn from Louisiana, and he was looking for books about the history of the area. He had wandered all the way down to Brighton and found the bookstore just steps away from the train station. Concentrating on the stack of books he had collected off the shelves, he collided into Sofia and dropped the stack of books in his arms. Catching a wicked spark that lit up his fiery-blue eyes, Sofia could feel a rush of blood surge through her body. She stared back at his curly mess of dark hair, boyish grin, and dimpled cheeks. He began apologizing for running into her as if he had committed murder against the pope and offered to buy her a cup of hot chocolate at the bookstore's bar. That sealed it for Sofia—a gorgeous man with a love of books and chocolate. *How could I go wrong?* she thought.

An easy decision, Sofia and Ben had been together ever since that day.

Now on the phone, she blushed the shade of borscht and agreed, "Yes, I do know. It's been too long." Not wanting to sound too eager, she added, "So I'll make us dinner here, and you can bring the wine."

It was close to nine o'clock when Ben finally rang the doorbell. Sofia rushed through the kitchen, making sure she had thrown out the jar of Newman's Own tomato sauce and the bag of pre-cut kale before letting Ben in. She combed her fingers through her loose ginger hair and tugged at her earlobes, heavy with the weight of gleaming diamond studs.

As Sofia opened the front door and peered down the hallway, Ben stormed out of the elevator holding a bottle of red wine and a bundle of delicate white lilies. He rushed at Sofia and began pecking at her with gentle kisses on her lips and throat. Sofia let her body melt into his as she purred with excited desire.

"Hello to you too," Sofia moaned and let Ben push his way into the apartment.

They rushed through their dinner of spaghetti and meatballs, made small-talk about Sofia's upcoming performance and Ben's latest tech project for his company, and made their way to the sofa in the tiny living room before Sofia could offer dessert. The furniture in her apartment still remained sparse but for a small woven rug and a collage of family photos and old posters of Baryshnikov on the white walls that colored the space with a warm, lived-in ambiance. Scented candles lit the room and cast a suggestive explosion of cinnamon into the air. Sofia placed the open, almost-empty bottle of wine and their two glasses on the coffee table, but Ben quickly grabbed her by her shoulder and spun her around to face him. In a matter of seconds, clothes and shoes and belts were flung across the room, and Sofia gave in to the flame that ignited her passion from deep inside her core. Sofia sighed and let her impulses take complete control of her body and mind.

Sofia didn't want to remember her first sexual experience, but she couldn't help it. The memory of Josh managed to seep into her conscious every time she had an intimate encounter with a man. The memory always began with pleasant and amusing images of the handful of suitors that called on her as a teenager in Ukraine. None of them were ever allowed by her parents to escort her farther out the door than down the street for an hour (or two, if the boy was lucky) to the local coffee shop where dozens of nosy neighbors gathered. Thinking of those young boys, Sofia exhaled a ragged breath of air and tried to tame the coming urge to push away. As Ben hungrily rocked his body against hers, Sofia let her hot breath skim Ben's ear, creating a bidding that she willingly invited and encouraged.

Then came the barrage of later images: the familiar ache in her belly and the throbbing in her head, the overwhelming thrashing of one stupid, impulsive, childish whim. Why had she made such a ridiculous choice to go off by herself? It was one year after arriving in America, young and carefree and newly transplanted into the Little Odessa neighborhood of her uncle, aunt, cousin, and fellow immigrant countryfolk. But she should have known she was still too naive to venture out to a place like Coney Island on her own.

She had moved halfway around the world, leaving behind her parents and friends, but Sofia's life had changed little beyond that. While she spoke perfect unaccented English, she still found herself often reverting to common Russian and Ukranian expressions.

Also, she still ate the same foods and danced in the best Russian-run academies. The collection of wooden Matryoshka dolls that filled the shelves along the living room wall of her aunt and uncle's cluttered, gaudy apartment—a blind mish-mash of random dust-collecting *tchotchkes*—made her feel like she was still in her parents' home back in Lutsk. She often felt the urge to knock those nesting dolls down as if they were mini bowling pins. Within a few months, Sofia had already begun to feel empowered, emboldened, and confident enough that she was ready to explore on her own in nearby Coney Island. Her older cousin, Nathan, had been promising to take her there, but she got tired of waiting around for him and his promises. So off she went on her own.

It was a Saturday morning, and Nathan had carelessly left his wallet on the living room coffee table—right in plain view—the night before. She swiped a twenty-dollar bill, turning her attention away from the fact that she was committing a terrible sin, especially on the holy day of Shabbos (but he had owed it to her, didn't he?), and ventured out of her familiar neighborhood for the first time by herself.

As soon as she left the apartment, though, all of her guilt for stealing the money and sneaking off faded away, and Sofia was pumped with childlike excitement and bravery. She had hopped on the D subway line all the way to the famous Coney Island, clinging to the edge of her skirt with one hand and the train car's handrail with the other. She got off and walked one way on Surf Avenue, where she stopped to have a hot dog and fries at Nathan's and then continued back up in the other direction along the boardwalk, all the while staring wide-eyed at all the noisy, flashy attractions and the chaotic swarms of people. Sofia blended right into the crowds, her face awestricken and her head in the clouds. As the sun blazed above, and the ocean breeze kicked up from the shore, Josh Reznik appeared out of nowhere.

Josh was from Manhattan and had been wandering around Coney Island looking for a good time. He found Sofia and followed her until they were both standing in the dusky shadow of the Ferris wheel. Looking up at the height of the wheel, both Sofia and Josh bumped into each other and simultaneously blubbered, "Oh, I'm sorry. I wasn't paying attention." Josh cast a crooked grin at Sofia. Sofia's freckles faded under the crimson blush that spread up from her neck, and that was it. Sofia was lost.

They rode the Ferris wheel together—Sofia beaming with awe at the vast world that unfolded beneath her when the ride jolted to a stop as they reached the top and Josh snuggling up against her, whispering words of cool protection and assurance every time she squealed with alarm. It wasn't long after the ride was over and they were both on solid ground again that Josh offered to drive Sofia back home. It was getting late; she had been out all day, and Sofia welcomed the kind gesture. But the ride home, she would soon discover, came with a price she was not willing to pay. Sofia had the innate sense to run. And run is what she did. Knocking into late strollers, and even once avoiding a near collision with a city bus, Sofia managed to escape Josh and the horrifying possible consequences of her brazen, careless choices that day.

For years after that, Sofia couldn't trust anyone; the slightest touch of a man made her squeamish and would send her into frenzied panics. It was her first experience with a man, and she had foolishly allowed him to control her decisions that day in Coney Island. It was only in hindsight that she realized how lucky she was to have escaped an unimaginable situation. With the strength her father had instilled in her—and the will of God (He must have forgiven her for stealing the money from Nathan, she believed)—Sofia had managed to make it back on the D-train with her wounded pride and a few scratches on her arm. She had been fooled by whimsical choices and weak decisions.

Little by little, she learned to control her fears and anxiety; through dance lessons and recitals, Sofia was able to temper those fiery embers whenever they were stoked. She had vowed that she would never lose control of her good senses again, nor would she allow anyone to influence her decisions or change her path. Things would be her way or no way. She was free, strong, and in control, and she would never surrender herself to anyone, ever again.

The following morning, after a night of consuming, thrilling lovemaking, Ben snored in peaceful slumber at her side. Sofia's feet began to cramp with pain, and all her muscles from her neck to her ankles burned with exhaustion. She watched Ben's broad chest rise and fall with calm, rhythmic breaths as Sofia deflated like a worn tire. She swung his arm off her belly and sluggishly unwrapped herself from the mess of sheets and blankets around her. Naked, she trudged to the kitchen and put a kettle of water on the stove. Then she crawled back to the bathroom and locked the door behind her. Staring at her smudged makeup and tangled hair, Sofia raised her eyebrows and made a fresh decision.

Throwing on a pair of underwear, an oversized sweatshirt, and thick, fuzzy pink bedroom slippers, Sofia made her way back into the kitchen where Ben was already sitting at the table looking through a copy of the *New York Times*. Sofia kissed him on the back of his neck and poured two cups of tea before taking a seat at the table across from him. She began to speak, but she had no idea what she was going to say. All she knew was that she wanted Ben to leave so she could be alone.

Ben raked his hand through his tousled hair, set down the newspaper, and nervously fingered the edge of the vinyl placemat. "What do you mean I 'have to leave'? I thought we could spend some time together today, or at least…" A wide, rascally grin spread across his face.

But Sofia was not amused with Ben's flirtatious innuendos. The more he protested, the more she just wanted him to go and leave her alone. His continuous whining and childish teasing weren't helping the situation either. She needed something more at the moment, something just her own, and there was only one place she could find it. She tapped her foot anxiously on the kitchen tile, quickly grabbed their teacups, and dropped them with a jarring clank into the kitchen sink.

Fishing for an excuse that would not offend him, Sofia reminded him of her cousin's accident and explained that she needed to visit Nathan. She wouldn't have another opportunity to do so for a while, and she had to take advantage of her day off. It wasn't true, but it was the only excuse she could come up with.

Red-faced with frustration, Ben finally gave in. "Fine. I guess I'll see you soon. Whenever you have a free moment, you know where you can find me." He exhaled a blast of air and nearly toppled the vase of sweet lilies that stood in the middle of the table as he stood up from his seat. Sofia thought she heard him slur something else under his breath, but she couldn't make out his words. Without looking back at her, he left the apartment, slamming the door behind him. Sofia exhaled a sigh, left the teacups in the sink, and got ready to head out to the studio. So much for time off.

8

Maya

The evening air is still sticky, hot, and electrifying, despite the receding sun. Deep breaths are hard to swallow, and I feel like I'm being strangled every time I try to fill my lungs with the briny sea air. I'm not sure if it's the sultry weather or the exhilaration of seeing the show tonight that tackles me as the bus whirrs down the seaside road toward Tel Aviv. Buildings as tall as the famed Empire State Building rise in front of me, creating a breathtaking skyscape against the azure ocean and the crimson setting sun, the architecture and colors more beautiful than art in a museum. We slowly make our way through the congested city traffic. My knuckles are stretched tight as I clench my backpack against my chest, and my jaw is clenched with anticipation as the reckless city drivers slither questionably close to the Egged public bus. They honk and threaten to scrape right up against us. There must be thousands of people ambling around the city as if it were designed for their personal needs and purpose, and the constant blasts of horns and wandering jaywalkers add to my jumpy impatience. I wish I had the nonchalant ease that these city dwellers seem to possess. Finally, the grand theater appears ahead of me, and the bus makes a sudden stop in the middle of the bustling traffic.

Irena and Ilan are home from their worldwide tour, dancing at the Tel Aviv Performing Arts Center again, and Irena has arranged two front-row tickets for me and Danny for tonight's performance. Danny, unfortunately, is on his mandatory army reserve duty this week, but the good news is that I was given a free weekend from the kibbutz to come by myself. Danny and I had argued about my coming on my own, but by the time he realized there was nothing he could do to stop me from coming, he gave up on the notion of my declining the invitation and even helped me pack my overnight bag. That's how things are between Danny and me these days. He never hid his disdain for my friendship with Irena, but this time, he was even more infuriated about my leaving the kibbutz…leaving Aaron…leaving him.

"Are you bringing this thing?" Danny asked, stuffing my bag with the piles of clothes I had laid out on our bed. He was holding up a daring black-and-red bikini I had bought last summer on a dare in Haifa. "Why do you need this if you are only going to the theater? Besides, it's the middle of winter!"

Did he not hear me tell him that the boutique hotel that Irena has arranged for the weekend has an indoor pool?

Secretly enjoying Danny's apparent jealousy and chauvinistic attention, I suppressed a provoking laugh. "Danny, you sound ridiculous." I grabbed the bikini from his raised arm and shot a glance at the cobalt-blue silk mini dress trimmed with silver sequins that was hanging on the back of the closet door. Irena had lent it to me;

she told me that a new Russian seamstress that the Haifa school had found for the costumes for their last show had made it for her as a gift. It was the most beautiful dress I had ever seen, and luckily, it fit me just right. I held my breath and hugged the dress in front of me. Smiling and blushing at my husband, I blew him an exaggerated kiss and folded the dress into its plastic dress bag. I was definitely going to need my duffle bag as well as my backpack.

"I still can't understand why you need so much stuff! And I don't like you hanging around with Irena. She's a bad influence on you." He bites his lip, knowing he has just said the wrong thing.

"I know you don't mean that. Don't you trust me?"

"Er, yes, er, I do trust you, but why can't Gali go with you?" Danny sulks. "She could use my extra ticket for the show." Danny's hesitant words and childish reactions say much more than he is intending, and I wonder why he is so doubtful of me now.

"Gali is pregnant again and is about to pop any day," I remind him, rubbing my own barren, flat belly. "The last thing she wants to do now is travel to a big, congested city and be away from her family and home." Ever since Gali married my older brother, David, Danny has become increasingly more irritable about their fast-growing family and our lack of one. I understand this. But it is his insinuation that Irena is a bad influence on me that rings in my ears and ignites a fury inside me. The amusement I found with Danny's discomfort from just seconds earlier fades behind the burning flames of anger that now blind me, and I feel my compassion for him drain away.

Why should this be any different than any other argument between us? For a few years now, our quarrelling about my desire to spend so much of my time dancing and my lack of ability to *stay* pregnant has become sharper and more constant with each passing tick of the clock. At times, it's all I can do from wanting to run away and audition for a proper spot with the dance troupe in Haifa. Only hiding myself in the studio there has offered temporary moments of refuge. And now with Aaron, I don't even have that.

I am going to Tel Aviv, come rain or shine. Whether Danny likes it or not.

The ballet performance is brilliant. Irena and Ilan are brilliant. Their recital is perfect. The packed audience rewards them with thunderous applause and waves of ovations. After the last curtain call, I find my way backstage where the atmosphere is charged with electric energy, glittery costumes, and dancers who flutter about in all directions. My blue silk and sequined dress fades in comparison with the bloom of stage costumes, but I try to imagine fitting right into the sizzling scene around me as if I were one of the dancers. I wait for Irena to change out of her costume as I work my way through the crowd and congratulate the dancers on the evening's performance. I look for Ilan, but he is nowhere to be found. Someone suggests that he might have slipped out before the reporters could find him.

Lost in my thoughts, I coo under my breath with surging nostalgia. I can't believe how many years have come and gone since my first audition and those golden, dream-filled days of local recitals and studio rehearsals. Oh, how I still longed for those days…

Suddenly, I am jolted back to the present—Irena is pulling me by the elbow and leading me out of the crowded backstage area into the crowded city. Changed into tight jeans and a seductive, tight white button-down blouse, her face scrubbed clean of the caked-on makeup and stage glitter, she is as beautiful and graceful as ever. "I'm so happy you're here with me tonight, my dear friend. Did you enjoy the show?" Irena's natural poise and animation flow effortlessly around her, and she does not wait for my answer. She really doesn't need to hear my praise. She is completely aware that she, once again, stole the show. Instead, she turns to the backstage door and says, "I know exactly where we are going to go now. Wait 'til you see this new bar. It's the talk of the town!"

Some reporters and even some local recognizable producers remain lingering in the darkened hallway leading out to the parking lot, their pens poised to note anything Irena might offer as a blurb for their stories. Irena obliges them and stops to offer a few soundbites before batting her eyelashes and making excuses for our hasty retreat. A mix of emotions gurgles up from inside my ribcage. If I didn't love and cherish my friend so much, I would have hated her at that moment, the chronic, selfish resentment pooling in my gut and slowly spreading through my veins. She commands the stage and the praise—in front of and behind the curtains—and she knows it. But I know Irena like I know Ilan. They are complete opposites. While Ilan hides from the public eye and prefers to let others take center stage, Irena can't hide that typical ballerina arrogance that springs naturally from her. I hide a smirk with my hand and swallow a small burp of air.

I stop cold in my tracks, just as a photographer aims his camera and snaps a stream of photos of Irena and me. It could have been me on that stage. Couldn't it? It could have been me they are all flocking around to see now. My knees buckle, and I feel like I am going to vomit. I reach out and grab hold of Irena's sinewy shoulder.

Blinking to clear my head, I smile for the camera and wave my hand like the Queen of England addressing her adoring constituents. The small crowd around us parts and creates an opening for us, as if they are making way for the country's beloved prime minister himself, and we are released from the pressing throng of fans like a cork popping from a champagne bottle. I have no time to entertain any more thoughts of "what if," so I push my way through the noisy mob on the proverbial coattails of my dear friend, desperately trying to regain my spectator's focus. My tongue is dry, and my toes spasm inside my three-inch stiletto pumps.

Twenty-five minutes later, after strolling our way on foot through the nonstop pulse of Tel Aviv, Irena and I arrive at a trendy, romantic wine bar near Habima Square. The cool winter air blowing from the Tel Aviv seashore makes our brisk walk refreshing and effortless, but I'm grateful that Imma lent me her velvet cape for the weekend. The place is packed with young, loud, carefree Israelis, all wrapped in the vibrating energy that a night out in the big city has to offer. It is everything Irena had promised, from a packed crowd that spills onto the street curb to the blaring music that pumps loudly over the animated conversations of the patrons, to the continuous pouring of colorful drinks in large glasses. Irena and I snatch a table near the front corner of the sidewalk patio. I immediately slide my squished feet out of my pumps, cross my legs, and dangle one shoe on the end of my toes.

A faint, relaxed sigh of reprieve hisses from behind my clenched teeth. It feels good to sit down after the walk from the theater, but I still feel a bit lost and out of place. I can deal with my aching feet (something all of us dancers eventually get used to), and I can lose all self-doubt when dancing on a stage (the egotism plagues us all too), but being in a vast crowd—in a big city—I am as uncomfortable in my own skin as a vulnerable lone rabbit lost in the woods. Taking in Irena's perfect posture and nonchalant composure, though, I quickly remind myself to sit up straight against the back of my chair and cross my legs subtly at my ankles beneath the table. I hang my mother's cape carefully over the back of my chair. This is the luxurious break I've been waiting for, and I intend to take advantage of every free and happy moment.

Irena's eyes are focused on something in the distance behind me, and she whispers through clenched teeth, "Don't look now, but I think we have a stalker. I saw this man lurking backstage at the theater before. He must have followed us here. He's a real cutie too!" She reaches for her purse, and I pray she is not carrying a small weapon in it. That would be all I need now—a fanatical, dramatic incident so that Danny could later claim he was right about his doubts of letting me come to Tel Aviv without him. I cautiously twist my head around in the direction of her stare, and my eyes bulge from their sockets.

Swinging a cascade of hair to one side, a puff of air escapes my parted lips. I grab my own purse and quickly retrieve two pills from the vial hidden inside the zippered lining. "God, what is he doing here?" I ask out loud to no one really, as if Irena even knows what I am talking about. She pulls out a small compact from her purse and carefully reapplies her red lipstick.

Suddenly realizing her error in judgment, Irena closes her purse and returns it to her lap. "You know him?" Irena asks with incredulity laced in her voice. Her eyes pop wide open, and she hits her head with the palm of her hand. Her other hand scratches her craned neck, and her purse tumbles to the floor.

"Yeah, that's Boaz. Danny's best friend." I haven't told Irena anything about my argument with Danny about coming to see the show and spending time with her in Tel Aviv. Of course, over the years, she has probably sensed his ill feelings toward her and our friendship.

"What on earth?" Irena's voice rises two octaves. Her eyes bulge in shock at finding a kibbutznik here in Tel Aviv—let alone one that shows up at the theater…alone.

"I'm sure Danny sent him to spy on us." I chuckle, trying to hide my own curiosity and sounding as blasé about it as I can.

Irena wiggles seductively in her seat and plays with the low-cut edging of her blouse's neckline. I could tell she wants to say something else. I know her better than anyone, and I could tell she was looking for trouble with Boaz. I put my hand up to my forehead as if shielding my eyes from the bright neon lights above us. A warm tingle fills my head, the pills taking immediate effect. Taking a quick look over my shoulder to where Boaz is sitting at the bar, I say, "Wait here a minute. I'll be right back."

Boaz is wearing his American jeans and a neat polo shirt. His curly hair is a mess, though, and his fingernails are rimmed with black grease. I look up at him just as he orders a beer from the bartender. I replace my shoes on my feet and stand up.

"Where are you going, Maya? Are you going to talk to Boaz?" She takes a sip of her beer and bats her long eyelashes.

I make my way through the crowd, and just as I get within arm's length of Boaz, he turns to face me and croaks, "Hello, Maya. Fancy meeting you here in Tel Aviv. How'd you manage to escape the kibbutz?" A nervous chuckle escapes his throat as he leans over to kiss the top of my head.

I inhale an exhausted gulp of air and blow it out through pouty lips. Throwing one graceful hand up in the air to get the bartender's attention, I point over to our table where Irena sits waiting alone, fixing her dark hair in her compact and shimmying her shoulders.

I pick up Boaz's beer from the bar and motion for him to join us at our table. Boaz follows, and I purposely sway my hips with exaggerated swagger. Boaz pulls out my chair for me and sits down in the chair next to Irena. He searches her face for any sign of recognition, but his stare shows he is coming up blank. "So what are you two beautiful ladies doing here tonight? Maya, Danny didn't tell me you were going to be in Tel Aviv."

"No, I don't suppose he would have told you. I came to see the ballet while Danny is doing reserve duty this week. Oh, how rude of me. Let me introduce you to my friend, Irena Plotkin. She's my dearest friend, but I'm sure you recognize her from the theater tonight. Irena, this is our friend from Gan Notzah, Boaz Gittleman." I lower my gaze and blink several times. Boaz clears his throat and takes a huge gulp of his beer. His eyes dart around the bar, landing on anything but me. He knows he's been caught.

"*Na'im me'od.* Very nice to meet you." Boaz wipes the frost from the rim of his beer glass and shuffles his feet under the table. He kicks the leg of my chair, and I let out a loud screech. Boaz makes a dramatic scene of excusing his clumsy manners.

"So sorry. I didn't mean…"

Ignoring the fuss he's making, Irena says, "So tell us, Boaz. I would never take you for a ballet enthusiast, but did you like the show tonight? I noticed you earlier at the theater." Irena stares right at Boaz, as cool as the winter wind blowing in from the Mediterranean Sea.

"Actually, I didn't see the show. I was only there to find my friend and his girlfriend so we could all come here." Boaz turns to me and adds, "You remember my buddy Doron from the army and his girlfriend, don't you, Maya? Well, I didn't find them at the theater, and they are not here now either. *Ani col-cach co'es*! I'm so pissed off!"

"What a shame. I wonder where they could be. Would you like to use my cell to call them?" Irena's words spill from her crimson lips like honey from a full beehive.

"No, that's okay. I have my phone. But it's getting late already, and I have a long drive back to the north. I'll call Doron and tell him we'll have to meet another time. Maya, if you want, I can take you back to the kibbutz."

Boaz catches me off guard. With the ambiance feeling more and more like a pickup scene, I feel like a third wheel at the table, and my attention has floated above the excitement of the partying crowd. Snapping back to the conversation, I manage to reply, "Thanks, but that's okay. I'm staying in Tel Aviv with Irena for the weekend, and I can get back home by myself." I bite my lower lip, cross my long, muscular legs, and graze the top of my exposed thigh with the tips of my fingers. The blue sequined fringe of my dress sparkles against my pale skin.

I lean forward and shoot a lighthearted sideways glance at Irena that says, *Let him go back without me tonight and tell Danny that he saw us hanging out and drinking in a bar…at midnight!*

Boaz reaches for Irena's hand and places it up to his lips. Scanning the crowded, shadowy space around us, I try to appear as if I hadn't a care in the world. I whisper, "It was a nice surprise running into you tonight. Have a safe drive home."

With that, Boaz finishes the last dregs of his beer and stands up. "It was a pleasure to meet you, Ms. Plotkin."

"Please, call me Irena. Any friend of my dear Maya is a friend of mine." Coolly, coyishly, and practiced, she smiles at Boaz and lowers her gaze.

As Boaz walks away from our table, head bobbing above the crowd, my mind begins to take flight. No matter how far I go to escape, I cannot hide. Things with Danny have been icy, at best, and I have run out of places to turn. Boaz's presence here in Tel Aviv tonight triggers an avalanche of emotions that I thought I could leave behind and forget about for a while. Chained to me still are all the doubts, the deceptions, the regrets.

I spend more and more time thinking about the studio, the stage, the lights, and the excitement of performing—the music, the dance, the freedom… My old dreams of pirouettes and adoring applause… It is me who is unhappy and unfulfilled with the choices I've made in my life, and it is not Danny's fault that my dreams don't really include children or an uninspiring job in the communal kitchen, cooking and cleaning up after a thousand other people. I know I should be grateful for what I have, but…

It's not what I want. I don't want to live a simple, satisfied life, just because it's safe and easy. Like my younger, wiser brother, Kobi, always says, "Even though it may be difficult to do, it is better to make the right choice than just the safe and easy one."

I'm afraid I made a mistake. I'm afraid I made the easy choice. The one that is safe and predictable but not the right one for me. I face that fear of my choices every time I look into Aaron's pudgy little newborn face.

On the other hand, I know I am responsible for my decisions—good or bad—and I have to make the best of the consequences. After all, it is I alone who made the choice to stay on the kibbutz, to get married, and to commit to a family. No one put a gun to my head and made me stay there. I could have chosen a different path.

But I didn't.

The added weight of my guilt and shame for selfishly wanting something more—something different—plagues me, and I fight to hide the lonely desperation that has lodged in my heart. I am trapped like a lightning bug in a glass jar, and I fear Danny is just as frustrated as I am with all the changes and threats that my dreams pose for us. Something is bound to snap, sooner or later.

Shouldn't I be grateful for what I have? Should I begrudge a safe and stable life with a loving husband and a wonderful son? A father and mother and brothers that would do anything for me? A community that works together for the greater good?

Yes, I am grateful. And it is never too late to be happy.

My choice.

The thumping bass music and the noise of the gregarious crowd compete with the rumbling in my head. A sudden explosion of laughter from the table to our right rocks my thoughts, and I am jogged back in the moment.

"Hey, Maya. I'm talking to you. Where are you, my friend?" The din of the music and Irena's words blur in a haze as I shake off my sullen trance.

"Sorry, I think I'm not feeling so well. What were you saying?"

"It is nothing important. Just kibitzing about Boaz and the kibbutz." Irena uses air quotes to emphasize the words *kibitz* and *kibbutz*. She lets slip an unladylike snort, amused by her own wit. Then she sighs and adds, "What's the deal with Boaz? Does he have a girlfriend or what?"

"Oh, no, Irena. Don't even go there. Boaz may be Danny's best friend, but he's a big chauvinistic player. He's cute and funny, and he knows it! He's quite the ladies' man at the kibbutz!" I try to shed the lack of confidence and confusion I am feeling, but the nervous bouncing up and down of my foot and the quiver in my voice expose my true insecurity. I close my eyes and take a swig of beer; a warm, familiar flow curdles under my skin. The pills.

Irena's thin eyebrows arch upward as she sputters, "Ladies' man, *shmaydies'* man! Who's talking about a relationship? I was just wondering… Well, let's talk about something else."

I shiver and wrap my mother's cape around my shoulders. Happy to steer the subject away from Boaz, I announce, "David and Gali are expecting their baby any day now. I think Gali will probably give birth within the week." I twirl the beer glass in front of me and take another long sip.

Irena quickly interrupts my pointless gossip and turns the conversation back to her. "So have I told you the good news? I think we might be going to America! Ilan says we have a good shot at being invited to perform in Philadelphia. I've never been, but I love the United States."

9

Sofia

The air was crisp and cool outside—the winter stubbornly making an early appearance—and Sofia was beyond exhaustion. On top of the relentless pushing from Boris to practice for her role in *The Dying Swan*, they had spent months traveling and performing all over the country. Two, three, four shows each week had become their normal routine, and when they were not on stage in front of an audience, the Tantsor troupe spent the better part of their days in rented studios rehearsing together for their big Christmas extravaganza of *Swan Lake*. It was a wonder Sofia could keep her head on straight with the intense schedule she was keeping, but the more she danced, the more boundless she felt. Dancing was the only place she felt in control, at home, perfect.

They had just returned from a tiring week in Dallas, but Sofia was in high spirits. Her popularity as a lead dancer—the prima ballerina of one of New York City's most acclaimed Russian ballet academies—was beginning to follow her, and the media devoured her at every turn. Time was strengthening her professional resolve, and Sofia was enjoying every minute of the ride. She was reaching the prominence in her career that her parents had always supported and expected of her. She had even received a nomination on the short list for the envious *Prix Benois de la Danse* award earlier that year. (Later, she would ultimately be beaten out by the ballerina assoluta from the American Ballet Theater in Manhattan, but even that did not dissuade her.) Sofia was certain her day was coming. *Just wait 'til they see me as the dying swan!* Sofia swore over and over.

It was a surprise to all of them then when Boris suggested they all take the night off and enjoy an evening by the ocean. The waves soothed him, he had said, and he was inspired by the notion of the rehabilitating effects that the sea would have on the minds and bodies of his company. No one blinked twice as some of the members of the cast began to quickly pack up their gear and happily suggested they all meet at the Brighton Beach boardwalk.

When her small group arrived, Sofia was relieved to see that the seasonal tourists were not yet crowding the area and that the spray of the ocean waves was indeed as therapeutic as Boris had suggested. She couldn't remember the last time she enjoyed the beach and the laid-back feeling of being "home." She grabbed Becca's hand and led her closer to the shoreline. Sofia breathed in the briny air and chuckled at the sight of dozens of old men playing chess on boards that lay precariously balanced between them on park benches. Boris stepped between the girls and led them to the popular restaurant that had just opened between East Boardwalk and Brightwater Court. The flapping green awning and yellow tablecloths of the newest hotspot on the boardwalk were inviting; Sofia grinned and relaxed her shoulders as the familiar vibe of her old neighborhood overtook her.

Another group of young dancers from the troupe at Tantsor had already arrived and had taken their seats at a large outdoor patio table. Loud and rambunctious, Christine, Patrick, and Nina waved their arms for attention from the patio, and Flora let out a shrill whistle through her two front teeth. "Hey, guys, we're over here." Chairs scratched loudly along the wooden floor planks as Sofia tried to position herself around the table set for eight as far away from Nina as possible, but she found herself standing directly next to her. By the time everyone found their places around the table and sat down, the only open seat left was the one directly to Nina's left. Sofia slumped into the open chair, purposely knocking her backpack into Nina's head.

"Ooohh, so sorry," Sofia offered, with a hand to her sneering lips. Nina scooted her chair over and glared up at Sofia.

"Watch it, clumsy," Nina snorted through clenched teeth and tight lips.

Taking the seat on the other side of Sofia, Becca was panting wildly as if she was going to hyperventilate. Sofia found herself stuck between competing distractions, like an animal caught in quicksand.

"Oy, vey," Becca blurted. "He's here. And I look like a *shmate*!" she screeched. She frantically clawed at the sleeve of Sofia's jean jacket.

"Let go of me, Becca. Calm down! *Who*'s here? And who cares what you look like? We're at the beach... We're home!"

Sofia followed Becca's wide-eyed stare and found Nathan at the other end of it. He was wearing a yellow apron over a light-blue button-down polo, a pen lodged over his ear. His face brightened with a beaming smile as he walked over to the table and stood between Sofia and Becca. "What a great surprise to see you here. How do you like Galina's new restaurant?"

Sofia turned her head up to her cousin and raised her eyebrows. "Hey, cousin, I think the better question is, what are *you* doing here?"

Nathan bent down toward her and kissed her on both cheeks. Then he winked at Becca and blushed a deep red. "Hi, Becca. You didn't tell her?" Not waiting for an answer, he continued, "Yeah, I got a job here in the evenings. It's great money, the tourists love it, and I'm finally getting back on my own two feet again. Just like you suggested, cousin." His sarcasm was erased by the sincere twinkle in his blue eyes. The scar over his left eyebrow danced as he winked at Nina.

Sofia looked at him with stunned surprise and annoyed shock. How dare he flirt with Nina! And right in front of Becca! Huffing, Sofia punched Nathan lightly in the stomach and brought his attention back home. "What's with Mendel Cohen and the pharmacy? Don't you still have a job with old Mr. Cohen? Don't tell me you've given up on your med school dreams!"

"No, I haven't given up yet. It would take more than a couple of broken ribs and a hospital debt to make me forget about my dreams. I still go into work at the pharmacy during the days when Mendel needs me. But I'm feeling much better now, and the tips here are pretty good. I could use the extra money to help Mom and Pop buy a new car. Besides, I thought a lot about what you said the last time you came by, so I got off my *tokhes* and 'found strength to carry on.'" He straightened his shoulders and waved his hand to his forehead, like a soldier saluting his commanding officer. Nathan was talking to Sofia but kept his eyes riveted on Nina.

Becca's color drained from her face as she smoothed her hand over her faded "I♥NY" sweatshirt. In a bashful whisper, she said, "Sorry I forgot to mention it to you, Sofia! I knew Nathan was working here, but we haven't had time to talk lately."

"I heard about this place all the way up in Williamsburg," Boris chimed in. "Is it as good as they say?"

"The locals seem to love it. Very authentic, quality dishes. We're constantly busy every night. And you gotta believe that if the locals here approve, it's gotta be good!" Nathan smiled at the group and removed the pen from behind his ear. "Can I get you all some drinks? Maybe a bottle of vodka?"

Nathan, proud and confident, suggested they try the *varenyky* dumplings, "One order with potato and mushrooms, one order with cherries and sour cream, since they're both so good." Boris, Becca, and Sofia helped the others choose a variety of ethnic favorites from the menu. Nina was the only one at the table to protest.

"Why is everything on the menu so fattening? Why did we have to come all the way here for this? I think I'll just have an unsweetened iced tea and a kale salad. You do have that here, don't you?" she asked Nathan with a dubious grin and a tweak of condescension in her words.

Sofia wanted to punch her in the gut. Instead, she picked up her water glass and stuck out her elbow as she slurped the water loudly. Her long arm jutted right into Nina's shoulder, and Nina jerked her slender body away with a shriek. "Hey, watch it, Sofia. What's with you? You've been getting in my way all night!"

Sofia stifled a laugh and considered the irony. *No, Nina. You got it all backward. It's you who is in my way.* "So sorry, Nina. This table isn't quite big enough for all of us, I guess."

As soon as Nathan reappeared and placed the dishes on the table, the rowdy group was finally quieted by their grumbling stomachs and their watering mouths. Sofia quickly grabbed her fork but dropped it on the floor between her chair and Nina's. This time, her clumsiness was not deliberate. She cursed under her breath and bent down to pick up the fork. In a split second, she was scrambling on all fours beneath the tablecloth and between the legs of the table. While under the table, Sofia couldn't help but notice that Nina had removed her revolting nine-hundred-dollar Gucci screener sneakers (with crystals!) from her feet. Sofia could see her pointy toes and the high arch of her perfect little feet. She wanted to barf! Still on the ground, swiping her hand across the dirty floor hoping to retrieve the lost fork, Sofia recalled the first time she had laid eyes on Nina Cassel. The tall beauty had stumbled into the Tantsor Russian Ballet & Dance Academy, nonchalantly introducing herself and announcing that she had an appointment for a two o'clock audition. In her perfect American accent, she stood out like a sore thumb in the heavily Russian-filled school. Sofia and Boris had been in the middle of a rehearsal for a recital they were performing that night, but they jumped to attention as Nina stared confidently and unaffected in the open door of the studio. Sofia could still remember how Nina danced for that audition and how Boris could not wipe the ridiculous grin off his face as they watched her glide effortlessly with wide, sweeping arm movements and poised, controlled steps. She hadn't perspired a drop through her entire routine, and her technique was graceful and flawless. Sofia had watched the audition, frozen with awe behind the large glass windows of the main studio, and felt ill by the time Nina had taken her final bow. She hated to admit it, then and now, but Nina Cassel was a picture-perfect ballerina. She had a long neck and long, slender legs and muscular shoulders (although a bit broader in the back than the other dancers in the troupe). The directors of the academy didn't waste a single day in announcing their decision to accept Nina's application to join the Tantsor's corps de ballet.

On the filthy floor of the restaurant, Sofia felt the *holubtsi* coming back up in her esophagus. In a split-second decision, she grabbed Nina's nauseating sneakers and shoved them into her backpack. Something poked at her knee, and she reached for the lost fork. As she crawled out from under the table, her head banged against the edge, causing all the silverware and dishes to clatter above her. "Found it!" she yelled, standing and holding up the fork like a trophy. Becca, on one side, chuckled at her friend's silliness; Nina, on the other side, huffed and rolled her eyes.

For the rest of the evening, the jovial group of dancers were served with more food than they could ever dream of finishing; they drank generous shots of vodka that flowed from a bottomless bottle and kicked up a noisy fuss of continuous laughter that floated all the way to the open waters of the Atlantic Ocean coastline. Sofia couldn't have asked for a more comforting place to be that night. She was surrounded by dedicated, talented dancers in a place of familial intimacy, swathed like a caterpillar in its safe cocoon. Not even Nina could distract her from her familial reverie. Sofia's cheeks ached from the constant smile plastered on her face, and her stomach thanked her for all the delectable food by sending up a constant string of tiny burps.

But Sofia was awoken from her entrancing calm when Becca tugged at her jacket and declared the evening had come to its end. "Hey, Sofia. *H-e-l-l-o-o-o*! Did you hear me? Nathan is finishing up with his shift and offered to drive us both home. Let's go before my parents throw a fit."

"Okay, Becca. I need to go to the bathroom first, but I'll meet you back at the entrance—"

Sofia's words were interrupted by a loud scream. "Shit! Damn it! Where are they?" Nina was cursing and hammering her fist against the bright-yellow tablecloth. She bent over and stuck her head under the edge of the table. Patrick and Flora did the same, sitting back up with confused expressions on their faces. "Where could they have gone? Weren't they on your feet? Your sneakers could not have just walked off on their own," Boris commented with a calm, drunken slur.

For the first time all evening, Sofia thought of her earlier stunt under the table. She quickly grabbed her backpack and slung it over her shoulder. "I wish I could stay and help with whatever your problem is, but we've gotta go. See you all at rehearsals tomorrow." She smiled and scurried into the restaurant without looking back. She could still hear Nina screaming about her lost sneakers as she reached the bathroom. Locking herself in the last stall, Sofia inhaled a deep, defeated breath and burst out in a fit of giggles. Without a second thought, she took the sneakers from her backpack and dropped them into the toilet bowl. She crouched down and stared at the once pristine sneakers, now saturated with grimy toilet water. Backing out of the stall, she let herself out and skipped over to the schmaltzy, gilded mirrors that hung over the sinks. A cool satisfaction tingled down her arms, and her eyes widened with an expression of approval as she stood in front of her reflection and pictured the sneakers in the toilet, soaked and ruined. She untangled the tight coil of hair tied at the nape of her neck and smirked proudly at her glowing reflection.

Feeling giddy and completely satisfied, Sofia quickly applied a layer of shiny lip gloss to her lips. A triumphant smile spread across her face. *There, Nina. That'll teach you!*

10

Maya

Aaron, still a baby, spends most of the week at the *gan*, the kibbutz nursery, under the care and tutelage of Hani. I am grateful for this service shared by the kibbutz's residents, but Danny sulks about it constantly, starting each day in a mopey mood. I've taken to waking up extra early just to beat him out of our cottage and get to my work in the communal kitchens instead of having to listen to him complain about us not spending enough time together as a family. It has become his morning routine to kvetch about the obligatory separating of children from their parents. This is the way we all grew up on the kibbutz, but for some reason, Danny is bucking the old system when it comes to the nurturing of his own son. For me, I'd rather start my days by dealing with the early-morning bats on my way to work and starting my day in the quietude and solace of the rising sun than spend it listening to a grown man whine like a baby. I pump some milk while Danny takes his morning shower, and I'm ready to slip out of the house before he even dries himself off. Danny is left with the task of walking the extra bottles of milk over to the nursery for Aaron each morning.

It's a bit drizzly this morning, but walking toward the old tailor's shed in my slumbering daze, I hear a low rumble of commotion coming from the front gates, and I remember Abba mentioning that we are expecting a new group of volunteers from the United States. Supposedly, they are all newly graduated from universities across America's "breadbasket" and are planning to spend time with us learning about our unique farming techniques and developing new agricultural equipment. While our almonds and sunflowers are cultivated during the summer months, it is never too early to start planning for the crops. This group of volunteers is coming to learn how we prepare for the season and how we generate new species of crops. Maybe they will even come up with more economical methods to produce our crops. Anyway, I know Danny is excited to show off the new truck they are using to harvest the almonds.

Car trunks slam open and shut, and Romi, our director of volunteers, organizes the group with a roll call of foreign names. A proud and deferential group of young kibbutzniks offers extra assistance by screaming ignored orders in Hebrew to the newcomers, telling them to follow them along to the dining hall. All the untethered energy and excitement of the arrival smacks me in the face as if I am walking into a surprise party. The drizzle of the early morning is subsiding, and I look up through the dewy bougainvillea bushes that border the path in front of me. The sun is beginning to peek through the clouds, but it is not strong enough to dry up the morning rainfall or warm up the chilly March air. I squint my eyes at the chaotic scene before me and jerk my body to a stop on the uneven cobbles of the path. I almost lose my balance, and I am stunned with a wave of youthful wonder of my own. How exciting it must be to travel halfway around the world and realize new dreams, adventures, freedom. A blinding sight for my very sore and tired eyes.

Romi and the other kibbutzniks finally guide the young and enterprising American volunteers to the dining hall while four more men from the carpool stay behind and stack suitcases and duffle bags on a soggy patch of grass by the gate. After my routine morning visit to Imma at the dairy, I enter the kitchen from the back door, and I can hear Romi in the dining hall calling out a long string of unfamiliar foreign names. He stutters through the pronunciations, clearing his throat after reciting each name and trying to sound smart and hip. The newcomers are not much younger than Romi or myself, but listening to their unleashed cries of wonder and curiosity, I understand why Romi might be intimidated by these young Americans. Through the pulse of their excitement, I try to decipher whether I hear the cries of adventure, the mysterious lure of the exotic Middle East, or the sincere desire to study our country's well-regarded agricultural trade.

Rivke approaches me just as I am cracking an egg over the edge of a giant metal bowl. Her shoulders are bent forward, and her face is dusted with white flour. "How are those eggs coming along?" she whistles from her puckered lips.

Startled by her sudden presence, I inadvertently dropped egg shells into the mixture in the bowl. "Oh, Rivke. You startled me. I'll have the eggs scrambled and ready in a jiffy."

"Yes, I can see you are a bit distracted this morning, but we have a big, new group to feed today, and I can't have you dawdling with the breakfast." Rivke smiles, and I prop myself in front of the countertop so she can't see the eggshells I let fall into the soupy mix. "What is it, my dear? Is everything okay?"

Here at the kibbutz, whenever anyone asks if everything is okay, I can never really tell if they are genuinely concerned about me or simply plying for gossip. It's a toss-up, but I like Rivke. She is kind and helpful and usually keeps to herself, so I answer sincerely, "No, everything's fine. I've just got a few things on my mind."

Truthfully, I have not been able to stop thinking about my weekend in Tel Aviv with Irena. I've caught Danny looking at me, wonder in his eyes, trying to figure out the unconscious smile on my face or my sudden bursts of giggles. It has been a month since my temporary escape from the confines of family and community, basking in the thrilling world of the city, ballet, and careless sunbathing with Irena. Carefree and unrestrained, I had felt like Irena had given me a wonderful opportunity—a gift—a whole two days of abandon, choice, independence. The freedom I experienced that weekend still soaks me with the same sensation as if I am a child opening eight gifts for Hanukkah all at once. The freedom and excitement of the city and of the ballet are all I've been able to think about. Sometimes I think that I might just be losing my mind.

I smile at Rivke and thank her for her concern. "I'm sorry if I seem a bit distant, but I guess I'm just preoccupied by the new volunteers moving onto the kibbutz today. I saw them when they arrived. There are about six of them, and they arrived in the rain." Recalling one of my mother's favorite *bubbemisers*, or old wives' tales, I ask,

"Isn't that good luck? When an event occurs in the rain? My Imma says it washes away all the bad stuff!"

A loud whine rings out from the dining room. One of the volunteers screeches, "Do they have bathrooms around here?"

Rivke clucks her tongue, ignoring my rant about the rain. "I can just imagine how they must be feeling. I remember when I first came here, and I was completely petrified. I was all alone, I couldn't speak the language, I had no idea what work I would be asked to do or where I would fit in…" Rivke drifted off into her own memories.

"I suppose it must have been a difficult transition. You made a huge move here from Ukraine, like many other families on the kibbutz. I'm sure the new volunteers are just as confused by the difference in lifestyle here." I am beginning to talk gibberish, and from the look of frustration that spreads across Rivke's face, I fear I am offending her with my indifference to her personal plight.

Before I can say another word, Rivke straightens her bent shoulders and says with a sigh, "Yes, but at least they made the choice to come, and they have the option to leave whenever they want. The choice wasn't so easy for me." Her words drifted off again, lost in the steam rising from the simmering pots on the stove. Rivke scuttles away from me and opens the oven door to check on the baking challah loaves, and I turn back to my eggs.

The swinging door into the kitchen from the dining room swooshes open, and Romi is standing there with a clipboard in one hand and a pencil in the other. His face is twisted with tension and impatience. "When is breakfast ready, girls? Do we have time to show the new volunteers to their cottages now, or should we just wait?"

Rivke answers with a huff, "Everything is going to be ready in a few minutes. The salads are all served on the tables, and the eggs and bread will be out in another five minutes. *Savlanut*, Romi. Patience." She clicks her tongue and pushes Romi back out the door.

When the door swings open, and Romi heads back into the dining room, I notice one of the volunteers sitting by himself on a table near the frosty, rain-speckled window by the front door. He is wearing a pressed white polo shirt, tight blue jeans, chunky black boots that look very similar to our army-issued boots, and a brown leather bomber jacket. If I had to guess, I would say he was about five years younger than me. He looks tired and anxious, his eyes scanning the dining room under drooping eyelids. His blond hair is pushed away from his face and puddles down around his thick neck. He has a boyish grin that rivals the magnetism of Brad Pitt in *Thelma and Louise*, and his complexion is as smooth and bronzed as a Greek god. But there is something off, not quite healthy, about his glazed stare.

"Watch it, Maya, you're in the way. Again with your head in the clouds? *Nu*, when are you going to learn!" Rivke is standing behind me with a tray filled with loaves of freshly baked challah and pita bread cut into triangles. She bumps the tray into my upper back, and I jump out of her way.

"Yes, Rivke. I'll get the eggs. I'm right behind you."

Later that day, I hurry down Gan Notzah's main road to the empty bus stop. The dirt road is muddy and puddled, and the early spring air is still sharp and cool, despite the competing sun's rays. My throat is raw from running, and I wonder if I'm alone because I just missed the bus to Haifa or if it is just a slow day for traveling. Cleaning up after breakfast this morning took longer than usual, and I found myself moving slowly and absentmindedly. As excited as I was to be going into the studio this afternoon, I was thrown into a dizzying daydream, and I had been barely functioning; I managed to finish my chores with my head in the clouds, as Rivke had said.

Just then, I feel the rumble of the bus approaching through the dirt beneath me, and I hike the strap of my backpack further up on my shoulder. The bus driver, whom I recognized from years of traveling at this time to Haifa, nods at me with a smile of acknowledgment as I climb on the bus and sit in the seat right behind him. Closing my eyes, I lean back in the plastic seat and rest my head against the cold window pane.

Grateful that the bus driver knows where I am going, I jump out of my seat when I hear him whistle for my attention. "We're here, sleeping beauty," he says with a friendly smile. His thick black mustache twitches under his nose, and I chuckle at his reference to Sleeping Beauty.

The one-story structure of the dance academy is small and hidden behind a crowded bus stop and a crush of people scrambling in every direction; the fading yellow-and-blue awning is the only thing that anchors the school's existence to the bustling street. It sits tucked between a busy falafel stand and a souvenir shop for tourists, selling everything from postcards and refrigerator magnets to olivewood carvings of the City of Bethlehem. I jump off the bus and land right in a slick pool of rainwater before I could thank the driver. "Gee, thanks," I turn back to say with a bitter sarcasm, shaking one boot at a time, and step onto the sidewalk.

Twenty minutes into my warm-up routine at the barre, Irena bursts through the studio door with a rush of energy. "My dear, you're finally here. I'm so happy to see you." With a look-over from the top of my head to the points of my slippers, she adds, "You look great…almost back to your old self!"

I am feeling great, if I had to say so myself. "Hey, Irena. I've got about an hour of practice time scheduled in the studio, but would you be able to get a coffee with me when I'm done?"

"Yeah, sure. I've got a class at six o'clock, but I want to talk to you. It's about a new show we're doing here. I think you should audition for it."

Irena takes me by surprise, and I stifle a sharp gasp. "Me? Audition? Oh, I don't know if I'm up to performing again. And besides, Danny may not be too happy about that either."

"Danny, *shmanny. Phooh*! We're doing a production of *The Sleeping Beauty* this summer, and you'd be perfect for the role of Aurora! Ilan and I will be in Rome at that time, but you could do this. I know you could!" *Apparently, the bus driver thinks I would fit the role too.* I giggle softly to myself as I look at my out-of-shape reflection in the mirror.

"Oh, I don't know, Irena. My brother and Gali just had their baby, and Danny is already upset that I don't spend enough time with him and Aaron." I flush with excitement and pride that Irena would consider me for the role in their new show. And not just any role but the *lead* role! I would do anything for the chance to dance in a professional show again. *What harm could it do if I just auditioned?* I consider the opportunity for a split second. Before I could protest any more, Irena turns to leave and waves an annoyed finger at me, cutting me off from my own thoughts. "It's your choice. We'll meet for coffee after your practice and talk about it," she mumbles and closes the studio door behind her.

11

Sofia

Sofia was oblivious to anything outside of her rehearsal schedule. She had been away touring with the troupe on the West Coast for several shows, delighted by the state-of-the-art theaters and change of scenery, but other than that, Sofia came home and was, once again, entrenched in her workouts at the academy. Boris had asked her to put in a few extra hours each day with the corps in order to coach and prepare them for the opening of *Swan Lake* later that year. But it was Becca who seemed to be acting all weird, and it was making Sofia more and more tense.

Becca had begun showing up late for rehearsals. She sulked around the studio, and the pallor on her heart-shaped face had gone from alabaster white to a sallow, ashy green. She continuously stumbled and cringed from the chronic jolts of pain in her leg caused by the car accident with Nathan, but Sofia pushed her harder with each day's rehearsal, hoping that whatever ailed Becca would soon pass. Her dance skills had suffered since the car crash, but was this something else?

An hour into their rehearsal on the third week of Becca's strange behaviors, Sofia scuffed over to the old record player, heavy and defeated, and turned it off. She twirled toward Becca, the chiffon of her skirt swishing behind her, her thin eyebrows arched way up on her forehead. "If you are not feeling up to backing me up for this show… Jeez, Becca. What's gotten into you lately?" Her frustration hung in the steamy air.

"Sofia, we have to talk. Can we take a break and go somewhere private?" Desperation was written all over Becca's blotchy red face, but Sofia was not willing to accept any more excuses for her slacking attitude. She picked up her towel and dried the sweat from the back of her neck. "If you think that talking will help, I'll go tell Boris that we're going for a late breakfast. And you better have a valid excuse for your shitty attitude and performance lately."

Sitting at the café on the corner of Oriental Boulevard, a barista kindly brought over two cups of coffee and a couple of warm chocolate chip muffins, placing everything on the table between them. Sofia watched the young girl walk away and touched the outside corner of her eye, mirroring the spot where the barista had three pierced hoops dangling from the side of her face. She scrunched the bridge of her nose, wondering about the useless reasons anyone could possibly have for undergoing the pain of making holes in their face. Becca suddenly broke her out of her arbitrary thoughts and reminded her of why they were sitting in that café in the first place. "Sofia, I have to tell you something. I can't hide it anymore, and you aren't going to be happy about it either."

That announcement immediately got Sofia's attention. She shook her head, putting the young barista out of her mind, squirmed in her chair, and bit down on her lower lip. Becca choked back a sob as tears began puddling in her eyes and then streamed uncontrollably down her cheeks. Barely audible, she lowered her gaze and whispered, "There's only one way to tell you this, Sofia, so I'll just say it. I'm pregnant."

What? Did Sofia hear that correctly? Becca is pregnant?

No. Just *N-O*. It couldn't be.

Becca was the most proper, most respectable, most upright person she knew… How could this be? Sofia was about to throw up her muffin. This was not the good news that a pregnancy should have been—normally would have been—under different circumstances, and it was definitely not the news Sofia wanted to hear now.

"I don't know what to do!" Becca let out a frantic, shrill bark, as if her fears were churning up from her gut, ready to strangle her to death. "You've got to help me." She placed a trembling hand on her belly.

What was Sofia supposed to do about this? Her first thought was of the baby's father, and she instinctively began spewing a roll of ridiculous questions at Becca. "Are you sure about this? I mean, did you see a doctor? Did you tell the father? Do you know who…" Still in a state of shock, Sofia sounded completely pathetic and misguided as soon as her words came out of her mouth. She squeezed her lips together in a tight line, lamenting the thoughts that were rolling through her mind.

Finally, Becca spoke up, "Of course, I know who the father is, Sofia. What do you think? That I'm some kind of common whore?"

In the blink of a wet eyelash, all their little-girl plans and dreams were washing away, simply because of a single choice with unanticipated consequences. Instead of celebrating what could have been her best friend's news, Sofia mourned the loss of their childhood innocence. "Well, what am I supposed to think, Becca? You're springing this on me, out of the blue, and you're not even dating anyone. What am I supposed to think? Who the hell did this to you?"

Becca didn't know who to blame, but she was sure it wasn't the baby's father. It had been her choice, her decision, her consequence to face. She felt totally scared and alone, but she had no regrets. If she was given the choice, she would do it again. There was no one to blame but herself.

Becca's only concern was how she was going to keep the baby and still maintain her self-respect and honor. This situation was not going to sit well with her parents. She was horrified to think of how they were going to react when she eventually had to tell them. Even Sofia looked now like she was going to explode with anger, or at the least, disappointment.

But she already loved her child, the tiny little person that was no more than a microscopic cell growing inside of her. There was no doubt in her mind that this baby was more than just a part of her, more than just a part of him, more than just the result of a heedless slip one night. Instinctively, she rubbed her shaking hand that rested protectively over her flat belly.

Becca's shoulders heaved up and down as she tried to catch her breath. She kept her eyes focused on her coffee in front of her, unable to look Sofia in the eyes. Zapped of courage and confidence, she exhaled sharply. Her next words flew out of her mouth with a ragged, strong, and indisputable edge, "I'm going to have this baby, Sofia."

"You what? You can't be serious, Becca. Do you know what you're saying?" Sofia let out a loud, incensed exhale. She bounced her head from side to side, checking that the other shop patrons were not eavesdropping on their conversation. The two of them sat in a tense silence that went on for what seemed like an eternity, trying to collect their individual thoughts about the reality of a baby and where to go from there.

Counting reasons against Becca's decision on her fingers, Sofia tried to rationally consider the argument. Breaking the awkward silence, she stared at Becca's petrified face and stretched her lips tightly over her own chattering teeth. Seething with anger, fear, and remorse, Sophia tried to control the mix of emotions bubbling up from her gut.

"Let's think about this calmly and rationally, Becca. There is no reason to make a hasty, rash decision about this. And there are definitely a million reasons why you clearly did not think this through. One, you're not married. Two, you're not even twenty years old, and you're still a baby yourself! Three, what about your dance career? And lastly…what are your parents going to do when they find out!" The list of concerns rushed from Sofia's lips like ballistic missiles raining down all around Becca. She wanted answers, but there were no responses that would change the situation or make sense out of the whole sordid mess. She looked up to see Becca's eyes teeming with tears again, and her puckered cheeks blew in and out with desperate gasps of air. Sofia dropped her chin to her chest in resignation and covered her head with both arms. In the end, it was Becca's choice, but she hoped she could convince her to make the right one.

Looking around the café again, paranoid that others were listening to their private concerns, Sofia lowered her voice and continued to make her case. "Have you thought about the consequences of this, Becca? No, you're definitely not a whore, but you definitely are crazy! You've gone mad! And your parents…oh my God! You do realize what this will do to them! They're going to kill you when they find out!" Sofia was typically less emotional, but now she was bowled over with confusion and fear for her friend, and her logic was being shoveled into the gutters of her mind.

"Why do you think I'm so confused about this? It's not the baby's fault. It's not the father's fault. It's mine. I made the choice to do what I did, and I'm so embarrassed with myself! Maybe I *am* a slut!" Becca blubbered, clutched at her leotard that was pulling taut across her still-flat stomach, and let her words hang in the space between them. She was coming undone—one minute she was a proud mother-to-be, the next she was a petrified little girl.

Sofia shuddered with the realization that Becca's whole life was about to transform. Nothing was ever going to be as it was before, and nothing was going to bring back the past. There were no "do-overs" and no second chances.

Suddenly, a white light blinded her eyes as a scene from six years earlier began to consume her. She felt her body lift and float, bringing her back to that frightful night. It was 2004, and she was only nineteen when she met Josh that night. She knew she was wrong to leave her aunt's and uncle's house that day on her own, taking such a bold, thoughtless risk. She was so young and still inexperienced in her new country. But once she was there, swarming with excitement and adventure in the crush of Coney Island, she couldn't resist all the obvious temptations that presented themselves to a young, carefree girl. Josh was so handsome and kind and funny, and she was not thinking about anything but the mustard clinging to his full, lush lips as he ate his hotdog and invited her to ride the Ferris wheel. The first time out on her own since arriving from Ukraine, Sofia had felt a soaring freedom wash over her. From the top of the wheel, she could see forever, and she felt totally invincible. She suspected Becca felt the same way when she…

"Okay, Becca. Let's calm down and think straight. I know this is not your fault. And no, you're not a slut," Sofia murmured, snapping out of her own twisted past. She hugged herself around her waist with her long arms. In a whisper, almost inaudibly, she asked, "Do you love him? The father, I mean."

Looking directly into Sofia's eyes for the first time that afternoon, Becca simply whispered back an unequivocable "Yes."

Sofia's initial insensitivity melted away, and all she could feel now was fear and sincere empathy for her little soul-sister. She imagined herself in Becca's shoes and wondered what would have happened if she hadn't been so quick, hadn't gotten away, and had gotten pregnant with Josh that one whimsical night at Coney Island. He had been a total stranger to her then, a one-time compulsion that ended in…well, nothing. What would Sofia have done if she had become pregnant back then? What kind of mother would she be? What could she give a child when she wasn't even sure what she wanted for herself? What would her own mother have done?

After what seemed like an eternity filled with a deafening silence, Becca tore into Sofia's thoughts. She had no idea about Sofia's long-ago tryst with Josh, but she pressed on the one invisible button she hoped would make Sofia see the reason for her final decision. "Sofia, think about it. How did you feel when your father disappeared, and your mother sent you away? How do you feel now without your mother and father? Would you really abandon your own child?"

Sofia had no answers. Becca's words cut right to her core, but she knew she was right. She had gotten used to her father's work "absences," but her mother was her best friend. The loss of her dear mother still twisted in her chest every time she thought of her. She could not imagine having to give up her child. The hope that one day her family would reunite and recuperate what they had lost was the only thing that kept Sofia moving forward. She heaved a deep, painful sigh.

It would be hard, but she would find a way to help Becca deal with her family and her washed-up plans for the future. She let out a slow exhale of resignation, opened her arms, and reached for Becca from across the table. "For now, we keep this between us and get back to the studio. Leave it to me, and I'll think of something."

12

Maya

I hate working the breakfast shift. I hate getting up at three thirty when it is still dark out, just to escape the brooding mood that has settled in our home, to cook and to prepare a meal for nine hundred early risers and workers, and be totally exhausted by ten o'clock in the morning. It's not until eleven thirty or so that I am officially done with it all—scrubbing up the last of the burnt pots and washing off the old Formica dining room tables. I look around the empty dining room, and the smell of mucky, industrial-strength cleaning chemicals tickles my nose. Wiping my hands on my filthy apron, I am eager to get to the vehicle pool.

When I get to the garage shed, I call out for Shmulik. A rough cigarette-induced cough and a baritone bellow hits me from behind. "What's your rush, little princess? Heading out to Haifa? I have only one car left for the day, so I guess you are pretty lucky."

I take the car keys that Shmulik's greasy palm holds out to me and throw my backpack into the back seat of a blue Toyota parked on the gravel driveway. "Thanks, Shmuly. See you later. I'll be back no later than six." I offer a lighthearted chuckle, circle around the car, kick at the dusty tires just like Abba taught me, and wiggle into the driver's seat.

It has been a month since my last trip to Haifa. I'm a little nervous to go back and find myself desperately wanting, coveting, the audition for Aurora. If I'm honest, Irena's suggestion that I audition for the role in *The Sleeping Beauty* has left me confused and hopelessly wishful. I haven't brought up the subject with Danny. What would be the point? He would just laugh it off like it was some big joke, or he would explode in another round of disappointment and accusations. "What's so important about dancing now, Maya? Don't you have everything you want already?"

I have everything I *need*, not everything I *want*. Two totally different things.

Like riding a bicycle, I travel the tree-lined road to the city that is clearly etched into my internal memory, and I navigate the whole way through the valley on automatic cruise-control. As I travel further away from Kibbutz Gan Notzah, I fiddle with the radio dial and feel my shoulders slowly relax.

Arriving at the dance studio, I park the car in the cramped lot behind the building and turn to grab my backpack from the backseat. Irena and Ilan will be surprised by my visit—I haven't told them I am coming today. I sit alone in the musty silence that fills the car. It feels good to be free and back at the academy again.

I can hear relentless musical beats pushing through the air from the back entrance of the studio—*one, two, three-and-four, five, six, seven-*

and-eight...despite the roar of the relentless traffic from the street. In front of the studio, a public bus holds up traffic and slowly chugs by. A loud honk from an impatient driver startles me, and I jump. I scurry around the building and into the glass doors of the studio.

Inside, the melding heat of dancing bodies and the hum of measured music puts me in a trance. One of complete serenity and joy. My toes are on fire, and my spine stiffens into a locked position. I hug my arms around my torso, suddenly very aware that I am still wearing my work apron and threadbare gauze dress under my oversized army-green sweatshirt. My fingers fumble under my sweatshirt to untie the knot of the apron strings around my waist.

A familiar voice calls out from behind the reception counter. "*L-l-a-a-h-h!* I can't believe it. If it isn't the one-and-only Maya Sharret. You finally came back! Irena and Ilan have been asking about you." The girl's reaction is a blatant display of sarcasm, but melodrama is truly a diva's main strength.

"Yes, it's me. In the flesh. Good to see you, Nadia." I can't contain the giggles that burst from my lips. Nostalgia hits me like a bolt of lightning, and a warm mist of steam rises from my chest and burns my freckled cheeks. Nadia had been studying at the academy in the younger corps' class for years, and I recall how she used to follow me and Irena around like a hovering shadow. Now, according to Irena's latest gossip update, Nadia is the newest up-and-coming star of the little studio and would have been my biggest competition for the role in *The Sleeping Beauty*. I'm reminded of how young Irena and I were the up-and-coming stars of the studio and were moved up from the younger group of dancers. Nadia is a simple reminder of how hard and long the journey is to becoming a "rising star" in the business. Irena made it all seem so easy. Back then, I wished I had more of Irena's gumption and grit. Today, I still wish I had Irena's gumption and grit.

"Have you seen Irena around?" I ask her. I am still clumsily trying to untie my apron strings and hide the dirty rag in my backpack as Nadia waves a delicate hand toward the row of small studios.

"Yeah, she is rehearsing with Ilan in room number 2. Did you hear the news? She and Ilan are going to Bucharest to perform in *Concerto DSCH* next week. Overnight sensations, those two. They're so good…and lucky!"

Of course, I had heard the news.

I offer a big, toothy grin, but still, I can't help the pangs of envy and resentment that poke at me when I picture Irena and Ilan journeying all the way to Europe. It's one thing to be asked to perform here at home, in Tel Aviv, but it's quite another thing to be asked to perform internationally.

Straining to keep my composure, I picture Irena and Ilan prancing gracefully in their colorful costumes across the spotlighted stage. I straighten my spine and tap the toe of my muddy boot. *I've got to get to the bathroom and change out of these disgusting clothes*, I say to myself.

Concerto DSCH is a major ballet choreographed by Alexei Ratmansky—the former director of the Bolshoi Ballet and a current dancer with the New York City Ballet. I still couldn't wrap my head around it. Yes, this is a really big deal. A true dream come true. I should feel nothing but pride and happiness for my dearest friends.

Shouldn't I?

"Well, as hard as they work, it's no surprise they've finally succeeded," I suggest to Nadia.

Luck, be damned.

"Maybe I'll get my chance soon too," she continues without even blinking an eye. "But you should go quickly now and see if you can catch their rehearsal. Irena and Ilan look fantastic together. Room number 2." Nadia's scuffed leather slippers scrape gracefully on the floor as she walks away from the desk and disappears down the hallway.

First, I had to get to the bathroom and change into my dancing gear. I didn't dare interrupt the rehearsal, especially dressed as a frumpy kitchen maid. Changed and standing silently at the door of the studio room, I watch the pair glide effortlessly, gracefully, beautifully across the worn parquet floor. Until…

"OUCH! Watch your step. You missed your cue again!" Ilan's face is red and sweaty, and his eyes bulge from their sockets as he glares at Irena.

"Let's take a break already, Ilan. Please. We've been practicing nonstop for hours today," Irena whines and rubs her thigh muscles. The duo hasn't noticed me standing in the doorway, so I hold my fist to my mouth and blow out a soft cough.

"Can I come in? I hear it's break-time."

After a loud, emotional show of hugs and congratulations, Ilan agrees that it would be a good time for a rest. "But I can't go with you girls. I have a class to teach in about fifteen minutes. You two should go have fun, *kibitz*, and gossip for a while, and you can bring me back a watermelon shake?"

I'm already changed into my dance clothes, but Irena and I saunter down the street to a nearby pedestrian thoroughfare filled with food kiosks, small art boutiques, and busy restaurants. Neither one of us reacts to the catcalls or stares as we make our way to the salad diner at the end of the street in our scanty leotards and tights.

My eyes widen, and my chin drops as I take in the energetic bustle of the crowds. Irena looks at me sideways and grins. Arabic music blares at us from all directions, and people wearing everything from traditional garb to modern fashion whiz by us. Young and old sit together in the fancy (and some not so fancy) restaurants lining the street. The mix of tantalizing aromas—fruity and nutty spices, salt from the sea spray from the nearby seaport—fills my nose. The city never fails to send me into fits of sheer euphoria and delight. *How do we manage to continue living such an antiquated life on the kibbutz?* I wonder to myself. We find a table on the sidewalk in front of the restaurant and plop into our seats.

Immediately, Irena regales me with all the studio gossip, and I fill her in on the latest news from the kibbutz. Putting down her glass of water, Irena opens her mouth wide and yawns. "You'll have to relay *dash*, regards, to Boaz from me. But now, tell me… You must be happy to be getting back on your feet again. Even if you are still on the kibbutz." Her derision is palpable. Her clear condescension whips at me like a burst of flames licking at my naked soul, and I bow my head in humility. I would never admit to Irena—or anyone, for that matter—that I often felt the same sentiments that she is spewing at me now. "Can I assume you have decided not to audition for our new performance?" Irena concludes.

My arms fly up around the crown of my head, and I twist my hair into a knot. I take a long swig from my Diet Coke, and crossing my legs under the table, I notice there's a hole in the knee of my tights. I make a mental note to stitch it when I get home. I lift my head and wink at Irena. "Yes, I mean no. I did decide, and I will not audition. The role is all Nadia's." I wonder if she can sense the jealousy and spite in my reply.

There was a time I would have arguably disagreed with what I know Irena is thinking: that my domestic issues are nothing more than a boring distraction from what's really important in life. But now I stop and wonder. We used to be dancers with hopes and dreams. The two of us were going to make it all the way to the top of the ballet scene. I can't remember ever wanting anything more. And now I never thought my life would come to this—filthy diapers, stained aprons, blistered hands... Who would have ever thought that I would be content with the life I am living now. Why should I be surprised or upset with Irena's sharp reaction?

Doubts and questions whirl in my head like a washing machine spinning and blurring the colors of my dirty laundry. I can no longer focus on Irena or her attempt at feigned interest in my life. I stare at her plate of salad and vegetables, still untouched in front of her. She doesn't eat a bite, while I devour my pita stuffed with crispy chunks of lamb meat and globs of tahini sauce. I let her talk more about her upcoming trip to Europe while I silently eat—greasy french-fry oil dripping precariously through my fingertips. The differences between us seem to grow more and more obvious by the minute. Swallowing down the last olive on my plate, I push my body away from the table. A heaviness pressing down on my neck and shoulders keeps me stiff in my seat. Irena is animated with details of their upcoming trip, but her words become white noise, sitting heavy between us. My head jingles between my ears and fills with envy, disappointment, regret, and emptiness. I can't bear the pressing weight of it all.

Danny and I had been inseparable since we were babies, like two proverbial peas in a pod. Born just two months apart, we were in the same childcare class in the kibbutz *gan*, children's nursery, since before we could even speak. Growing up, we remained attached at the hips. When he went on the swings, I followed. When I went for a drink of water, Danny was right behind me.

We shared each other's secrets and most private feelings, like when we graduated high school and were getting ready to leave for our mandatory military service; I wasn't as scared about the future when I discovered that Danny was experiencing the same fears as I was. It was Danny who was always there for me, whether it was to soothe my nerves when I needed to walk past the "bat attack" pathway or to help me study for my academic exams.

But Danny was more scholarly and serious; I leaned more toward frivolity and theatrics. We were a match made in heaven—opposite forces operating interconnectedly. His yin to my yang. Back then, Danny even supported my interest in ballet and had encouraged me to join the national dance troupe that performed for the military around the country. Back then, Danny understood my dreams, my desires, my passions. Or so it seemed. And as we grew older, more aware of the intimacy of our friendship, more aware that there was something much stronger than playground fantasies, there was no doubt in anyone's mind that we would be together forever. Danny was as vital to me as the air I breathed. And I was his "shining guiding star." It was simple. Easy. A no-brainer decision.

So what happened to us? I guess we're not the same young lovers we used to be.

Our waitress comes by and clears the dishes from our table. Thoughts of the past fade, but I can't help but think to myself, *I should have auditioned for Aurora.*

I wipe my fingers on my shredded napkin, and I reach for my backpack lying at my feet. It is crammed with two damp bandanas, a rusty set of car keys, a balled-up work apron, an old pair of sunglasses, and a comforting vial of pills. I tip two pills into my palm and place them on the tip of my tongue. I tilt my head backward, swallowing them before the rim of my water glass even touches my lips. I flash a contrived smile at my dear friend and let her pick up the check.

Sofia

As expected, Becca's parents did not take the news of her situation well. Although it was 2010— the twenty-first century!—the Kaplans still believed in the ancient, unyielding beliefs of their forefathers and their age-old convictions. To Mr. Kaplan, a daughter's "bad" reputation could destroy a family, and he could not bear the impending evil stares and the ill-spirited whispers of the neighbors that he was certain his family would come to bear from Becca's pregnancy. There was no other choice for him but to demand Becca leave their home.

"Jakob, Becca needs us now more than ever! She's still just a child! Our child!" Mrs. Kaplan begged in defense of their oldest daughter. Her nonstop crying and blubbering had not put a damper on her desperate pleas. Nor did it discourage Mr. Kaplan's rage and humiliation. Mr. Kaplan was unbending.

"She brought this on herself, Sima. I can't have her humiliate our family this way. She was old enough to make her bed, and now she must lie in it!"

Her husband's stubborn and cruel choice of words was not lost on Mrs. Kaplan. Screaming and choking on a flood of tears, she pleaded on. "But where will she go? What will she do? You are her father, Jakob. For good or for bad. Have you no pity?"

There was only one choice left to make. If Becca continued to insist on keeping the baby, Sofia saw no other way out. Maybe she was stepping in where she had no business doing so, but she needed to support and protect her dear friend. It was going to disrupt her own life and routine, but what else could she do? Three months in and Becca showing the undeniable signs of natural maternal glow and slight "mommy bump" with nowhere else to turn, she dared to utter the words she was dreading for a while.

"Alright, Becca, you can come stay with me," Sofia groaned, and that settled it.

The sweltering summer saw Becca grow more swollen, and her usual graceful stride turned into an uncomfortable waddle—the secret of her pregnancy no longer remaining hidden. She was only five months along, but her raging hormones played havoc on her normally petite frame and delicate features. Her only saving grace was that Becca was still able to smile through it all and even get in a brisk dance practice every day. The doctors had assured her it was safe and encouraging for Becca's state of mind. Boris even let her stay on and teach a group of younger students in a new hip-hop dance class they had recently opened at the academy, even though Becca struggled with her own skills since the accident with Nathan.

Sofia was living a somewhat double life—one as an up-and-coming prima ballerina, a rising star in her lifelong fantasy, and another completely different life where she had transformed into Becca's mother and had to tend to all her *tzores* and constant care. She wondered if she had it in her to continue being strong and supportive enough for both her friend and herself. Her will was tested, her purpose questioned, but somehow, she kept on going.

"Sometimes, good people make terrible decisions," Aunt Anika reminded her one Shabbos evening. "But she'll make a good mother, and you are being a wonderful friend."

The right choice was not always the easy choice.

The Saturday night before her twenty-sixth birthday, Sofia posed in front of her bedroom mirror while Becca watched, perched on the edge of the bed. Clothes were strewn all over the floor, but Sofia proudly admired her final choice of outfit—her new Oscar de la Renta floral minidress. The flowing, gauzy fabric hung on her muscular frame as if it were painted right onto her skin. Sofia tossed her hair from one side to the other and slipped into a pair of red pumps.

"You look stunning in that dress. Ben will love it." Becca stood up and began picking up the discarded outfits from the floor. She touched her hand to her lower back and let out a rumbling groan.

"You think so? I have a feeling tonight is going to be special." Sofia paid no attention to Becca's soft, painful moans.

"You're so lucky, Sofia. You've got an amazing career, a handsome boyfriend who loves you, and the beauty of a movie star. How do you do it all?"

"You are just as beautiful as any movie star, and you will dance again—" Sofia stopped talking when a sudden random thought entered her mind. With no consideration to diplomacy or correctness, she blurted out the one unanswered question that remained burning in her mind, "Becca, are you ever going to tell me who the baby's father is? You said you love him, but he isn't around? At least, I haven't seen any men hanging around or calling to see how you are. How can you love a guy who seems to have vanished in thin air, just when you need him most! I must admit, I'm very confused…to say the least."

Becca plopped herself back on the bed and turned her eyes toward the open window and the fire escape outside. "I haven't told him yet. I want to have this baby, but I can't make another mistake and ruin another person's life with my decisions. No, come to think of it, I don't think I want to involve the baby's father in all of this. Not now, anyway."

Sofia sucked in her cheeks and brushed more blush over them. "So are you saying that you think that having this baby is a mistake? Bad timing? You would rather suffer alone and possibly lose the man you love? I don't get it, Becca. Which of you is going to be 'ruined,' as you say? This man of yours? Your child? Or *you*?" Sofia felt her cheeks flush with heat, her not-so-discreet rebuke spitting from her ruby-red lips. She drummed her fingers on the dresser to shake out her nervous energy. She still had no answer about the father and was more irritated about the coming consequences for her friend. She couldn't contain her nagging misgivings any longer. Pointing her mascara wand high above her head, she turned and glared at Becca.

"You're trying to be so selfless about this whole thing, but you're just as self-righteous and stubborn as your parents! Whose argument are you fighting here, Becca, the father's, your baby's, or yours? How are you going to love and financially support this baby? Have you thought about that? You're not thinking this through!"

"Of course, I've thought about all that, Sofia! I've thought about nothing else for the past four months!" Becca yelled back. "I haven't been able to think of anything else since I found out I was pregnant. But don't you see, dear friend?" Becca lowered her voice and stared softly at Sofia's back. "I will have to deal with my own choices. If I tell him now, it could ruin his future. I love him too much to let that happen. I know it won't be easy, but it's right. I know it is!" She punctuated her last sentence by rubbing her rounded belly and throwing an air-kiss at Sofia's reflection in the mirror. As if reading Sofia's mind, Becca added an afterthought, "My future is now all about this baby."

Sofia took one last look in the vanity mirror and grabbed her purse. She had no intention of continuing this ongoing argument and ruining her own night out with Ben. It was a free country, and so she continued to wrestle with the sense that she had to respect her friend's free will and just let it go. Sealing her mouth shut, she reapplied a thick layer of red lipstick over her lips, and smacked them open and closed a few times. "Well, I can't say I understand you, but I hope you know that I love you, and I'll support whatever decision you make. Now grab my earrings from my jewelry box, the diamond studs that Ben gave me."

Ben came to pick Sofia up but wouldn't tell her where they were going. He was used to her busy schedule, but tonight he insisted on having her all to himself "for a special birthday celebration." He had made it perfectly clear beforehand. "No interruptions, no uninvited guests or tag-alongs." Sofia got the hint. When she left the apartment, Becca was on the couch, munching loudly over a bag of Doritos and watching reruns of *Bewitched*.

As soon as she got into Ben's car, a new red Audi A5 he had just recently purchased, Sofia was swept off her feet. He had told her it would be a night of surprises, but she wasn't expecting anything. The first surprise Sofia got that evening was a bunch of red roses that greeted her from the passenger seat. "How romantic!" she swooned, laying the bouquet in her lap. Ben smiled and pecked her on the cheek with a wet kiss, but he didn't say another word. Twenty minutes later, they were crossing the Manhattan Bridge. Finally free of Brooklyn, Sofia felt a rush of excitement tingle over her skin. She loved the romance of it all, and going into Manhattan with the man she loved—as she normally had little time to go on her own time—in a fancy new sports car and a bouquet of roses was already more than she had anticipated. She sat, gloating in Ben's silence, her forehead plastered against the glass window, mesmerized by the sparkling lights floating over the East River.

After a heavenly meal at a new restaurant near the Plaza Hotel, Ben left the car parked in the hotel's parking garage and led Sofia by the elbow up toward Sixty-Fifth Street and across Central Park. "This is the downside of having a car in this city," grumbled Ben with a deceiving smile on his lips. "There's never enough parking, and you wind up walking everywhere anyway."

"No worries," answered Sofia. And she meant it. After a romantic dinner, a stroll through Central Park with her handsome, intelligent, loving man was making Sofia feel lucky and light-headed. Despite the summer mugginess, the teeming mosquitoes that seemed to find and follow her, and the pinch of her stiletto pumps, Sofia let out a satisfied sigh. "The walk will help our dinner digest." She slapped at a mosquito that had landed on her bare forearm.

"The mosquitos like your blood," Ben said with a grin. "You're sweet." Sofia gave him a playful punch on the shoulder as they continued to walk hand in hand. Ben leaned over and kissed her ear. Sofia purred with pleasure.

Suddenly, Ben threw his arm out in front of Sofia and brought them both to an abrupt stop. Sofia teetered in her stilettos and grabbed Ben's forearm to regain her balance. Looking down, Sofia realized she was practically standing on top of the tiled memorial to John Lennon. Strawberry Fields. Bunches of wildflowers so colorful she could still make out each hue in the darkness of the night were strewn all over the ground in front of her. A reverent hush surrounded them, hugging them into a cozy stillness. Without a word, Ben pulled Sofia to a nearby bench where they both took a seat.

At first, neither of them said a word. Ben and Sofia sat side by side in a comfortable, relaxed silence as they watched an old woman feeding a cluster of pigeons on the next park bench and a young couple sitting on a large red blanket, giggling and sipping slowly from plastic wine glasses. A bicyclist whirred by and broke their spell.

"Do you ever get tired?" Ben asked, his Southern drawl suddenly sounding more prominent.

"Tired of what?"

"Tired of all the traveling and performing and demands of the ballet and the theater." Ben rubbed his temple and hid his shifty gaze behind the shadow of his hand. His fingers were trembling in the dim light of a nearby lamppost. Tensing his shoulders, he leaned closer to Sofia.

"No," Sofia replied without pause. What was Ben getting at? Why was he acting so funny? "I'll never get tired of my dreams. Ben, is everything okay?"

"At first, when you and I first met at the bookstore, I have to admit that I had some doubts about dating you. After all, you are a 'famous' ballerina (Ben used his fingers to sign air-quotes when he mentioned the word *famous*), and I'm just a transplanted country bumpkin. But I decided to take my chances, and…well, I'm glad I did. I didn't expect it, but I started to fall in love with you…really fall in love…with you." Ben was stuttering like a bullied child on the playground of his school. "But now it just seems that you have time for everything and everyone else but me. So I was just wondering if you ever get tired and feel like you want to take time off. You know, for me. *With* me!"

Sofia narrowed her eyes and waited, taking some time to process all that Ben was asking her. She pleaded with him in her head. *Please don't ruin our night with this crap now. I don't need any more surprises.*

After a long pause, Ben continued, "Okay, I've got another question for you. You're turning twenty-six next week, and… Well, do you ever think about your future?"

"It's all I think about, Ben. Why do you think I work so hard at the academy?" Sofia's gaze fell on the center of the tiled memorial, the word "*Imagine*" faintly glistening in the moonlight.

Ben's cheeks were glistening under the moonlight as giant beads of sweat slid down the sides of his face along his jawline. He twisted around in his seat and reached into the pocket of his jeans. Sofia felt Ben slither off the bench and crouch on the ground in front of her.

Oh, my God! Is this what Ben meant when he talked about a night of surprises?

Sofia put her hand up to her mouth and suppressed a startled gasp. A small blue jewelry box rested in the palm of Ben's outstretched hand. "Sofia," he began again with labored breathing. His Southern twang that he worked so hard to hide since moving to New York sharpened as he continued, "As we celebrate your birthday with this night of magic and surprises, there is something else I'd like to propose we celebrate. Our future. Together. I love you, Sofia. Will you marry me?" Ben's eyes glistened in the soft moonlight with anticipation and hope.

14

Maya

We are sitting on the front porch at my parents' cottage. Danny has just come in from his shift in the fields, and David and Gali are here too. My sister-in-law, eight months pregnant again, waddles and paces back and forth on the grass yard, too uncomfortable with her swollen belly to sit still. Also present is Baruch, the director of the kibbutz, whose parents helped in the founding of Gan Notzah in 1934.

"Kobi warned us that things are going to get worse for us." It is Abba who breaks the uncomfortable silence. A look of panic on his pale face, his voice cracks as he states the obvious, "The stress in our country is heightened more and more each week, and our finances are being used up for defense and building more shelters."

"Yes, Noam. We have implemented a stricter security protocol. But we are not here to talk about that now. We need to concentrate on business." Baruch takes out a yellowed hanky from his breast pocket and wipes at the sweat beading around his pudgy neck.

"What can we do to help?" Imma asks. "We've had our ups and downs before, but we've managed to pull through. Can things really be that bad now?"

"I'm afraid so, Shula. The kibbutz is losing money every day, and the banks will not extend our credit any more. I've asked for this little meeting to see if we can come up with a new plan to boost our economic interests. I'm open to anything."

Danny offers an idea to increase our almond production, and David suggests that we start selling some of the sunflowers to floral shops instead of just selling the seeds. "It may not sound like a lot, but in the long run, I think it can help."

Suddenly, Imma lifts her head, and her eyes pop open. "Why didn't I think of it sooner?"

My mother usually stays out of business matters; that's more my father's job. She takes us all by surprise now with her sudden outburst, and we all grow silent as we wait for her to continue. "Every year, more and more young people are coming from all around the world to volunteer here. Maybe we can interest them in something other than agriculture." Taking a moment to gather her next thoughts, Imma beams with pride and erupts with a burst of excitement. "Maybe we can convince this younger crowd—people from this area and also our own people—to come to the kibbutz for dance lessons…from Maya!"

"Oh, Imma. Please." I interrupt. What could she possibly be thinking?

"Let me finish. We can open a real school—a proper academy—right here on the kibbutz. And we can invite locals to come in for lessons from surrounding towns. You are certainly qualified, and we can charge them for weekly or monthly schedules. God knows I've been paying an arm and a leg for these lessons at the Russian Ballet Conservatory in Haifa all these years!" When did my mother get so crafty and wise?

Before I could protest, Baruch rubs his chin with his fat fingers and smiles for the first time that afternoon. "Sounds like a good idea. What do you say, Maya? I think it may work. Let's give it some consideration before we say no. Deal?"

Gali waddles over to us and stares at me with widened eyes. Rubbing her extended belly with one hand, she points a finger of her other hand at her temple. I turn away from her. I know exactly what she is thinking. After all, Gali has known me all my life, and it is no secret that my passion for dance has never left me.

"I think Danny and David have better ideas. After all, we are an agricultural society, no?" As the words are coming out of my mouth, I begin to wonder if my mother's idea could really have some merit. I could give up my kitchen duty and concentrate on full-time, professional lessons with students who share my passion for dance. Leave it to us women to come up with the solution for our communal problem. *Yes, I think I could do it!* I say to myself, the missed audition at the Russian Ballet Conservatory in Haifa sitting like a stone in the middle of my chest. My heart begins to race with the idea, and my feet shuffle lightly against the cement porch floor. I look back up at Gali and then at Imma. My face twists with mixed doubt and excitement.

"Okay, I'll think about it," I promise with a wink at my mother. Danny turns his back and walks away from the group.

"This sounds great. I thank you all for your time and input today. Maya, I hope you really consider this dance academy thing… It certainly seems like an easy and lucrative move for us, and you can start right away. Please give it some serious thought, and tell me you'll do it. We need you, Maya."

I don't know if Baruch really likes the idea or if he is just desperate enough to try anything, but the wheels in his head are visibly spinning behind his bloodshot eyes as he hefts himself out of his seat. Imma smiles discreetly and lowers her gaze to the bib of her soiled overalls. Abba stands and leads Baruch back to the cobblestone path in front of the cottage.

Meeting is adjourned. For now.

Despite the fallout I expect back home with Danny, I can almost taste the sweetness of the words coating my tongue. *My own dance academy! It's a dream come true!* The thought of it pops like electric fireworks all around me. Maybe it is time for us women to stand up and make a difference around here for a change. I'm in.

The reality of our charming little academy on Gan Notzah takes off and is scheduled to officially open a month after our first discussions. I could barely contain my excitement of modernizing our little corner of the world. Danny wouldn't let me see anything while he worked on the building, but when he finally announced that the new space was complete, I ran to Gali and David's cottage so we could see it for the first time together. I will never forget that first moment when we all rushed into the studio, out of breath and speechless in the doorway, my eyes soaking in the little academy. Gali grabbed my hand and raised it in victory. Not even trying to hide his irritation, Danny huffed at our excitement. The kibbutz's board of directors had printed posters and flyers to publicize the school as *Lirkod Gan Notzah*, but all of us on the kibbutz adapt a different name for the studio: *Maya's Dance Palace*.

Imma found a box with all my old posters and photos of Baryshnikov and the other ballerinas I had grown to idolize, and Danny has hung them on the newly painted walls of the two-room studio. On the back wall of both classrooms, Danny and Boaz have installed floor-to-ceiling mirrors and a wooden barre that runs the length of the mirrored wall. A brand-new sound system is also installed, and speakers hang high above and out of reach in the corners. The floor is covered with smooth blond planks of wood and is sealed with a shiny, smooth varnish. Soon enough, the sheen will fade, and the wood will darken from the wear of leather slippers and metal shoe taps. But for now, everything gleams with purpose and perfection. I couldn't be prouder.

This afternoon, though, I am standing in front of the mirror that hangs behind our bedroom door, wondering if I could really pull this off. Can I make a triumph of Maya's Dance Academy? Can I really make a difference that would help the kibbutz? There are so many people relying on its success. On *my* success. I startle when I hear the front door suddenly open and slam shut—Danny is home from work. Quickly, I peel off my leotard and squeeze into a pair of old jeans and a T-shirt.

"There you are, my darling *motek*. I have a surprise for you." Danny's sudden flirtation surprises me, and I squint my eyes suspiciously at him. He holds out a bundle of sunflowers in one hand and a small burlap bag in the other.

"Shalom, Danny. What's in the bag?" I grab the bundle of sunflowers and the bag from him as we come together in the living room.

I can immediately smell the sweet, earthy aroma of freshly picked almonds, and I do not have to open the bag to know that he has brought me my favorite snack. We stand there, awkward, not knowing what to do next, when I say, "*Toda*, thank you, Danny. I love almonds, and the flowers too."

I stare at Danny's chiseled face, his square cleft chin, his strong, muscular shoulders, and I think to myself, *I really am lucky. And stupid.*

Gracelessly, I add, "But I'm in a bit of a rush now." The words tumble coldly from my lips, and knowing I can't take them back, I try to cover up my brashness. "Remember I told you last night that I have to go to the post office in Afula today to pick up a package of music CDs I ordered. It arrived two days ago, and the clerk at the post office keeps leaving me messages, reminding me to pick them up."

"Yes, I remember." Danny lets out a deep groan and drops onto the couch. The disappointment and frustration that mark his stare kick me right in the gut.

"The flowers and almonds are not my only surprises," he informs me. "I also have a car waiting for us. I want to take you to Afula and have dinner there. A romantic night out, just the two of us. Boaz told me about a new place that opened there that serves great *sabich*. I'm starving. What about you?" He scratches his forehead and waits for my response.

As much as I love Danny, I relish the few times I can find some alone time for myself, away from him and everything else at the kibbutz. It's those little moments I manage to carve into my hectic schedule that I relish the most. It is also during these times of selfish indulgence that I find myself daydreaming and fantasizing about a life I do not have—because I made other choices. Simple, safe choices.

I don't want to disappoint Danny, but I just can't make him understand. I could do without the sandwich (which is usually eaten as a breakfast meal anyway, but I don't dare to remind him of that now), and I had been looking forward to going out this afternoon to simply get away and enjoy some peace and quiet, even if the chore would take me just a ten-minute bus ride away into the tiny nearby village. Danny's gentle caramel-colored eyes are pleading now, and his mop of dark curls bounce around his face. I smack my lips and tell him I think it's a grand idea. He smiles and murmurs, "Come on, then. The post office will be closing soon."

The drive to Afula is short. Leaving the front gates of Gan Notzah, we pass Omar, a friendly local orange farmer and neighbor, standing on the corner of the dirt road. His pyramid stacks of oranges are piled high, glowing like melted circles of sun trapped inside his crates. No one but locals and kibbutzniks drive this road, and I wonder how Omar manages to make a living and support his family with these oranges.

A young boy caked in mud and dried manure walks on the side of the road, holding a stick in one hand and pulling a tired, dusty donkey by a rope with the other. He is wearing a stained Beatles T-shirt. Our car kicks up a red cloud of dust, and the boy with his donkey disappears in our rearview mirror.

Once we reach the little village of Afula, Danny finds a parking spot on the one main road. The post office is just ahead, and the new restaurant in town is across the street and down a narrow alley. I scout the area, my eyes darting up and down the street, and I see a crowd of men on the sidewalk outside the post office. "I wonder what's going on over there," I say to no one in particular. Danny looks up, sees the crowd, and raises his eyebrows in serious concentration. Like most Israelis, we are both quick to react with caution whenever there is a commotion or possible disorder. Large, noisy crowds in the middle of an otherwise quiet street always make us nervous. Danny reaches into the glove box and pulls out a small object bundled in a grease-covered cloth. Tucking the bundle into the waist of his pants, we get out of the car. I don't ask any questions…there's no need. Danny adjusts his shirt, and I let out a deep breath of air I don't realize I'm holding in.

After picking up my parcel at the post office, Danny and I walk close together to the sandwich shop. The crowd of men we saw earlier is gone, and the street lights begin to flicker on. I let Danny carry the package, and I shuffle slowly beside him. Danny and I find the restaurant and request a table outside. One family—a mother, father, and four fussy, dirt-stained children—are the only other people in the small space, but they make enough noise that could drown out a sold-out rock music concert. Danny cautiously takes another look around us, raises his hand, and whistles to the lone waiter, a young Arab boy wearing pants that are too short. In his broken Arabic, he asks for two beers, two plates of sabich, and a large order of chips. The boy quickly brings us our beers and the order of french-fries that are dripping in hot, spicy oil.

When the young waiter moves out of earshot, Danny takes a long swig of his beer and says, "Maya, I want to talk to you about something."

"Uh-oh." I tsk. This doesn't sound good. Keeping my composure and a cool expression on my face, I ask, "Sure, what's up?"

The dishes of sabich—my sandwich on pita and Danny's on *laffa* bread—are stuffed with fried eggplants, hard-boiled eggs, chopped salad, parsley, amba and tahini sauce. The smell makes my stomach gurgle. I wonder where my husband manages to find the space in his belly for all this food. He eats with his heart, as my mother would say. But the heavy aroma of Iraqi seasonings and oil assaults my nostrils, and I cover my mouth to suppress a low, nauseous burp.

Eyeing the food in front of him, Danny licks his thick lips, ready to attack the treat he has been waiting for. In short bursts between big, sloppy bites, he explains that, despite my time and effort with the dance academy, Gan Notzah is still not showing enough signs of digging out of its economic hole, and he is worried about the future finances of the kibbutz and its residents. He tells me that he and my father have already discussed the meager revenue that the dance studio is generating at the moment, and they both share the opinion that it might be years (years that we don't have to spare!) before they could see the kibbutz scrap its way out of the red. "It might have been a bad investment for us." I listen to Danny, wondering if he is referring to the investment as bad for the kibbutz or bad for us in particular. Sweat is now edging around my neck like a noose.

My attention is momentarily diverted. A foreign-looking man in jeans, a white polo shirt, and muddy work boots takes a seat at the table in the far, dark corner of the restaurant. A pair of Ray Ban sunglasses are perched on the top of his head. I bounce backward as soon as I place his face and remember he is one of our volunteers. What is he doing here in this dump of a village, in this dump of a restaurant, all by himself? I can't peel my eyes away from him.

Danny, oblivious to the lone volunteer sitting in the corner, hammers his large palm on the table, and I jump to attention. His frustration is written all over his face, and his shoulders slump down in defeat. "Maya, are you listening to me? *Hello…*" The plates and silverware on the table shake from the slap of his hand, and I am brought back to our conversation. He is obviously not paying any attention to the man sitting next to us; Danny's eyes are glued on me, and his cheeks are glowing crimson with exasperation. "I'm worried, Maya. I really am. The kibbutz is in trouble. *We* are in trouble." His chest heaves unevenly as he squeaks out the word *we*. "Don't you even care? Our agricultural research and the dance studio this year have cost more than we thought, and just like I originally thought, the dance classes are not really helping as much as we thought they would…" His rasping accusations trail off.

Danny's outcry screeches in my ears like a sudden car crash. "I know we have had a slow start, but I honestly believe we are doing better now. I mean, the classes are all full, and I teach three classes a day. What more can we…I…do?" The look that spreads across Danny's face makes my chest flutter and my toes wiggle inside my sweaty sneakers. Maya's Dance Palace is hardly Broadway or even Tel Aviv, but I know the income from the academy has to be bringing in *some* profit. Even though the kibbutz is still operating in the red, according to Abba, the income from Maya's Dance Palace has got to be offering some breathing space for the kibbutz. I blow out a stuttering, frustrated blast of air.

Apparently, all my efforts have not been enough. I have not been enough. All the planning and worrying are washed down the drain like dirty dishwater. Have my personal hopes and dreams not been enough to make a difference for our community? I stare over at the lone volunteer sitting at the next table, and my heart skips a solid beat. No, I can't give up. Hopes and dreams are all I have, all I can offer, and too many people are counting on me. The muscles in my thighs spasm, my spine straightens, and my mind swirls with pirouettes. "We can't give up now. Just give me some more time, and I'll come up with something."

*"When we are no longer able to change a situation,
we are challenged to change ourselves."*
—Viktor Frankl

15

Sofia

Sofia hurried out of the shower and got dressed. She was sure this Shabbos was going to be unlike any other. Aside from the hullabaloo she was expecting from her family for her birthday, she also had big news to announce. Becca was coming along too, and that was certainly going to add to the tumult of gossip. It would be Becca's first time back in the old neighborhood since her father ordered her to leave their house, but at least Becca's presence this Shabbos at Tyotya Anika's and Dyadya Sol's would deflect some of the shock Sofia was expecting from her sudden announcement about her engagement to Ben.

As an added birthday-slash-engagement surprise, Sofia and Ben had spent a few days in the Hamptons at a gorgeous beachfront bungalow. It was a special perk, reserved by the tech firm where Ben worked, for "special" clients, and his boss had graciously allowed them to use it for a few days to celebrate the announcement of Ben's engagement and Sofia's twenty-sixth birthday. It was a small blessing that Boris gave her time away from the academy, considering the brutal rehearsals he was imposing on the cast for *Swan Lake*. Anika and Sol did not approve of Sofia going away with a man alone ("*Oy, gevalt*, what would your *mamoh* say!" Anika had protested), but Sofia had no intentions of letting them ruin her first opportunity to vacation in the Hamptons. She knew Anika did not really like Ben that much either. It didn't help that he was not Jewish or that they thought that he flaunted his newly-gained money too much ("He's like a monkey in a silk suit," Sol had said, adding fuel to Anika's fire).

Well, what do they know? challenged Sofia. She decided she would tell her aunt and uncle about the engagement that night over Shabbos dinner. She was not a little girl anymore; after all, she was turning twenty-six! She was old enough to make her own decisions, regardless of what they thought.

Sofia and Becca had to get on the city bus before the evening rush hour, or they risked being late. The Sabbath always started when the first three stars in the sky after sundown could be seen, or at precisely 7:56 p.m. this particular Friday night. Uncle Sol had called four times that day to remind her. "Remember, *meidele*, when you're on time, you're late," he sang to her and then added, "It's better to be five minutes early than one minute late!" If they were not there on time to light the candles with Tyotya Anika before walking together to *shul* for evening services, it was likely to cause World War III in the Fridman home.

She wore her navy-blue dress—one of the few dresses modest enough for Shabbos—with sleeves that concealed her arms to her elbows and a hem that hung matronly over her knees. The boatneck collar was the only thing that conveyed a hint of skin at her clavicle.

This was the one thing Sofia loathed about the Sabbath—the hypocritical ruse of dressing like a wolf in sheep's clothing. Who was she kidding in that dress? Who was *anyone* kidding in their Friday night getups? But she recalled how her mother always insisted that "perception was reality" and that "tradition needed to be respected." Sofia never put much credence in her ancestral traditions, but her religion was more than just a bunch of Jewish rituals—it was a way of life. Even more so after moving to New York, Sofia noticed. "Here we have the freedom to live as we should according to God's word," Dyadya Sol had professed over and over. "It's not like it was in the old days back in Russia." She could hear her mother's words ringing in her ears now too as she stared down at her hand and twisted the two-carat diamond ring on her finger.

Becca knocked on her bedroom door and burst in without waiting for Sofia to invite her in. "Come on, Sofia. Hurry up. We can't be late." In her hands, she swung a white bakery box. "Fresh and hot bow-tie cookies for dessert," she said with a grin, holding the box out toward Sofia. "My mom makes the best *kichel*, but I bought these from Raisa's Bakery. I'm sure Anika baked a birthday cake for you too, but you know I had to bring something." She clutched her free hand at her chest and held her breath.

While the Fridmans went to shul for Shabbos services, Becca stayed behind and waited for them to return, not wanting to run into any old acquaintances, or God forbid, her parents. While she waited in the warm apartment, she set the table for the big dinner, but as soon as the Fridmans returned, she grabbed Sofia by the arm and dragged her into the kitchen. She was desperate to hear about her family. "Did you see my parents? What about my brother and sisters? Did they say anything to you…about me?"

Sofia was distracted by the sight of her aunt's famous chocolate rum cake and the intoxicating smells of all her favorite dishes—roasted chicken, glazed carrots, and sweet noodle kugel. They were the same smells that always brought Sofia home, her real home back in Ukraine with Mamoh and Tatoh, and she barely heard Becca's pleas for attention and comfort. Suddenly, Sofia was standing in the kitchen back in Lutsk with her mother and father, the bolt of tradition freezing her in the moment.

From her earliest memories, Sofia could recall her father bursting through the front door just in time for Mamoh's delicious Friday night family dinner. He would appear, rushing from God knows where, carrying armloads of gifts for her and her mother. (Sofia's favorite gift, she still recalled, was a small doll of fine white porcelain. Her hair was made of gold thread and pulled into a tight knot with a shiny blue ribbon. The doll wore a white leotard, a crinoline tutu, and white satin fabric wrapped around her two pointy feet.) Tatoh would grumble with a smile about his heavy workload and how grateful he was to be home with his family at the end of a hard, long, and distant work week. By Sunday morning, Tatoh would be gone again, but Mamoh and Sofia would carry on, finding more dance auditions and stage productions to perform, until Tatoh returned to them again.

The Fridmans gathered around the table where candles burned brightly and two loaves of freshly baked challah waited to be uncovered and devoured with a prayer. After four courses of rich foods, several cups of wine, and the singing of "happy birthday" in three languages, Aunt Anika and Nathan emerged from the kitchen with coffee, a bottle of vodka, a homemade birthday cake, and the box of cookies that Becca had brought.

It was Becca who finally found the courage to address the elephant in the room. She spoke up, but her voice was barely audible. "The baby is due at the end of the year. I've been thinking of names, but of course, I don't want to talk about that yet." She burped back her embarrassment and covered her mouth with her trembling fingers.

"*Ptooh, ptooh,*" hissed Aunt Anika. "Don't even mention baby names. It's too early to speak of that!" She pretended to spit through her front teeth, crinkled the space above her nose as if she just smelled something foul, and turned her gaze away from Becca.

"Since you brought up the subject, Becca, I have a question." Nathan laid down his fork and wiped frosting from his lips. "Did you even consider a Plan B?" Nathan choked; but it was his words, not the cake, that was stuck in his throat. He covered his mouth with his fist and coughed as his face lit up like a menorah on the eighth night of Hanukkah, and his eyes darted back and forth. He was speaking to Becca, yet he couldn't bring himself to make eye contact with her.

Becca bit down on her lower lip, and Sofia kicked her cousin under the table. Uncle Sol swallowed hard, as if he would choke on the bite of rum cake he had just shoveled into his mouth. Nathan looked around the table and continued, "I guess, it's too late to consider now, and I don't mean to make you feel uncomfortable, but it might have been something you could have considered. I mean, after all, you are not married, and—"

Sofia cut him off, pounding her fist on the table. The crystal wine goblets and scattered silverware rattled. "Nathan, that's enough! It is none of your business, and quite inappropriate, I might add, to be talking like this to Becca. She obviously wants to keep this baby and doesn't need to hear your know-it-all solutions."

Becca's cheeks turned crimson, and her eyes puddled with tears. She took a quick gulp of coffee and slunk down in her seat.

"I'm just saying I could have helped." Looking directly at Becca, Nathan nodded his head with empathy. "I could have gotten the morning-after pill for you at the pharmacy…or even the RU-486 abortion pill without a prescription. Mendel would have kept quiet about it, and no one would have known."

Becca turned away from Nathan and cleared her throat. "I'm fine, really. Sofia is right. I decided I am going to have my baby. But thanks for your concern. Really." Becca did not want to keep repeating the argument she had been fighting with Sofia for months and feeling like she had to defend herself to everyone, but like Nathan said, she was the one who brought up the subject. She just needed to get it all out in the open, and now though, she was going to end it. She smiled faintly at Nathan and looked down at her hands resting in her lap. "I've discovered there is a very fine line between good and bad decisions…right and wrong choices…but it is how we deal with the consequences that really matters. We all make bad choices sometimes, and the consequences are not always clear or easy to deal with. But sometimes good decisions are the hardest ones for us to make. They are not easy to make, but they are right, regardless of the consequences." Without making eye contact with anyone in particular, she excused herself and ran to the bathroom.

Both Sol and Anika shot scolding glances at their son. "Now look what you've done. Can't you keep your big mouth shut, big shot! This is Becca's business, not yours!" Anika scolded.

"And you're being rude. She is a guest in your house," Sol added.

Sofia was furious with Nathan and temporarily forgot her own announcement about her engagement to Ben. She stood behind

Nathan's chair and bent over him to whisper in his ear, "You know Becca is like a sister to me. How could you talk to her that way? You're not a doctor, and you're not her savior! What you are, though, is an insensitive, cruel ass! Mind your own business from now on!" Sofia's fists balled up at her sides; she could not control the sense of protectiveness for Becca that flowed through her body.

"You're right, and I'm sorry if I embarrassed Becca. As it is, I have a bit of my own gossip to share tonight." She wasn't sure she could handle any more drama and scandal for the night. Just then, Becca returned from the bathroom, taking deep breaths of air and swiping at the black eyeliner that was smudged under her eyes.

Sofia watched her friend sit back down at the table and admired her pride and courage. She picked up her empty wineglass and willed her mind to blank out all her growing worry. Love seemed to be more costly, more painful, more disenchanting than it was made out to be. Her parents were nowhere to be found, Becca was going to have a baby without a husband and without a father for the child, and Ben… Well, then there's Ben.

She reached for the bottle of wine next to Nathan and waited for him to elaborate about his pending announcement. "So what's your news, cousin? What's got you acting like such a *chutzpahni* tonight?"

Nathan nibbled on a bite of his *kichel* and picked up his glass of wine. "I've got good news for you all." He stopped for theatrical emphasis before he continued, "You are all looking at the next college-bound Fridman." Looking around the room, he pumped up his chest and pointed his chin up to the ceiling. "Yup, I've been accepted to pharmaceutical school in Chicago!"

Becca rubbed her hand over her tight belly.

Uncle Sol yelled out, "*Mazal tov*, my son! I knew you would do it!"

Aunt Anika's eyes filled with tears of pride and happiness. "Oy, now he's your son, Sol? A minute ago, he was only a rude boy." Turning to Nathan, Anika said, "What *nachas* and joy you bring us, Nathan!" She looked at Nathan with pride and stood to give him a tight hug and kisses on both cheeks.

"You're going where? You're leaving New York?" was all Sofia could cough up.

"I sure am. I'm out of here! I applied to the University of Illinois, to their department of pharmacy practice. Mendel graduated from there and wrote me a letter of recommendation. If I'm lucky, I might even get to work in their research center." Nathan's eyes sparkled as he spoke of his longtime dream. He had always wanted to study medicine, and now his dream would be coming true. "It won't be easy, especially so far away from you all, but I have to admit, I can't wait to go!"

"When are you leaving?" Becca's four words were faint and garbled.

"The fall semester begins in August. I plan to leave sometime in the next two months." Nathan bowed his head and swallowed hard.

The night was turning into a bigger show than even Sofia had anticipated. A night for confessing dreams. A celebration to toast the future. A moment for facing fears and dealing with consequences.

Cheers!

But Sofia wasn't about to let anyone else steal her show. After all, it was her twenty-sixth birthday. "Well, I thought I was the only one with shocking news tonight. Hold on to your seats, and let's all raise our glasses one more time." Sofia sucked on her lower lip, held up her half-drunk glass of wine, and irrevocably blurted, "I'm getting married. *L'chaim*!"

16

Sofia

She couldn't help it any longer. It was turning into a situation she hadn't bargained for. Sofia rebuked herself for her fading empathy, but her nerves were slowly unraveling; if the conversations were not about Becca's swollen legs or the tweaked muscles in her neck and back, the only thing they had to talk about was the growing concerns about Becca's persistent headaches and queasy stomach. Sofia really wanted to be supportive, but all she could think about was how she had become a 24/7 nursemaid. It wasn't what she signed up for when she offered to help her best friend.

But now, thank God, five months into the pregnancy, Becca was beginning to regain some of her strength and vivacity. She started teaching classes again with the younger academy students, and their lives slowly morphed back into a steady routine.

With the anticipation of her engagement and upcoming wedding to plan, she was glad to recover her time in order to focus on

Ben. Becca and the dance studio had been consuming every minute of her time, and Ben's frustration with her lack of attention was growing more obvious and bitter. Sofia's vigorous rehearsal schedule occupied every moment during the long summer days, but at night, she tried to dedicate her time and efforts on Ben. Becca seemed to understand, and she slowly loosened her dependency on Sofia.

Sofia concentrated on Ben and remained open to his considerate and affectionate suggestions for ways they could spend time together; they attended shows on Broadway, took rides in horse-drawn buggies around Central Park, and rummaged through trendy, hipster art galleries in Brooklyn. The only places Sofia refused to go with him were Brighton Beach and Coney Island. And the more she rejected those ideas, the more Ben pleaded.

"Aw, come on, princess. I'm still a bit of an outsider in this city, and I would love to ride the Ferris wheel with you! I hear it's a real thrill," Ben begged.

"No way, Ben, I already told you. I'll go anywhere in this whole world with you, *except* there."

To placate him, Sofia arranged a family get-together at Galina's Restaurant in Brighton; it was the first time she would be introducing Ben to her family as her fiancé. And sure, as she suspected, the evening turned into a total disaster.

Uncle Sol had been pleasant enough, but Aunt Anika had left Sofia to drown in disapproving derision. There was no doubt that her aunt didn't like Ben, and Sofia was starting to question her decision and future with Ben too.

The boardwalk was relatively quiet. It was a balmy August night, and even along the seashore, the air was stifling and repressive. The summer months saw native New Yorkers as well as glitzy tourists, looking for cooler, more luxurious, vacation spots outside of the city. So sitting on the seaside terrace of Galina's restaurant, drinking shots of vodka, and noshing on bowls of pickled cherries, Aunt Anika squirmed restlessly in her seat. She was not impressed with Sofia's choice for her future husband, and she wasn't afraid to let everyone know what she thought. Ben got up to go to the bathroom, and Aunt Anika seized the opportunity to let her tongue fly. She squinted at Sofia's engagement ring and scowled, "You know, *meidele*, it's not so good to rely so much on a man. Especially one that is not cut from the same cloth as you are."

"What are you getting at, Tyotya? Why don't you like Ben?" Sofia rolled her eyes toward the beach and continued to play it cool with her aunt. But she knew exactly what her remark was referring to, and Sofia finally let out the words that encompassed her own fears and doubts. "I know he's not Jewish, and that bothers you and Uncle Sol. But you don't know him like I do. He's a good man, and I love him!" Sofia looked around to see if anyone was paying attention to her tantrum.

Truth be told, Sofia had begun to have her own misgivings about Ben and thought that her aunt might be right about him after all. Now engaged to be married, her husband-to-be, Jewish or not, had started to let his true intentions slip out. One evening while walking hand in hand across the Brooklyn Bridge, Ben proposed the notion that Sofia's days in the theater would come to an end once they were married and started a family of their own. "I may be an old-fashioned Southern boy, but I'm sure you'll agree…your family's old-world traditional ways…that a wife needs to be home, available, and loyal to her husband and children." Sofia had never heard him express such thoughts before. *What does he know of my family's traditional ways or just how "old-world" I was?* She fumed. *Was he kidding?*

Aunt Anika clarified her statement, softening her tone and lowering her watery gaze to her purse resting on her lap. "Just think about what I'm saying, Sofia. I think you're rushing into this without thinking clearly about it. You just turned twenty-six, and you still have time for romance and marriage. You are still becoming who you are meant to be. And what's that, *nu*? You're destined to be a ballerina. A star. That's what you are! It's what you've always been. Are you willing to give it all up for a man? For Ben? And what about your parents? What would they say about you abandoning your traditions and your people?" Anika clicked her tongue and adjusted her girdle under her linen skirt. "Mark my words, Sofia, Ben might be a nice guy, but he's not the one for you."

Her aunt's words hit her like a sucker-punch in the gut. Sofia knew her aunt was upset about her stubborn determination to marry Ben, but worse than that was the sadness and disappointment she saw in her eyes. Maybe her aunt was right, and Ben wasn't the guy for her. Traditions or not, Ben couldn't possibly expect her to give up her career, her dreams, her future, just because they were getting married.

Could he?

Images of her past played like an old black-and-white film in her mind. She saw her mother compromising her ambitions and vowing allegiance to a marriage that stole her dreams of working in the theater. She had heard her mother talk about personal freedom, responsibility, of Tatoh's work and responsibilities to his family; there was always a trace of resentment and remorse in her words. Sofia sensed that as long as her father was loyal to his job, her mother would have to remain trapped in an empty world of uncertainty. Mamoh had given up her own dreams and aspirations in order to take care of her family.

Sofia knew her mother loved her father, but what did that really mean? She always wondered about the sacrifices she had had to make in the name of love. Tatoh's work and endless absences from home seemed more important than Mamoh's dreams and passions. Was Tatoh the reason Mamoh gave up on her own aspirations for the theater? Was love about compromise or sacrifice?

Who controls the choices we make in the name of love?

The questions drudged up by Aunt Anika's words now grew prickly around them, and Sofia shuddered against the salty ocean breeze. A knot tightened in her chest and squeezed the air out of her.

Anika broke through Sofia's silent thoughts. "I understand your infatuation with him, *bubbeleh*, what with all those diamonds he gives you and that fancy car of his, but I just don't get the feeling that you've thought this all the way through. Just promise you'll think about it some more before…" Anika poked her finger at her jaw, and her eyes glazed over. Her last words hung in the air, suspended by the salt and grime of the sea waves crashing nearby.

Is it too late?

Anika remained silent for the rest of the evening and showed Ben nothing but good manners and indifference from that point on while Ben and Uncle Sol bonded over their combined praise of the Yankees and their respectable differences of opinion on the subject of the high-tech market.

Sofia was becoming more and more restless as she waited for Becca's dance class to end. They had plans to have lunch together at the new Russian diner down the street, and she was starving. Just thinking about lunch made her mouth water and her stomach growl. She stood there, her *kishkes* vibrating in her stomach from the hip-hop commotion escaping from the studio, and contemplated all the food awaiting them and how lucky she was to have been blessed with an abnormally fast metabolism that allowed her to eat beyond the limits of her fellow dancers. At that thought, she giggled out loud and hugged her arms around her rumbling belly. A woman turned to look at her and crooned in a heavy Brooklyn brogue, "Not for nothin', but aren't these kids *so* cute! Is your kid in this class too?"

Sofia let out another deep chuckle and said, "Yes, mine is the older, round one in the front of the class."

Just then, Sofia was distracted by a large masculine shadow looming by the back studio, usually reserved only for Boris. Noting that it was his day off and that it couldn't be him she was seeing, she watched the lurking silhouette pace back and forth at the end of the hallway. The rambling woman at Sofia's side was insulted by her sudden lack of attention and flashed her a frown before skulking away.

Sofia barely noticed the woman leave her side. She was no longer listening to the pounding beats of the music either. She kept her suspicious eyes pinned to the shadow and watched as it slowly came into focus. It couldn't be him. But it was. Ben.

Sofia slipped past the thickening crowd of the dance class's onlookers gathered in front of Becca's studio and half-ran-half-skipped down the hallway. Approaching with jumbled curiosity, she said with a shocked pant, "Ben? Is that you?"

Hearing his name, Ben spun around to face Sofia. In a dark-blue suit, red tie, and shiny brown leather moccasins, Ben smiled innocently. "Oh…hi, Sofia. I looked for you, and since I couldn't find you, I thought I already missed you. Didn't you say you were going to lunch with Becca today?"

"I'm waiting for her to finish her class. But a better question is, what are you doing here?" He had shown up, uninvited, on her turf, and Sofia did not appreciate his intrusion in her personal space. She wrestled with the momentary idea that she was overreacting, but her fury (irrational as it might have seemed) rose from her hollow gut all the way to her head.

She tried to disguise her annoyance with a smirk and a playful poke to Ben's belly. Her own belly sizzled with the creepy sense that Ben's sudden appearance there—in the middle of the workday—was inappropriate (at best) and threatening (at worst). *Was this the beginning of his hidden agenda to control and manipulate her?*

"I had a meeting with a client around the corner, so I thought I'd come by and see if I could catch you for an impromptu lunch date. What do you say, princess? I'm sure Becca wouldn't mind if I joined you two." Ben's poise and self-confidence blared like a siren and knocked Sofia off-balance. Yet it was very much in character for Ben to surprise her with random treats and attentions, so why should it alarm her so much now to find him there for an impromptu lunch date? Sofia shook the suspicion from her head and clucked her tongue.

"I'm sure Becca wouldn't mind, Ben, but I did promise I'd spend time with her today." Just then, Nina Cassel sashayed into the hallway, almost as if on cue. Her long legs glided down the narrow hallway, and the scent of her flowery perfume hung precariously between Sofia and Ben. Sofia choked out a dry cough and said, "Hello, Nina. Have you two met yet? This is Ben. My fiancé." The words barely squeezed past her clenched teeth. Sofia swiveled her whole body toward Ben, but kept her eyes pinned on Nina. She fidgeted with the diamond ring on her finger.

Nina grinned until the corners of her heart-shaped lips nearly touched her ears. "So nice to meet you," she whispered, extending a graceful arm toward Ben.

"Nice to finally meet you too," Ben replied in his polite Southern drawl. He took Nina's hand in his and shook it up and down as if he were pumping water from a nineteenth-century water pump. Sofia noticed he was holding her hand a moment longer than necessary.

"*Finally*, huh? So I take it that Sofia talks about me?"

Sofia snarled. *Can she really be so narcissistic?* Nina continued to stare deep into Ben's eyes and drew her finger down an imaginary line from her chin to her collarbone.

An idea popped into Sofia's head. "Ben came to have lunch with me and Becca. Would you like to join us?"

"Really? Sounds great. I'd love to! It'll give us all a chance to get acquainted." Nina was speaking to Sofia, but her eyes remained locked on Ben, whose jaw dropped, flabbergasted by Sofia's invitation. Smooth as cotton candy and just as sickly-sweet, Nina went on, "I'll need a few minutes to change my clothes. Tell me where you're going, and I'll meet you there."

"Becca and I were thinking of going for a burger at the Beer Barn. You know the place on the corner by the new IMAX theater. They have good salads there too. Oh, here comes Becca now."

Without waiting for a response from Nina and grabbing Ben by the cuff of his jacket, Sofia swiveled on the balls of her feet and headed down the hallway toward Becca and the dispersing hip-hop class. She waved her hand above the crowd, signaling for Becca to hurry up. Ben and Becca followed Sofia out onto the sidewalk, but instead of turning right in the direction of the Beer Barn, Sofia led her unsuspecting cohorts to the left, steering resolutely toward the new Russian diner down the street.

17

Maya

I never felt so panicky, so inadequate, as I have these past months. Kibbutz Gan Notzah is drowning in debt, and our dance academy venture is not helping as we expected. So much of our survival has been placed on my shoulders, and for all of my efforts, nothing is working. I am plagued with nightmares that keep me up all night, and I walk around like a zombie all day. Danny and I are drifting farther and farther from each other, and Aaron is spending longer days at the nursery. Feeling useless and invisible on our communal enterprise, I have never felt so lonely and lost. The medicine bottle I left sitting on top of the record player glistens in the afternoon sunlight.

Standing in the entry of Maya's Dance Palace, I look around and take in all the vintage artwork and posters hanging on the walls. I remember when these collectibles represented the passion and inspiration of my dreams—that one day I might become a first-class prima ballerina. Once wallpapering the walls of my bedroom, now the décor of our small but professional kibbutz academy, the displays seem old, worn, and misplaced—a poster of Baryshnikov performing an aerial pirouette, a ceramic set of comedy-and-tragedy theater masks, a black-and-white photograph of the great American Ballet Theater in New York City. I yawn and swallow two pills from the bottle.

I'm on pins and needles, fluttering about the main studio as if looking for the secret entrance to the Cave of the Patriarchs, when I hear the front door swoosh open. Classes will begin in a few hours, but I am not expecting anyone this early in the day. I spin around to see Mr. Movie Star standing in the doorway, blocking the rays of the early afternoon sun. He is wearing the kibbutz uniform of khaki shorts, white T-shirt with the kibbutz logo on the front, and work boots. He interrupts me from my own musings, and I inhale a huff of exasperation by the dirt he is dragging into the entrance. His expensive glasses rest lopsided on the bridge of his sunburned nose. His gold hair is matted with sweat, and his skin is glimmering gold. Mr. Movie Star quickly removes his glasses and stares at me without saying a word.

"Hi there," I say, trying to keep my smile friendly, my wide-eyed stare confused. He can't possibly be lost; he's been here for five months already. I think maybe he's not feeling well. "Can I help you with something?"

"No. I mean, yes. Well, maybe. I just finished the project we were developing with the cultivation plow, and I have been curious about this place. I've been hearing a lot about your studio. Do you mind if I have a look around?"

"First of all, what is your name?" I never realized before that moment that the group of volunteers had been with us for nearly half a year, and I still don't even know their names. I had simply referred to this guy as "Mr. Movie Star" since the day he arrived.

"James. James Turner. But people just call me Jim." Jim takes a step toward me and holds out his hand for me to shake. I had guessed him to be in his midtwenties, but his mannerisms seem a bit stiff and uncomfortable. I detect a slight twang as he speaks, but I can't place it. I reach out to take hold of his long fingers, and an electric bolt shudders up my arm and down my spine. I pull my hand back as if I had been stung by a bee and wipe it on the gauze of my skirt. Jim flushes a deep crimson and stands, rocking uneasily from one foot to the other.

Quickly, I recuperate my composure, and I continue to throw more questions at him. "Okay, Mr. Turner…Jim, I mean. What exactly have you heard about Maya's Dance Palace, and why are you so interested in our little conservatory?" My words are overly stiff and professional (mimicking the formality of my visitor's demeanor) and suggest a tinge of pride in the compliment of his notice, but my reservations about his sudden intrigue is evident in my shrinking posture. I back away from him and let a low guffaw escape from between my grinning lips. "Are you a dancer, by any chance?"

"Oh, no. Not me. But my sister is a dancer. Jazz, mostly. She would love this place, and it does make me feel a bit homesick," he offers with sincere emotion in his eyes. "If I didn't know any better, I'd say I was back in Seattle, picking her up from her lessons." He smiles warmly at the memory, and adds, "Her name is Rosie…" His dreamy gaze scans the surroundings again before resting back on me, and suddenly, we are connecting beyond the formality, on a completely different plane, as if we were friends for decades.

Unexpectedly, I am feeling self-conscious and giddy. I haven't felt this frisky since I performed in my first ballet recital as a teenager. My muscles are flaming hot, and my toes twitch and tingle inside the cotton-packed toes of my ballet slippers. To my pleasant discovery, James Turner, the volunteer with the Brad Pitt smile, is also kind and sensitive and compassionate.

Jim follows me on a tour around the building as I obligingly show off our studios and classrooms. He listens attentively to my inane anecdotes about some of our students—like the time Anat, our youngest pupil, tripped on a loose floorboard during an important show for the municipality's leaders and sailed halfway across the stage, face-first into the piano. Jim laughed and told me about the time his little sister was performing for an annual Christmas party in Seattle's main concert hall and had lost her tutu when it came untied in front of the full audience. Jim amuses me with more stories about his family and his studies in agricultural college in Iowa. Strolling around Maya's Dance Palace, side by side, laughing until my cheeks hurt and stealing occasional touches on each other's shoulders, I forget all that I was worrying about, and my head begins to swim with renewed fantasy, passion, and longing. I make a new friend, and the feeling comforts me like an old, worn blanket.

The path is pitch-dark and eerily silent. The only sound I hear is the menacing scratches of claws digging into the wooden beams of the old tailor's shed. It's still early for the bats to come alive, but all the same, I know they're there, lurking and waiting for me to make the wrong move and fall right into their reach. I know this path like I know every contour of little Aaron's pudgy face, but I walk cautiously, careful not to trip over any pebbles or broken slabs of concrete. Looking down at my feet, I remember that time when I was just nine years old, and one of those pesky bats flew into my hair and wouldn't let go until Kobi came to save me from the attack. He waved his fists and screamed like a wild banshee until the bat finally disappeared back into the darkness of the shed. I stifle a quiet giggle and grab my loose strands of hair, holding them in a tight fist behind my head.

"The things we'll do for..." I don't dare finish that sentence.

I feel a swift tug on my arm, and I jerk to a stop in my tracks to face a silhouetted figure. I smell a familiar scent—a soft mix of engine grease and Halston cologne. Without a word, Jim pulls me off the path, and we step slowly away from the shed and over the dewy grass until we reach the edge of the sunflower field. It is a moonless night, and Jim's hand rests lightly on my forearm. The encroaching scent of the sunflowers mixes in the air and makes my head dizzy.

"You scared the shit out of me, Jim! What are you doing out here?" I punch him in the shoulder with enough force to make him wince.

Jim doesn't waste any time and pulls me closer to him, his breath whispering gently in my ear. "Maya, I have to talk to someone, or I'm going to explode. What I have to tell you isn't easy. And I need to know that you won't say a word about it to anyone."

"Don't be silly, Jim. Of course, you can trust me. What's this all about? And why did you need to meet me here—in the middle of the field at night? My husband is going to have a fit if I'm not home to have dinner with him..." That last thought trails off into the shadowy night, and I can hear the bats' claws scratching against the wooden beams, even standing yards away from the tailor's shed.

"The past year here at Gan Notzah has been like heaven for me, Maya. This place is like a little oasis in a big desert. I didn't want to bring this up at all, but I can't hold it in any longer. You have become a trusted friend to me, and I need to talk to someone." I pull away and scrunch my nose in wonder at Jim. I still can't imagine what could possibly be so urgent. I listen to Jim's whispered words, glad that he thinks of me as such a trusted and worthy friend.

Tired and anxious to get home to Danny and Aaron, I reply, "I really have to get back home, Jim. I don't want to sound insensitive, but meeting out here is kind of…well, weird? So tell me. What is it that has you so upset? What can I do to help?"

Jim heaves a big gulp of air and stares me right in the eye. "Okay, here goes. I have a huge confession to make to you." Stopping as if to consider his next words, Jim pinches the bridge of his nose and continues, "I have AIDS—"

"Stop it, Jim! Stop right there. If this is your idea of a joke—"

Jim cuts me off, "This is no joke. My immune system is completely shot to hell, Maya, and the doctors…well, the doctors…that's why I've come out here. To Israel. I wanted to do something special and important before—"

Now it is my turn to interrupt Jim. My jaw drops open. I want to shout, but nothing comes out of my mouth, and all I could hear is the rustle of the wind between the sunflowers. "Surely the doctors have some treatment…some medicine to cure this, no?"

Jim grabs my shoulders and gives me a quick shake. "No, there's nothing. All the drugs and treatments so far have been Band-Aids. There is no cure for me. What's done is done. I am at the end of the rope. No, I just have to deal with the consequences now. I don't mean to burden you with this, but I had to talk to someone. I don't want anyone else to know about this. It has to stay our secret. Please promise you won't tell anyone else!"

Nothing is making any sense to me. Jim is too young, too smart. He has so much more to achieve. Still stunned by Jim's news, I don't know what else to say. Before I say anything really dumb, I close my lips into a tight line.

"Maya, you have become an inspiration for me. You have shown me that even when times are tough, we have a choice to pick ourselves up and keep moving forward. We all have problems, but it is how we deal with these problems that make the difference. And you have given me the strength to deal with my future, no matter how much time I have left. Being strong and fighting through the hard times is what really counts."

My throat is clogged; I can't breathe, and no sound will come out of my mouth. My head spins, and I can't see anything through the blackness clouding my vision. In just a few months, Jim has become an enjoyable companion and a welcomed friend. He can't be dying. Not now. Suddenly, I find myself missing Kobi, and the only words I can utter are, "You remind me a lot like my little brother. You never met him, but I bet you would have liked each other."

"If he's anything like you, he must be pretty special, and I am sure we would be good friends."

A tear rolls down my cheek, and Jim swipes it away with his thumb. Through hiccups and gasps of air, I say, "Jim, you invented an engine-thing that will revolutionize the almond industry for us. If anything, you are the one who is my true picture of inspiration! It is me who is thankful for your friendship!"

"That's just it, Maya. Maybe you should take a better look at yourself the next time you're dancing in front of that mirror of yours." Jim laughs and begins to cough into his fist. "You don't even recognize your own gift. Your own inspiration."

"What on earth are you talking about, Jim? Please, you have to shut up for a minute and let me soak this all in!" Jim's selfless comments make me feel more guilty, more inadequate, more useless than ever. Here he is, telling me that his days are numbered and that I have given him new hope and strength, and then he's talking about my *gift*? What the hell is he thinking? This conversation should not be about me; this is all about Jim. Wiping my nose with the back of my hand, I consider this untimely, heart-wrenching news. I cluck my tongue and swallow down a sour clot of bile.

Wrestling with the fear and doubt and pain of Jim's revelation, I hear him whisper, "You've been a great friend to me, and I am grateful for our time together, even if it was only for a few months. I may be out of luck, Maya, but you're not. You still have a choice. You've got to perform your ballet."

Embarrassed, angry, and awkward, I bend over and clutch at the sharp jab in my stomach. How does he know about my ballet? I haven't shared it with anyone except Irena, and that was many years ago. His grip on my shoulders becomes weaker, and he breathes through another admission. As if reading my thoughts, he says, "I've been watching you practice, Maya. And trust me, my friend. You *must* dance. Of course, it's still your choice, but your family and friends here at the kibbutz need you. It's your time to shine and make a difference!"

"Yeah, but—"

"But nothing! Maya." Tears begin to pool in his eyes, and his voice rises and breaks with a raspy hack… "I am leaving in three days, and we'll likely never see each other again. I will think of you, but I need to know you will not give up. That you will make the choice to help yourself and Gan Notzah. That you will not compromise your passion. I know it's hard to make difficult choices, but the difficult ones are the best ones. So please, Maya, promise you won't give up on your dreams and that you'll dance."

18

Sofia

It had been easy for Sofia to persuade her aunt to meet her at the new espresso bar near King's Highway that morning. As the Jewish New Year and holiday season of that month came to an end, this was a perfect excuse to escape the long and frenzied religious obligations in their overwhelming Brighton Beach community. Her mother's younger sister, Tyotya Anika, was only in her late forties and was adept at getting around the city on her own. She had no reservations about hopping on a bus and riding unaccompanied into the heart of Brooklyn. Courage, strength, and vitality were in their family's DNA helix.

The café was located halfway between Bay Ridge and Brighton Beach. Sofia figured she would meet her aunt there on her way to the academy that day, where they could enjoy a nice coffee and chat, and then they could head back to Brighton together—Sofia to the studio, and her aunt to Uncle Sol and their cozy little apartment. Anika took the seventeen-minute bus ride and stopped at Avenue U, then walked a short distance to West Sixth Street. Sofia was already there waiting for her to arrive (her father's words about being late etched into her mind). She marched back and forth on the busy sidewalk, searching between the crowds of commuters for sight of her aunt's arrival. As Anika approached the café, Sofia caught her patting a cautious hand on her handbag, a large black tote with sparkly sequins and shiny beads forming a collage of sea shells.

Spotting her aunt's purple scarf wrapped around her alert face, Sofia yelled out, "You made it, Tyotya. I'm so happy to see you." Sofia stood on her toes, reached up, and leaned her body forward for a kiss from her aunt's fuchsia-painted lips.

"Of course, I made it. What do you think? I don't know how to ride on a bus?" Aunt Anika's old-world accent always seemed more distinguished when she was outside of the environs of Brighton Beach's Little Odessa community. She planted a forceful kiss on Sofia's forehead and chucked her on the chin with a bony knuckle. "You look as gorgeous as always, my *sheine meidel*."

"Oh, Tyotya." Sofia smiled and blew out a puff of air that lingered in the icy air. "Let's go inside and grab a table. This place will be packed with people before we know it." Sofia led her aunt to a table and motioned for her to sit. They took off their puffy coats and hung them on the back of their chairs. "I know you prefer hot tea, but you have to try the espresso here. It's to die for! I'll go get some for us while you wait here."

"Oy, vey! What drama you young people make about coffee! I doubt I will die if I don't drink your espresso, but I didn't come all this way to your 'to-die-for' coffee shop just to order a little tea. So let's see what all the fuss is about."

Sofia couldn't help but grin at her aunt's good humor and quick wit. Anika was younger than her mother, but she had been nothing short of a loving and generous substitute parent to Sofia since she arrived in the United States eight years earlier. Sofia was eighteen at the time, but it wasn't until recently that she became keenly aware that a person never outgrows a mother's love and guidance. She was glad to see her aunt in such good spirits that morning. Especially since their conversations lately, mostly revolving around Ben and her upcoming marriage, usually led to arguments that rivaled nothing short of nuclear explosions. This morning, Sofia was hopeful for a pleasant change of pace.

When she returned to the table clutching two hot cups of espresso with steamed milk between her scorching fingers, Anika reached for her bag. "Look what I brought for you. It's *syrnik*, straight from Rina's ovens of the Homemade Cooking Café near your uncle's market. The line of customers went down the block, but I know how much you love this cake." It was an extravagant gesture that made Sofia feel guilty. Her favorite pastry, cheesecake covered in chocolate, was not only decadent for the tastebuds but an extraordinary expense for her aunt's pocketbook. Anika placed the bakery box in the middle of the table, untied the purple floral scarf from around her head, and licked her cracked red lips.

Sofia plopped down in her chair and spread paper napkins like placemats on the table in front of her. She grabbed the cake box and inhaled the sugary aroma. "Yummy. Tyotya, thank you. Is this the surprise you told me you were bringing today? You really didn't have to do this."

"I have to admit, I couldn't resist the cake when I smelled it in the bakery. But it is not the surprise I wanted to share with you today." Anika stared up at the ceiling, patted her heavy purse, and waved a hand in the air as if brushing aside Sofia's concerns. Hesitating for a minute, she began bragging about Nathan. "You know, your cousin called from Chicago last week. It's a shame he can't come more often to visit in person, but he calls every Friday before the start of Shabbos."

"Oh? How is he doing?" Sofia felt a dull pang of jealousy. Nathan had never called her since he left for the university. Her favorite cousin seemed so far away now, and she wished he was still around. *The things we take for granted…* Sofia sulked.

"Apparently, classes are going well, and he's getting all set up there in his new apartment. He's living with two other *shmegeges* he knows from New Jersey. He told us they found a shul not too far from his apartment, and they all attended services there for Yom Kippur."

Anika talked, and Sofia listened. Her aunt was animated with detailed stories describing which Brighton Beach neighbors were losing business and which were celebrating another grandchild's bar mitzvah or graduation. It seemed like everyone in Brighton Beach had some story or other that was worthy of juicy gossip, and Anika seemed privy to every detail. Sofia felt like she was watching a familiar rom-com movie as her aunt sketched out the details of the community's frivolous daily affairs. And then she just had to interrupt and ask, "Tyotya, tell me truthfully. Are people talking about Becca? What do you hear about the Kaplans?"

"Oh, you know how the people are. Of course, they are talking—they see Becca coming and going from the academy, and she can't hide her growing belly anymore. I hear that her father's barbershop has been losing business. It's sad, no?" Anika's last comment is more of a discouraging observation than a question.

Sofia wrinkled her brows and considered the sadness in her aunt's comment. "I can just imagine what everyone is thinking, even when they don't say it out loud. I feel so bad for Becca, but she will never give up this baby. No matter what people say about her, no matter what her family does."

"Yeah, well, we'll never stop the *yentes* from talking *lashon hara* against others, but her own family! It makes my kishkes shake in my stomach to think they would turn their backs on their daughter. Shame on Jakob, that *shlub*! They should never know from losing a child!" Anika choked on that last escaped sentence, and a few pastry crumbs flew from her mouth. Putting her hand up to her lips, she went on speaking, "You know, Sofia, people can be so terrible to each other. We are a community. A family. We are supposed to support each other, without judging each other. We're not supposed to kill each other with our words and personal views. People will point a finger at anyone, not realizing that, at the same time, they have three fingers pointing back at themselves." Anika held up her hand, pointed her index finger at Sofia as if she were pointing a gun, and wiggled her other three fingers that were nestled in the palm of the same hand.

Anika snorted and stopped talking long enough to let her words settle around them. Her smile suddenly receded behind the laugh-lines that surrounded her mouth, and her eyes glazed over as if she were opening a distant crevice in her mind. Crumbs clung to her greasy burgundy lipstick. Long seconds later, she cleared her throat and stared at her young niece. "It's the same old, same old, Sofia. What more can I say? You young people are moving away, and the rest of us are all getting older…but here we are, me and you, in this expensive 'to-die-for' café, drinking 'to-die-for' coffee, and noshing on this truly 'to-die-for' *sorik*. This is what we have, meidel, it's shitty to grow old, but this is the life, no? So let's enjoy while we can!" She whimpered, grinned, and shook her head as if she were trying to release her mind's eye from a view of something past and rejoining the stability of the present.

Sofia recognized her aunt's rehumanizing melancholy creeping up on them. Kvetching about getting older and reverting back to using native Yiddish insults was not a usual part of Anika's buoyant personality, but if it were an Olympic event, Anika would have won the gold that morning. Memories—good or bad—always brought people to these duplicitous places of wonder and remorse. "Oh, Tyotya. You're not old, and I am still here with you." Sofia assured her aunt that there was no reason to let her memories ruin her present mood.

As if suddenly remembering what they were initially talking about, Anika asked, "So how is Becca doing these days anyways?"

"Aside from throwing up a lot and getting headaches, she's okay. The doctor keeps telling her that it's all normal stuff, but that she needs to eat more spinach and fish. Something about having low iron and possible anemia." Changing the subject, Sofia asked, "So what was it you said you wanted to share with me today?"

Anika tsked and reached for her handbag. Like a magician reaching into a magic hat filled with tricks, she pulled out a stack of letters tied together with fraying red twine. The envelopes looked worn and faded with time, but the neat lettering on the front of each was clearly recognizable. A faint hint of Chanel, her mother's favorite perfume, wafted up in the air and tickled Sofia's nose—a light floral, fruity scent that made the hair on the back of Sofia's neck stand and prickle. "What's all that?" Sofia spit out with dazed confusion.

"These are from your mamoh. I've been holding onto them for years, and I think it is time to show them to you. Here is one, the last one we received, I think you should read now." Anika tugged at the envelope on the top of the stack and slid out its contents. With a trembling hand, she passed the folded piece of stationary across the table to Sofia.

It took Sofia a moment to collect herself as she stared down at her mother's familiar handwriting. Why had her mother written all these letters to Tyotya Anika but had never bothered to write to her? The reality stung her as she began to read—her lips moving, her mother's voice lodged inside her throat.

May 17, 2002
Lutsk, Ukraine

Dearest Anni,

I hope this letter finds you, Sol, and Nathan healthy and happy. Unfortunately, I am writing to you with questionable news of my own. I'll try to get to the point quickly, but first I must tell you what has led me to this terrible day and this frightful news.

As you know, for the past eleven years, things here in Lutsk have been more or less quiet and happy. It has been eleven years since the fall of the Soviet Union and the great fight for independence in Ukraine, and Avrum, Sofia, and I have been comfortable and content. We always have enough food, we are not harassed in the shul, we work, and we are able to indulge Sofia's love for the ballet. That is, as long as we continued to keep our heads down and our Judaism hidden from sight, which we have learned to do quite well over time.

As I have told you in previous communications, Avrum is called away from home a lot for work. I don't know where he goes, and I don't dare ask any questions. He only tells me his absences are duties he must perform for his engineering business with the government and that I have nothing to worry about. I learned not to interfere with Avrum's business and not ask too many questions. Mamoh and Tatoh used to tell us that happiness and security never come to anyone who complains or makes too much noise. Remember when they would tell us? So we have kept to ourselves, and Avrum always comes back home to me and Sofia—happy, safe, and content.

Here, Sofia stopped reading and took a moment to absorb her mother's words. Reading Mamoh's careful script brought back images that pounded in her heart and crept up her veins to the piece of paper trembling in her fingers. Yes, they were happy and content. So why did Tatoh disappear without a word? And why did Mamoh send her away to live in America? Sofia looked up at her aunt, then stared back at the sheet of paper quivering in her fist. She continued reading…

And so here I get to my point. It has been almost one month (twenty-seven days today, to be exact), and Avrum has not returned home, nor has he contacted me. I have not heard a single word from him, and when I call his office at the energy plant in Moscow, no one there can give me any answers either. As much as he has disap-

peared often without explanation in the past, this is not like him. I must admit that I am quite worried this time.

Sofia is becoming a strong, wise young lady now—she will be eighteen years old in two months. But the time has come for me to make a painful decision. I have applied for permits for Sofia and me to leave Ukraine. The acceptance for Sofia came quickly, but I am still waiting for my papers to be approved. So I am asking that you can take Sofia into your home until further arrangements can be made. I only hope Sofia will forgive me for my desperate choice to send her to you alone and that she will come to understand that all I want is to protect her and provide a better future for her.

Our government has been very generous with us. Avrum's engineering education and training has been a lucky benefit for us. I am thankful for Avrum's work and the generous opportunities we have been given, especially as Jews here. But now, as Sofia's mother, this is the only choice I have to protect and love my child. Enough said.

Please, tell me you will take her in and watch over her for us.

I expect our spirited young Sofia will not be happy about this decision I've made, and she will unquestionably protest my motives. She is a typical teenager—too young and stubborn (like her mamoh!)—to understand these things. She is currently dating a nice, young, hamishe boy she met at our shul, and her dancing career is advancing quite nicely now. I'm sure she is hating me for making her give this all up. But she is also clever and brave, and maybe she will accept this decision and see it as an adventure. I must think only of her safety and make a wise (if not difficult!) choice to send her to you. Whether she understands this decision or not, only time will tell.

One last thing, sister. No matter what happens to me, please promise me you won't let Sofia give up on her dreams of dancing! Not for anything or anybody. Life without dreams and choices is no life at all. It's not always easy to make the right decisions, but with courage and determination, we can have the opportunity to make wise choices. She is a rising star, and we must give Sofia the encouragement and the chance she deserves.

We will all be together again soon, God willing, and life will go back to normal. But for now, I need my baby to stay safe. For this, I remain forever in your debt.

Your loving sister,
Riva

Sofia could not believe what she was reading. By the time she got to her mother's signature at the end of the letter, her eyes were burning behind pools of tears. Her throat was dry and spiky as if she swallowed a handful of poisoned thorns. For almost eight years, she had believed that her mother and father had deserted her, thrown her out like garbage, not even trying to contact her or find her again. Looking at the pile of letters sitting in front of her aunt, Sofia struggled to make sense of this news. For eight years, Sofia wondered and waited, consumed with feelings of unwanted abandonment, and now she felt like she would unravel, like the tied-up stack of old letters. All these years later, and it was her parents, after all, who were lost.

Did Tatoh ever return home? Did Mamoh ever get her permit to immigrate? Were they together again, somewhere out there? A lump clogged her throat and pushed a well of tears up to her blurry eyes. Sofia stifled a sob as tears spilled down her flaming cheeks.

Sofia and Anika sat in a blanket of silence for what seemed like hours, neither knowing what to say or do next. The café buzzed around them, but all Sofia could hear was her mother's voice and whispers of resigned admissions.

19

Sofia

The elevated trains rumbled overhead and the autumn winds gusted around them. Sofia and Becca pressed their way through the scurrying crowds and sidewalk vendors who were peddling *tchotchkes* and junk no one needed but everyone sought. Everything was for sale, from sugarcoated peanuts to handmade toys to hand-knitted doilies and *schmates* (cleaning rags as well as decorative headscarves). Sofia didn't know who was more weighted down, Becca with her ever-growing belly or herself with renewed sadness and confusion over the news of her parents. Becca could still disguise her girth with an oversized sweatshirt, but Sofia could not contain the grief she wore in the sour pucker of her lips and the downward crinkle in the corners of her eyes. It had been three weeks since her aunt shared her mother's last letter with her, the one that put finality to the puzzle of her parents' demise. It had been the last letter any of them had received from Sofia's parents. The rest could only be surmised.

Becca thought that a walk through the old neighborhood would bring Sofia back around and out of her blind stupor. She had managed to avoid the old neighborhood and the prying, nosy gossip of her family's community for almost six months, but she was willing to go back if it would help Sofia out of whatever she was dealing with, away from the studio, away from Ben, away from the obvious vexation in which her best friend found herself drowning. At the Tantsor Russian Ballet & Dance Academy, more often than not these days, Sofia was showing up late for rehearsals and leaving early each afternoon. At home, Becca would find Sofia locked away in her bedroom, hardly eating, never speaking more than a few grumbled words at a time. It was only four days earlier that Sofia finally opened up to Becca and told her the unadulterated details of her encounter with her aunt and the disclosure of her family's demise.

"Look over here, Sofia." Becca hoped to put a smile on Sofia's face and led her straight toward a small nail salon. The blinking red lights of the store's gaudy marquee informed them in both English and Russian that they were standing on the threshold of the finest nail art salon in two continents. (At least, that's what the sign above the door promised.) "I think we should go in and get manicures. And pedicures! Doesn't that sound wonderful! I haven't been able to bend down to see my toes in weeks now." Becca wasn't sure if she really wanted the manicure or if she just wanted to get off the crowded streets and hide away from all the disparaging stares.

Sofia couldn't resist a chuckle at her friend's expense. And it was true that they could both use a warm, bubbly soak in a footbath. Giving in to her friend's willfulness, Sofia reluctantly agreed. "Okay, let's go in. But I am not getting any shmaltzy designs on my nails."

She looked down at her short fingernails and picked at a chip in her pale-pink nail polish.

Sitting side by side in matching pedicure chairs, Sofia relaxed her shoulders and gave in to the comforting vibrations of the warm water at her feet. In front of them sat two Russian-speaking girls, each no older than twenty years old, with bleached, straw-like hair covering their lifeless blue eyes and freckled cheeks. They both wore matching black T-shirts that displayed the name of the salon (*Regina's Famous Nails*) over the left breast. The girl with the DD-size chest bending over in front of Becca left her customers nothing to the imagination, and the girl who was perched in front of Sofia had bedazzled her T-shirt with red and silver rhinestones. Sofia looked over, eyebrows arched, and saw Becca rubbing a hand over her belly and purring like a kitten with her eyes closed. She was taking deep, counted breaths, obviously enjoying this spontaneous, spoiled indulgence. Sofia ignored the Russian banter between the two young manicurists and closed her own tired eyes.

But no amount of pampering was going to ease her loneliness and pain. Sofia's chest heaved, and she rubbed at the prickles under her skin on her arms. She couldn't help but wonder for the millionth time, *Is it remotely possible to believe her parents might still be alive, somewhere out there?*

The last thing Anika had revealed to Sofia that afternoon in the coffee shop was that she had, indeed, enquired of the Russian government as to what had happened to Avrum and Riva, but even the three Russian embassies in New York, Houston, and Washington, DC, had not been able to supply any evidence of their whereabouts after 2002. A secreted bank account Riva had wisely opened in Manhattan was secure and would be fully turned over to Sofia when she had a child of her own or when she turned thirty. Whichever came first.

Sofia felt a light brush against her forearm, and she jolted out of her trance. "Are you okay, Sofia? I thought I heard you breathing a little too hard. And I thought I was the one with a bowling ball striking at my ribcage."

Humbled by Becca's persistent optimism and happy demeanor, despite her own muddled situation, Sofia was only too glad to steer the morose mood in her mind in another direction. "Have you heard from Nathan lately? I've only spoken to him once this whole month. I guess he used up all his spare family time during the early holidays this year."

A gleaming set of teeth shone across Becca's face as she broke out in a fit of school-girl giggles. "Yeah, he called the other day when you were at rehearsals." Her eyes found a faraway place, and she giggled some more.

"How am I the only one who always misses his calls? So tell me. How is he? Does he miss us yet? Is he settling in to his new life as a student?" She shook her head and rambled on with a devilish glint in her eye, "Remember when we went to Chicago for the production of *Giselle*? Man, that city really rocks!"

The two manicurists finished up with the pedicures, and it was time to move on to their manicures. Sofia had grown restless despite the hypnotic vibrations of the pedicure chair, but it was obvious to her that Becca's relaxed grin and slow-moving shuffle to the nail station was going to keep them in the salon for a while longer. Waddling carefully behind her in her paper slippers, Sofia suddenly beamed with an idea.

"Would you mind if I left you here for a bit? I forgot I have an errand to tend to while we are here in this part of the neighborhood."

"You mean you aren't going to get your nails done? Come on, Sofia. Your hands look like shit, and I thought you said you would get a manicure as long as you didn't get any *fancy-shmancy* nail art. You're making me feel guilty for wanting this!" Her words came out harsher and more reproaching than she meant.

"Don't get upset with me, Becca. If I can deal with my nails… and Ben can deal with them…you should be able to deal with them too. Besides, like I said, I forgot I had an errand to run. I'll meet you back here in less than twenty minutes. Enjoy your manicure. You deserve it." Sofia kicked off the paper slippers from her feet and shoved carelessly, without thinking about her still-wet pedicure, her feet back into her socks and sneakers.

"You're going to ruin your pedicure, Sofia. Can't you just sit still for a while?"

"Don't worry, I only used a layer of clear polish on my toes. I'll be back in a jiffy."

It didn't take Sofia long to come back to the salon and meet up with Becca again. The sun was beginning to set behind the elevated tracks, and Sofia had promised Boris that she'd meet him back at the academy for a late rehearsal that evening. She knew she had to start focusing on the upcoming performance; she was due to perform her most important role in *The Dying Swan* in a little over a month. Without realizing it, time and energy were gradually slipping away from her. Between Ben hanging onto her every free moment, the loss and guilt over her parents, and Becca's approaching motherhood, Sofia had become perpetually frazzled and completely out of focus. She swooshed through the front door of the salon, noting Becca already waiting for her with her hands held up in front of a small table fan.

"I told you I'd be back fast. The wind is picking up out there, though, and the sun is beginning to set fast. We better get a move on it." Sofia swung her windblown ponytail behind her shoulder and clenched tightly to a brown paper bag she was holding in her fist. A coy grin spread across her face, one that Becca recognized easily of her closest confidante. It was obvious Sofia was up to something.

"Fine. Let's go," Becca said. Her efforts in raising her friend's spirits that day seemed to have been all for naught, and she was silently regretting her promise to go back to the dance studio with her that evening. "Let's stop and get some khachapuri before we get on the bus. I'm starving!"

"You're always starving these days, my dear. You're gonna turn into a fat pig if you keep eating like this."

"Easy for you to say, skinny-minny. I wish I could eat like a horse and never gain an ounce."

They made their way through the rush-hour bustle between Second and Third Avenues and made it in just enough time to catch the approaching bus that would take them back to the Tantsor Russian Ballet & Dance Academy. On their harried way to the bus stop, Sofia pivoted her head back and forth to catch any sign of Uncle Sol in her peripheral vision. He would surely be part of the crunch of people heading home from their shops and work in the area, but she had no intention of running into him tonight. She concentrated on the faces of each passerby and appreciated their eagerness to return home at the end of a long, hard day of work instead of stopping her or Becca to engage in typical communal kibitzing for gossip's sake. The air, although chilly, felt oppressive with the mixed odors of sweet and savory foods and exhaust from the roaring elevated trains above their heads. Finally, they were sitting on the bus, lucky to find two seats opposite each other.

Plopping down hard in the tiny seat, Becca eyed the paper bag in Sofia's fist. "What's in the bag, Sofia? Is that what was so important that you couldn't sit still for a manicure?"

"Oh, you'll see. Anyway, I wasn't in the mood to stay any longer in that place. What's the big deal anyway if I didn't want a manicure today!" Sofia's question was more of an annoyed statement. She was not like Becca, and she did not feel comforted by pedicures and manicures. "Don't you know what I'm going through now? Cut me some slack for not wanting a *forshtunkenuh* manicure!" Sofia just couldn't contain her agitation for one more second.

Becca leaned her head against the cold glass window and glared impatiently at Sofia. She snorted and said, "Look, Sofia. I do know what you are going through. I just lost my parents too. In a way. Look, I'm not trying to compare situations, but I do understand you. But I have to say that you are not considering the other side of the coin here. At least your parents loved you till the very end." Becca stopped and closed her eyes to take a minute to recall the contents of the letter that Sofia shared with her. "I mean, after all, your mamoh had to make a very difficult choice to send you away. She loved you and needed to protect you and make sure you were safe. As a woman who will be a mother very soon, I can honestly say I would have done the same if you were my daughter and I thought you might be in danger. No doubt your parents loved you very much."

Sofia cut her off before Becca could say any more. "I would never leave my child or send them away. I would—"

Now it was Becca who stopped Sofia in mid-sentence. "Don't talk nonsense! You don't know what you would have done in the same situation. It is not always easy to make the best choices in life. Sometimes the right choice is the hardest one to make." Becca paused for a moment and opened her eyes wide. She hoped her words would sink in for Sofia. "No one can make decisions for you, Sofia. But no one will love you or want the best for you more than your mamoh and tatoh. And your tyotya, for that matter. You have to believe that."

Sofia let out a slow blast of air that she had been holding inside her cheeks. She hated to admit it, but Becca's words made sense. In her own young, naive way, maybe Becca had a point. Sofia squeezed her eyebrows together and bit down on her lower lip. The only thing that blurted out of her quivering lips like a steamroller out of control was, "Well, fine. But when Ben and I get married, I'm not going to have any children. That way, I won't have to worry about making these kinds of hurtful, deceitful decisions."

20

Maya

I have three months to put it all together. Baruch and the other board members of Gan Notzah are all in agreement that we should be patient and wait through the lengthy Jewish holiday season and also take advantage of the country's tourist season that always booms in December. They seem to think this strategy will work. I can't say I am as optimistic. After all, who am I to expect my ballet to make a difference. But it's all I have, so I keep my fears and insecurities hidden from everyone.

It is Baruch and my mother who insist that we do the show right here on the kibbutz. The rec center will somehow have to be transformed into a fitting and expedient theater, with all the proceeds from the event going straight into the coffers of our community. I have been given leave of my duties in the kitchen in order to spend ten hours each day practicing and drilling my best students for each part in my debut ballet. I am running on 100 percent adrenalin. I visit the rec center daily, wondering how I am ever going to manage it.

It is one late afternoon in the rec hall that my attention is suddenly diverted as I listen to the screech of Nirvana's "Heart-Shaped Box" from the crackling speakers in the social hall. It is then that I realize I haven't heard from Jim in a while. After his return home to the States, I had received a steady stream of letters—each one with explicit details of his visits to the doctor, his interviews for jobs with the prominent tech firms in Seattle, and his sister's latest dance recitals. Clearly, he is trying to follow his own advice and choosing to live fully and optimistically, as hard as it may be. His tone is always amazingly confident and cheerful in each of his missives, but our connection seems to have abruptly gone dry. I find myself missing him—his contagious laughter, his spring of optimism, his encouraging friendship. I wonder if he is truly happy. I speculate about his health and the limited hope the doctors have given him for a positive recovery. Danny has noticed the subtle cageyness in my mood, but I blame it on the pressure of the upcoming show. I can't let my fears and doubts about Jim interfere with my commitment to the show and the kibbutz. It's a triple dose of anxiety—one for my friend, one for the survival of my family, and one for my own success. I do my best to remain strong for all three. Between the punishing dance rehearsals and the tension that is growing between Danny and me at home, I wonder how I am going to make it through the next few months.

The next day, two hours into my morning routine drill, I hear a tap on the glass window of the studio. I look at my reflection in the mirror that covers the length of the back wall and frown. Strands of hair that have escaped my tight bun are frizzing around my hairline, and my pallor has gone saggy and gray from lack of sleep and constant worry. Purple bags puff out from under my eyes. "I'll never be able to pull this off," I huff.

Shutting off the music blaring from my portable boom box, I leave the studio and make my way to the building's entrance. Standing in the hallway, Danny leans on the counter and stares over at me.

"Oh, it's you. I heard the door, and I got nervous."

"Yes, your nerves have been on edge lately," Danny snickers.

I wipe the sweat from my chest with my hand and move slowly toward him. If I look exhausted, my husband looks like he just came back from the battlefield. "You look beat, Danny. Have you had lunch yet?"

"I just finished working on the truck. The gears are stripped, and the valves need to be replaced, but it's all we got."

"By the time the next harvest begins next year, we'll have that new vehicle you need." I move closer and put my hand up to Danny's dimpled chin. "Just hang in there—"

Danny takes a quick step backward and snaps, "Yeah, sure. I'll just hang in there."

The blood drains from my sweaty cheeks, and my extended arm hangs limp in the air in front of me. Tilting my head to one side, I ask, "What's wrong, Danny? Did something happen today?"

With an impatient swoosh, Danny reaches into his backpack and pulls out a stack of envelopes. From where I am standing, I could see that they are all marked with international stamps. My letters from Jim.

"Where did you find those?" I ask with a sigh of indignation.

"Never mind where I found them, Maya. What's going on with you? Is there something you want to tell me about?" Danny's face reddens deeper with each word.

Grabbing for the stack of envelopes in his outstretched hand, my anger and resentment flare. The insinuation, the blame, the accusation in Danny's glare makes the hair on the back of my neck stand up. "No, Danny. I have nothing to say. Jim is—was—my friend, and that's all." Should I tell him that Jim is sick? Would it help the situation if I tried to explain to Danny about Jim's illness and our mutual bond of support and encouragement? Should I betray our promise to keep our secrets just between us?

"This doesn't sound like that's all. For months…no, for years now…since Aaron was born, you've been moping around here like you could give a shit about anything or anyone but yourself and this ridiculous dance studio! I think you do have something to tell me, Maya. And I'm not leaving until you do!"

"Is that a threat, Danny? It sure sounds like one." Both of us are now yelling, and I look around to assure myself that we are truly alone. "I'm telling you there is nothing going on. Jim and I—were only friends. Don't you trust me?" I notice that I am using the past tense to talk about Jim, and my eyes fill with tears.

"It's not a matter of trust, Maya. I just feel like I've lost you, and I don't know what to do to get you back." Danny puts his head between his hands, and sobs begin to rack his shoulders.

"You haven't lost me, Danny. I'm still here. But are you willing to see me?" I stop to let my words sink in. Can Danny hear the sincerity in my pleas? I think back to the time when I had my first dance audition in Haifa and how proud and excited Danny was for me.

But that was then, and this is now.

"Danny, I am a dancer. It has been my dream for as long as I can remember. You always knew that, and one time you were just as encouraging of my passion as I was. Getting married and having Aaron does not change that. Jim saw that and pushed me to recapture my dream." I take a breath and then continue to dive into the truth that is pouring from my lips. The whole truth. "Jim is dying, Danny. He came to me for hope and inspiration. He offered friendship and support in return."

After I finish spilling the whole story about Jim and his ultimate fate, Danny looks up at me, his eyes twinkling with new regret and guilt. "I am so sorry to hear about his illness, really. He is a good guy. But still, Maya. Damn it, I am your husband, and I thought I was your friend too. You should be coming to *me* for friendship and support, not a total stranger!"

I hear the critical accusation of betrayal in Danny's words. I see his eyes begin to puddle with tears, and I sense an intensity in his plea. Danny's right; I should have been able to rely on him for support, understanding, and friendship. But the truth is I just couldn't reach him. Instead, a perfect stranger had come along and had offered me something I didn't even know I was looking for. I had needed Jim's nonjudgmental understanding of my desires, his brave zest for life, and his unconditional faith in me. I had needed someone to tell me that I was capable and worthy. Even with the impending knowledge that his own days were numbered, Jim had shown me more strength and appreciation than I had ever known. It has been a long time since I have felt these assurances with Danny. A sharp pang of irritation—mixed with a bit of guilt—stabs me in the gut. I wrap my arms around my torso and bite down hard on my lower lip.

"I can't argue with you there, Danny. But if we are both going to be honest about all this, we have to also agree that you have not been overly supportive of my dreams. You think I've changed just because I am a wife and mother, but I haven't. My ambitions and passions and drive are still all about dancing. The ballet is my life, and I may not be a prima ballerina or a famous performer, I may not be able to save the kibbutz from economic ruin, but I don't want to give up on my dreams, on me…not for you or Aaron or anyone. It's scary and confusing for me. The kibbutz is counting on me, you and Aaron count on me. I get it. And I doubt I'll ever reach Irena's fame or be as good a ballerina as Baryshnikov, but please don't ask me to stop dreaming. Please don't ask me to make a choice between myself and my family. You have your own vision of what you think is a perfect family and a perfect life, but you can't see what I've been missing, what I need. Don't force me to make a choice, Danny. That's just not fair!"

All the air is expelled from my lungs as I come to the end of my tirade. I keep a cool distance from Danny and begin to play with the hem of my skirt. I can't believe—after all these years—I finally found the courage to stand up for myself! To admit my feelings and reclaim my own identity. Danny cannot look me in the eye. With a look of defeat, he turns away, slumps his shoulders, and throws the pile of letters down on the counter. He scuttles out the front door leaving large black scuff marks on the wooden floorboards.

21

Sofia

"What the hell is the matter with you, Sofia? What were you thinking!" Boris blew out a sharp, jagged breath, his first break for air in his twenty-minute tirade. Sofia had never seen him so angry before, yet she couldn't bring herself to feel guilty about her rascally antics.

Truth be told, this latest strike for revenge didn't even have anything to do with Nina, per se. Nothing more had changed since the day Nina walked into the academy and their life, yet she continued to claw at Sofia's every nerve. She flirted shamelessly with every man that crossed her path, she pushed her way up the ranks of the troupe faster and easier than all the other hardworking ballerinas, she finagled the position of Sofia's new understudy the second she heard about Becca's pregnancy, and she continuously stole the spotlight from Sofia (the last time was when the editor-in-chief herself came to interview the company for *Dance Magazine* about their upcoming show at the Montefiori Factory-turned-Theater). No, there was no new trigger that led Sofia to act up now. Except that Nina was a perfect target for Sofia's resentful wrath.

It was the news that came by way of the concealed letter from her mother that was really making Sofia increasingly more difficult and moodier these days; it seemed like all hope of her parents' safety and their conceivable reunion had been single-handedly derailed. She was old enough and wise enough to know that her dreams of reuniting with them was just a childish fantasy, but obviously, she was still just a jealous, resentful child when it came to her colleague.

Sofia offered her best excuse, "I really wasn't thinking at all. It was only meant to be a joke."

"A joke, Sofia? Are you kidding? Nina has been trying to fit in here for a year, and all you do is make her feel like shit! Like an outsider who has to fight every day to earn your respect. God, Sofia. When are you going to grow up and learn to be a team player? Nina learns and practices as fast as any dancer we've ever seen, and she has put up with your childish and petty jealous 'jokes,' as you say, since the day she arrived here! Whatever it is, Sofia, get over it!" Boris counted out Nina's praises on his long, slender fingers as his face grew redder with each point he made. Sofia only heard white noise rumbling in her ears. *Blah, blah, blah!*

Sofia had noticed the stink-gag in one of the crowded novelty shops under the elevated train earlier that same day. The store was a catchall for every piece of worthless junk in the neighborhood; it sold everything from rusty old skates to postcards from the Old Country to key chains to stickers and outdated books for kids. While Becca wandered around the aisles of baby products, Sofia happened to catch a glimpse of a barrel full of dusty packages of "fart bomb" spray. On the front of each package were the bold words "the best smelly, nasty, stinky prank." Plainly put, *Nina*!

So it was while Becca was finishing her manicure at Regina's Famous Nails salon that Sofia had returned to the trinket shop and strategized her next attack. Sofia thought back to that afternoon and pictured Nina's priceless expression when she entered her dressing room—her green eyes tearing and swelling shut from the irritating stench, her alabaster skin turning a blotchy red, her perfect, heart-shaped lips puckering and pouting while Sofia giggled mischievously in the hallway with anticipatory victory. *After all,* thought Sofia, *nobody was more smelly, nasty, stinky…or deserving than…Nina Cassel.*

But Boris was serious, and his threat boomed in Sofia's ears, "I want you to go home, Sofia. No, wait. First, I want you to clean up the mess you made in Nina's dressing room with that crap, and make sure the smell is completely gone by the time I come back from the theater later tonight. Then I want you to apologize to Nina. And swear you will never bother her—or *me*—with this kind of shit again! Geez, we're supposed to be professionals here, and yet I'm dealing with this childish bullshit. We have a major show coming up, and I don't need this kind of horse-play! You ballerina divas are real pieces of work!"

Sofia knew that last statement was not meant as a compliment. Scolding her like a child and making her apologize to her arch-enemy was as degrading and humiliating as she had felt in a long time. But it had been worth it. She hadn't thought about the demise of her parents all afternoon. She disguised her giggle with a sputtered cough.

Sofia finally made it home, but she was restless, now consumed with the nervous energy that came to her before each new stage appearance. Her big performance of *The Dying Swan* was scheduled to open in three weeks, and Sofia was feeling the weight of fear and failure—that uncontrollable jittery state of mind that came with each big show. And she had just lost an entire day of rehearsals because of a pedicure and a stink bomb. At eight o'clock that evening, Becca was still at the studio teaching her last hip-hop class of the day, so Sofia decided to take advantage of her free time and energy and called Ben. If she was lucky, she could still get him on his cell phone before he got on the subway. She scrolled through her favorites in her contact list until she found Ben's name and hit the call button. With a crackle, Ben's voice answered on the third ring.

"Hi, Sofia. What's up? I'm about to go into the subway."

"Good, then I got you just in time. I got the night off, and I was wondering if you wanted to meet me for some sushi."

"You got the night off?" Ben's voice sounded incredulous. "What happened? Is everything okay?"

"Yeah, sure. I'll explain everything when I see you. Can you meet me at Suki-Asia in an hour?" It was more of a command than a question. Sofia ended the call without further explanation. She was suddenly flushed with embarrassment and regret for her childish prank. She was a woman on the verge of marriage, and she would have to admit to her fiancé that she was reprimanded at the academy like a misbehaved schoolgirl. *No matter.* She clucked her tongue out loud. *Aach! Ben loves me, and he'll understand.* In the two years since they met, she hadn't really divulged much of her past to Ben and had recently avoided mentioning anything about the latest discovery of her mother's last letter. *Maybe it's time to come clean about my past*, she thought. *After all, we are getting married, and he has a right to know about who I really am.*

While contemplating exactly what and how much she wanted to share with her soon-to-be husband, Sofia showered and dressed in a pair of jeans and a thick wool sweater. She tucked her feet into her UGG boots and hurried to the subway station at the corner of her street. The sun had already set, and the street lamps illuminated the bustling streets. By the time the train stopped on the tracks in front of her, Sofia had finally settled on revealing some of the details in the letter from her mother, explaining her recent sour mood that led to planting the stink bomb in Nina's dressing room that afternoon. But she would leave out all the parts about her father's work and his possible (probable?) involvement with the Russian government. She would stick to her generic and long-standing story of how she lost her parents to pneumonia during her last frigid winter in Lutsk, since that part of the story is still a mystery, even to her. She had repeated that version of the story so many times that she almost started believing it herself, making the uncertainty of her parents' survival sting even more. The invented version of her missing parents, at least until reading the letter from her mother, had left a dangling thread of hope that her Mamoh and Tatoh would one day recover their health and find the path back into Sofia's life again. But that was all over now.

Sofia walked into the dimly lit restaurant and saw Ben already sitting at their favorite table near the koi fish tank. He had gone ahead and ordered a small ceramic flask of Sake, a small half-filled *ochaku* cup already poured in front of him. Sofia slinked into the chair facing him and flashed him a satisfied smile.

Half standing out of his seat, Ben leaned over the table and gave Sofia a peck on the cheek. He smiled brightly at her and, using two hands, poured her a cup of the rice wine. Sofia relaxed her shoulders and wrapped her cold fingers around the warm cup.

"Your call tonight was a surprise, Sofia. These days, you haven't had much time for anything but the show. Are you sure everything's okay?"

It was true that Sofia had been ultra-aloof and distant, wrapped up in her rehearsals and strategizing for the big opening of *The Dying Swan*. It was the niggling twinge of guilt and sympathy for Ben that made her call now. Sofia picked up her menu and pretended to peruse the offerings, running her short, unpainted fingernail down the list of Japanese dishes. She ordered takeout from there so often she could almost recite the menu by heart. She just needed a minute to put her thoughts in order before divulging the details of her disastrous day. She looked up to see Ben's confused stare begging for answers.

Sofia inhaled deeply and rolled her eyes up toward the low ceiling. "I just can't stand that Nina Cassel. She is such a conniving little b-i-t-c-h!"

"What did she do now? Did she show up in the same leotard you were wearing? Did she sneeze just as you were attempting a tough pirouette?" Ben could hardly suppress his bemusement. He had become acutely accustomed to accepting Sofia's trivialities as ingratiating and entertaining. Ben let out a chuckle, a second too late before noticing the look of consternation on Sofia's face.

"It's not funny, Ben. She drives me nuts. And I guess you still think it's funny how she shamelessly flirted with you that day I introduced her to you for the first time."

"Sofia, you're just being overly sensitive. She's harmless. My heart belongs only to you."

"Oh, you obviously do not know women too well. Or maybe it's just city-women that breathe fire and spit venom."

"Are you making fun of us Southern bumpkins again?" Ben's expression suddenly turned serious. He had come to New York as a naive country boy, but he liked to believe he had developed into a confident, sensible, progressive man-about-town. He took a long swig of his Sake.

"No, I'm not making fun of you. Actually, it's really not about Nina. Although she did cause quite a stink in her dressing room today and somehow managed to blame everything on little ol' me. She managed a sincere giggle at her own play with words. Boris chastised me for the mess like a child and sent me home for the night… but not before making me clean up Nina's room!" Sofia tried to keep up a serious demeanor while she indulged Ben with the sordid details of the smelly spray, but a devilish smile remained pasted across her face. "It was only meant to be a joke, but Boris and Nina didn't see it that way," Sofia finished with a heavy sigh.

"So if this whole thing really isn't about Nina, as you say, then what is it? Is something else bothering you?"

Just then, as if on cue, a waiter appeared and placed a bowl of salted edamame in the middle of their table. He whisked out a pen from behind his ear and waited to hear what the couple wanted. Sofia and Ben gave their order to the waiter and watched him walk away before speaking again.

"What is it, Sofia? This isn't about Nina or the show next month…but you haven't been yourself for weeks, and I'm starting to wonder. Is it the wedding? Have you decided you don't want to marry me?" Ben held back a muffled little laugh, but his eyes glowered with worry.

The date they had chosen for the wedding was April 17, 2011. Despite her aunt and uncle's continued silent protests, Sofia loved Ben, and she was not about to betray their two-year relationship with a sudden change of heart. Her decision was made, and she was going to stick by it, despite her aunt and uncle's disapproval, despite her own doubts and concerns.

Sofia grinned coyly, considering the country bumpkin she had met just two years earlier and how he had turned out to be quite the quintessential New Yorker he was today. "Of course, I want to marry you, Ben. I made a commitment to you, and I plan to keep it."

"Oh, so I'm only a 'commitment' to you now? Like an obligation?"

"No, I didn't mean it like that. Oh, geez, everything I say and do today is coming out all wrong." She ran her tongue over her teeth and clenched her jaw. "What I mean is that I will always be devoted to you. Ben, I love you." She didn't bring up the fact that having children was completely and totally out of the question for her—a fact that would definitely be a "deal breaker" for Ben when (or *if*) he ever discovered her long-held opinion.

Sofia took another long swig of her Sake and bit through a pod of edamame. Ben sat silently, waiting for her to continue with a 'but' after her professed love for him. Instead, she began the telling of her practiced tale with the coffee date she had with her aunt and didn't stop rambling until she reached the sketchy parts about the letter she read from her mother. "Imagine, Ben. All these years, I hoped my parents were still alive, somewhere out there. I had no idea of the sacrifices they faced…and how stupid I was to believe they might have just abandoned me and dumped me on my aunt and uncle. Life just sucks, and there's nothing we can do about it!" Sofia choked on her last words and belted out a loud cough. Ben patiently listened, waiting for Sofia to come to the end of her story. "I've been holding on to the naive hope that they would come back for me someday, and we would be a family again. Now I know that will never happen, and all I have left is my ballet." When Sofia finished, she stared down at her shaking hands, and fat tears tumbled down her cheeks.

"Wow! What a bummer." Ben tried to ignore her last comment, but uncontrollable anger and resentment burned in the pit of his stomach. What did Sofia mean by saying that she only had her ballet? Weren't they planning a future together? Didn't she just say she loves him? Ben was at a loss for words, so he pinched his lips together and remained stoic. He tried to imagine what he would have felt if he had been sent away from his home, never returning, or seeing, his family again. Finally, he mumbled the only words he could think of. "I think I understand, Sofia. But I'm still here for you. I know family is everything, but sometimes we have to make hard decisions to protect the ones we love."

Sofia sniffled and grumbled, "Don't I know it."

22

Sofia

Walking as fast as her aching feet would carry her, Sofia headed out for the Seventy-Seventh Street subway station. She shivered under her parka from the icy wind, and a slight drizzle pricked her cheeks. Irritated by the miserable weather, she hefted her backpack higher on her shoulder. Her feet cramped from the fifty-hours-a-week rehearsals she had been putting in for the upcoming performance, and every muscle in her body begged her to give in and simply let Nina perform in her place. The "white acts," or second acts of most romantic ballets, had kept her en pointe for most of that time, and when she wasn't spinning across the hardwood floors, she endured long periods of just standing in place and keeping a position.

Over and over...1-2-3-4-5-6-7-8...

Finally submerging underground and out of the rain, Sofia pushed her way through the throng of passengers waiting on the platform and let out a relieved whistle just as the R-train pummeled to a stop in front of her. Sofia shoved her way through the open doors and plopped into the last available seat, saying a silent prayer of gratitude for the lucky break in procuring a seat for the whole forty-five-minute ride. *There is no way I'm going to make it*, she thought anxiously to herself as the train jerked into motion and darted north.

Because of Boris's recent annoyance with Sofia, he had suggested she visit the theater and begin rehearsing by herself in its little studio before the actual show. If Sofia didn't know any better, she would say he was just trying to get her as far away from Nina as possible. The rest of the cast would begin rehearsals at the theater the following week, but Sofia was actually glad to get a jump start on things and check out the venue for herself. Because of the small size of the theater, the cast for the show had been cut in half, but Boris and the Tantsor Academy made up for the cuts with extra lavish stage sets and costumes. Still Sofia wondered how the reduced cast would affect the visual appeal of the performance.

Sofia stretched and rolled her legs to relieve the tight knots in her thighs and accidentally kicked the old man sitting across from her on the crowded train. "Sorry, sir," she whispered a bit insincerely, her eyes focused on the graffiti-covered advertisements above their heads. She twirled her ankles until she heard them crack and then moaned loudly. "*Aah*, that feels better." The old man pushed his thick glasses higher on the bridge of his bulbous nose and shot Sofia a look of disgust before turning away from her.

After switching over to the F-train, Sofia finally emerged from the damp and steamy subway and headed for the center of the Dumbo district on foot. In front of her, she could see the Brooklyn and Manhattan bridges on the horizon. Between the bridges lay the skyline of Manhattan, the Statue of Liberty, and Staten Island all sprawled out in breathtaking views; Sofia's knees buckled, and her breath caught in her throat. After eight years in the city, anything outside of her Brighton Beach community still made her feel like a first-time visitor in New York. The rain had stopped, and the icy air had tempered with the rising midmorning sun. She stood frozen in reverent silence before dodging her way forward through the hurried crowds on the flagstone sidewalk.

From the Water Street entrance, Sofia walked around the rustic brick building until she found the corner entrance to the Montefiori Theater. A big placard covered the entrance door, reading:

> *To celebrate our 30th Anniversary, join us for* Swan Lake...*and a special performance of* The Dying Swan... *Tantsor's Russian Ballet will rock the Montefiori Theater with an intimate, one week only...*

Sofia's stomach roiled, and a wave of nausea rose to the back of her throat.

This was the real deal. The *really* big stuff.

Sofia stepped into the theater and immediately felt her lungs collapse. She felt constricted, small, inadequate. The theater, in general, was smaller than she had envisioned, but it was swallowing her now with its authority and grandeur. Strutting around the tiny studio room, she placed her backpack in the corner and threw her parka jacket next to it. As if on cue, a scruffy, curly-haired, pimply faced boy appeared. He wore a faded David Bowie concert T-shirt and jeans with holes in the knees. His sneakers squeaked on the wooden floor as he introduced himself as the sound technician. "And you must be Sofia Brenner. They told me you were coming this morning. Just call me Curtis."

With a nod of her head, Sofia took in the young tech from head to toe and snarled. "Okay, Curtis, do you think you could show me around a bit? I'd like to see the stage and the dressing rooms."

After a quick inspection of the theater, Curtis led Sofia back to the stage area. "I was told there would be no live orchestra, but we have all the musical arrangements prepared for you on tape. The sound system here is really slap. Would you like me to play the music for you now?"

"*Oh God*," Sofia murmured just loud enough for the boy tech to hear, "*Tchaikovsky in the hands of an incompetent. What next?*"

Harrumphing, Curtis disappeared, and the musical score for *Swan Lake* began pealing through the air. "I need you to play the other solo score!" yelled Sofia into the empty space. "The four-minute piece by Camille Saint-Saëns!" Sofia knew *The Dying Swan* had been performed a plethora of times since her mentor Ana Pavlova's introductory staging of the ballet created especially for her, but she was determined to make her rendition of the performance the best anyone had ever seen. Now she was feeling more insecure and unsure of her vow.

Three hours later, Sofia heard the rhythmic clanging of rusty church bells telling her it was already two o'clock. She had agreed to meet Ben for a late lunch. Overcome with doubt and insecurity about the hand movements of her solo act, she swore under her breath and padded back to the dressing room. She had her technique down to near perfection; it was the expression in her upper body movements that were causing her insurmountable stress. She had even mastered the most difficult steps—the small *pas de bourrée suivi* steps of the dance—but the necessary dramatic gliding motions of her hands had her jammed with anxiety and fear, much like her emotional state had been for the past month. While making her way past the bathrooms from the stage, Sofia twisted her diamond engagement ring around her swollen finger.

She wiggled on a pair of leggings, collected her belongings, and slid into her parka. *One last look at the stage and the audience hall*, she mouthed, changing out of her ballet slippers and into her UGGs. Standing in the shadow of the dressing room door, she reached into the pocket of her coat and fingered the plastic bag she had been carrying around for days. Sofia stared at the mirrors framed with white light bulbs. She sniffed at the air heavy with the mixed aroma of makeup powder, sweat, and cheap cologne. Stepping further into the room, Sofia grabbed a red feather boa hanging on the back of a chair and wrapped it around her neck. She stood in front of a mirror and entertained herself as she pranced and strutted around. Her eyebrows arching high, a giggle escaping her pursed lips, Sofia reached into the pocket of her coat. Her fingers fumbled with the plastic bag. Speaking to herself in the empty dressing room, Sofia hissed, "*Nah*, I couldn't do it! Could I?" The plastic bag contained a dollop of fine powder, a powder that the store manager promised would cause a person severe discomfort. "Just sprinkle a little on a person's clothing and watch them wiggle and scratch like a suffering animal," the little Russian man had said.

Scattering the powder to see Nina squirm and itch would be a great gag, but this time, it might cause more problems than it was worth. She had to consider the consequences and make a better choice.

Enough with your childish horseplay, Sofia. You are a professional! Boris's words broke into the noise rumbling in her head, and his face, red and bloated, appeared behind her in the mirror.

With mischief clouding over her open stare, Sofia tossed the boa on a chair and threw one last glance at her reflection in the mirror. Blowing herself a kiss, she winked at herself and shrugged her shoulders. She found the bathrooms and dumped the itching powder down the sink.

Proud of her decision to control her naughtiness this time, Sofia exited the theater and stood frozen on the sidewalk facing Water Street. She glanced around in all directions, unsure and not so proud of her choice about meeting Ben today. The show was really causing excessive anxiety and stress, but Ben and the wedding plans were adding to her tension with untold ferocity.

Sofia lost herself in the memory of the conversation that began at dinner that night at Suki-Asia, over salty rows of sushi and bottles of intoxicating Sake. At first, Sofia tried to ignore the coolness of Ben's reactions, attributing both his insensitivity and her insecure nature to her upcoming performance anxiety. But her concerns had not dissipated, and each conversation with Ben since then had been nothing but tense and cautious. Neither one of them brought up the hapless comment Sofia made about her future as a dancer, but the subject loomed between them like a storm cloud waiting to crack open and soak whatever lay beneath it. But Ben had innocently suggested that they should meet for a quick bite after her rehearsal in the theater, and Sofia was not going to be the instigator of more tension by not accepting the invitation. In fact, Sofia's stomach began rumbling with hunger, and she could smell the aroma of pizza and beer tickling at her nose. A quick bite might be just what she needed then.

Suddenly, a hulking figure in an expensive wool coat and leather gloves stood in front of her, blocking her view of the nearby waterfront. "Ben, you scared me. Where'd you come from all of a sudden?" It was not the kind of greeting expected from a loving bride-to-be, and Ben squinted his eyes with resentful dissatisfaction.

"I saw you from across the street, and I thought you saw me too," Ben answered. "I didn't mean to scare you." He hesitated, then leaned forward and pecked Sofia on her forehead with a dry kiss. Christmas decor from the surrounding storefronts was now reflecting off the slick pavement, making a vibrant and festive setting in the afternoon swarm of shoppers. For a moment, Sofia felt relieved.

"Never mind. Where are you taking me for lunch today? I thought we might get something light, like a salad or some fish." She was lying. She would have preferred the pizza and beer she could still smell from the bar on the corner, but her diet these days had to be closely regulated for the ballet. She chucked Ben on the shoulder and followed behind him past the theater.

Sitting in a dim booth at the York Street Taverna—a watered-down version of a Greek bistro—Sofia ordered a lemon yogurt appetizer to be brought out with a salad of kale, caramelized onions, and cucumbers, topped with shrimp and crumbled feta cheese. Watching what she ate didn't mean she couldn't oblige her hearty appetite. Ben ordered lamb chops with lemon potatoes. When their orders were placed, and the waitress brought them a basket of breadsticks and two glasses of water, Ben broke through the stale silence that encased them. "So tell me. How was the theater? Were you able to rehearse much this morning?" He stared deep into Sofia's eyes.

"Yeah, but I still don't feel comfortable with the solo. My feet are okay, but I don't know what's wrong with my hands!" Sofia twirled her foot at the ankle, remembering the grumpy old man from the train that morning. She nudged Ben's leg with her toes under the table, smiling playfully, but Ben remained as serious and unimpressed as the man on the train had been. He simply twisted his napkin on his lap and ignored her gesture. Ben's stare was blank, and he seemed a million miles away.

"Yeah, and the costume is made of rainbow sequins," Sofia lied. She wondered how much he was actually listening to.

"Really? Rainbow, you say!"

"No, Ben. Not really. One costume is white, the other is black. I showed you the YouTube video of the performance… It's *Swan Lake*, for Christ's sake! What's up with you? Can you please just cut through the shit, be honest with me, and tell me what's up with you? I have enough shit on my mind, and I don't need to be worrying about you too!" Sofia hated walking on proverbial eggshells, and Ben's moodiness was testing her last nerve.

Ben snapped to attention, the palm of his hand slamming the table and rattling the silverware. His eyes remained lowered, not daring to look up at Sofia. "Fine. Here it is," he muttered through tight lips as if unsure he should say anything at all. "I'm starting to wonder about us." Stuttering, he shut his eyes and clarified, "If you and I are really made for each other." Sofia could not look at Ben. She was shocked—no, mortified. Feeling very foolish and a little self-conscious, she fiddled with her diamond stud earrings and then moved her fingers to the diamond engagement ring on her finger. She wanted to spit out the hate that had risen in her chest, but a wet sob clogged her throat and held it all inside. Her tongue was feeling more and more like sandpaper, and her eyebrows knitted together in a pained, disappointed frown.

Sofia sat up straighter in her chair; her eyes widened with shock, disbelief, confusion. "What? Did I hear you right? What do you mean you're wondering now if we're made for each other."

"I mean, we come from two different worlds, Sofia. And I'm not sure we want the same things anymore." Ben fidgeted with his tie, his eyes remaining glued to the bread basket in front of him.

"Oh, not this again, Ben. I don't care if you're a country bumpkin or a cowboy or a—"

Ben cut her off. "No, it's not that." He took a deep breath and raked a trembling hand through his hair. "I've been thinking a lot about us. And, well, you still seem to feel that the future is only about you and the ballet. I was hoping that if we got married, you'd come around and change your focus… that I would be enough for you, and you could start thinking less about your career and more about our family." His shoulders slumped, and he lowered his voice before continuing, "I know you don't want to have children, Sofia, but I do. I need a family. And I need to know you want one too." He took a sip of his water and spilled some on his tie. Ignoring the droplets, he reached across the table and grabbed Sofia's hand.

Sofia recoiled and stared at the drops of the water that were staining Ben's tie. They both cleared their throats and waited in the uncomfortable silence. Finally, Sofia said, "It's not that I don't want a family with you, Ben. I just don't want any children. I don't think I'd make a good mother, and besides, I never said I would give up my dancing." She chuckled, but Ben remained dead serious. Hers was a nervous reaction, she knew, but Sofia felt like she was being slapped across the face.

"We can't deny it… It seems like we've reached a stalemate. What if you never change your mind? What then? I can't risk betting on the chance that you'll change your views." He hesitated and turned away from her. "This is a deal breaker for me."

"So this is it then? It's over?" Gathering her thoughts and reaching for the right words, Sofia pinched her lips together and squeezed her eyes shut. "Ben, you have to know that you can't expect to change others or make choices for them. That's not fair. I have never lied to you about my plans or my future, and I thought you had accepted me *as is*. You've always known about my passion for the stage and our different beliefs about family." Suddenly, Anika's words seemed to all make sense.

The waitress came and placed their dishes on the table. Sensing she had interrupted something, the young waitress, with armfuls of colorful tattoos, fumbled with the plates and hurried off. Sofia stood abruptly and whispered something about the bathroom. If she waited one more second, she would have vomited all over their lunch.

How was she supposed to face the reality that her life with Ben was truly finished? Just when she should have been sitting on top of the world, everything was suddenly crushing down on top of her. She should have listened to her aunt earlier. Maybe Aunt Anika didn't have all the facts, but her instincts were certainly correct. Anika never cared much for Ben, and it was unfair of her to judge him. But Sofia should have known that her aunt, her substitute mother, would not steer her in the wrong direction. She would not try to influence her decision if it were not for good reason. Sofia should have trusted her. But she didn't. It had been her choice to accept Ben's proposal, and she was too stubborn to let anyone else—even her aunt—tell her what to do.

Her life, her passion…everything suddenly threatened to implode all around her. She had just lost hope of ever reuniting with her parents, she had just lost the man she thought she would spend the rest of her life with, and tonight she was about to screw up her entire career because she couldn't get her hand movements just right. She had to pull herself together. Everyone would be there—crammed into that small yet momentous theater—for what was supposed to be the most spectacular artistic performance of her life. She couldn't bear to lose one more thing. This was supposed to be her night.

The red carpet was littered with dozens of art patrons, photographers, wealthy philanthropists, and directors of competing dance academies. Ben had graciously agreed to appear with her for the evening, putting their personal issues on the back burner. Tonight was going to be all about Sofia Brenner—the biggest, shiniest light in the limitless sky.

She was the dying swan.

Ben, sporting a rented Emilio Zegna black tuxedo for the occasion, got out of the limo first and reached back to take Sofia's outstretched hand. She hoped the cameras would not capture the quiver that rattled her core all the way down into her fingertips or the feigned pride painted on Ben's face. Her dress was a long white sheath, studded with tiny pearls and shiny silver sequins, that fell off her slender shoulders to a plunging V neckline. Gracefully, she slid out of the limo and stood next to Ben while the photographers flashed photo after photo of their arrival. Sofia spotted the editor of *Dance Magazine* and nodded her head in acknowledgment. The powerful editor nodded back with recognition and acceptance. Sofia relaxed her shoulders, squeezed Ben's sweaty hand in hers, and waved to the roaring crowd.

The performance of *Swan Lake* went well. Aside from a few missed cues and an unnoticed stiffness in her fingers, the costumes and set were as exquisite as had been promised. It had been both technically and artistically challenging for Sofia to dance the double role of Odette and Odile, but she had little trouble switching in and out of her roles throughout the performance, while Nina, Andrew, and Becca looked on from the left wing. Boris was brilliant as Prince Siegfried. Anyone watching him on the stage that night would never doubt he had had issues with Sofia's professionalism or that he was not truly in love with her—especially after his last scene where he had to jump in the lake (a show of blue lights) to his ultimate demise.

Pushing past Nina, Sofia hurried to change into her costume for her final solo act. The moment she had been waiting for since she was a young beginning dancer around Russia and Ukraine had finally arrived. The solo dance of Pavlova's *The Dying Swan*. A dream about to come true. The music arrangement for her solo started up again, and Sofia took one long, deep gulp of air before gliding onto the waiting stage.

A disquieting howl resonated from the left side of the stage; Sofia stumbled off her mark, and her toes recoiled inside her slippers. For a moment, she felt her lungs collapse and her eyes blur, but somehow, Sofia managed to stabilized her equilibrium. She quickly spotted an older man sitting in the front row of the audience and concentrated on the wisp of frizzy hair that hung down onto his forehead. She had to keep going, but what was that noise? Sofia had never heard anything like it, and the piercing groan continued to ricochet off the eighteen-foot-high light beams.

Four minutes later, the music came to a full stop, and the audience roared with praise. On their feet, no one seemed to have noticed the commotion brewing behind the curtains. They whistled and cried out for an encore. Sofia took a final bow and leaped from center stage toward her left. From behind the thick velvet curtains, she could still hear the thunderous screams from the audience and feel the vibrating pulse of their applause. "Brava!" they called, as Sofia considered whether to return to the stage or find out what was causing all the fuss in the wing. A mass of feathered swans gathered around a lump of tricot, velvet, and sequins was splattered across the floor. Bowing low for the third time before finally exiting the stage, Sofia panted as she bounced and swished toward the curtained wing. What on earth is going on over here? Did they see how brilliant the performance was? Were they listening to the adoring audience, still pleading for more? She pushed her way through the blur of tutus and satin slippers and fell to her knees on the hardwood floor just in front of the heaped muddle. Her breath caught in her chest as she stared down at a colorless face, bloated with bulging glazed eyes and contorted with pain and fear.

An unnatural groan escaped her crimson lips, "No, Becca. No, no, no."

23

Maya

"I need a drink! Where is that kid?" My voice shakes with impatience. Ever since Jim came and went—a time that lasted a mere blink of an eye but affected my life in so many big ways—I have no more tolerance for these young volunteers. They come to have "an adventure," not realizing that they are intruding on real problems, real lives, real people. I hope that another beer will be enough to smooth my bristling edges.

I am still wearing my dirty apron, and Danny is late. He said he would meet me here tonight, which caught me by surprise since we haven't spoken a word to each other since the fight we had in Maya's Dance Palace. Aaron is spending the evening with his grandfather. Abba loves to play with him and tell him stories about his childhood in Russia. Aaron, of course, doesn't yet speak or understand a thing, but he is Abba's best audience.

I shift uncomfortably on the barstool; my legs dangle, barely reaching the footrest, and my neck struggles to hold up my throbbing head. A movie is playing on our latest collective pride and joy, an enormous new Samsung TV—long time in coming to our small community—that covers the entire wall like a giant movie screen. A small crowd of young kibbutzniks is gathered in front of it, sitting on wobbly folding chairs, watching *Indiana Jones and the Temple of Doom*. To my left, a half-open slatted partition scarcely blocks the music that is screeching from an antiquated, staticky sound system. (I have to remember to talk to Boaz about fixing this in time for the show.) In about one hour, the makeshift wall will be folded back to accommodate an improvised disco, and the TV will be turned off for the night. It is dark, and the place smells of wet soil, smoke, and stale beer. I sit at the bar, slim and erect, trying to imagine this room's transformation over the next twenty-four hours. Nervous tension escapes my lips with a loud, sloppy burp.

I look around the place for the thousandth time, making mental diagrams of my surroundings. More chairs will have to be brought in, I think, and the crude wooden platform near the back wall will have to be moved, sanded, and raised higher in order to serve as a suitable stage. A small orchestra, a group of older musicians, have agreed to accompany the performance, and Boaz has already been working on making the necessary adjustments to enhance the lighting. In just twenty-four hours, me and my young protégés will perform *Le Cygne Solitaire*. Almost twenty years in the making and my life's ambition will finally be revealed to an audience, even if that audience is here on Kibbutz Gan Notzah, in this hole-in-the-wall we call home.

It's all up to me now.

Everything is hinging on the success of my very own, original ballet. A white light suddenly blinds my vision, and my body stiffens. Forward, backward—a discord of emotions flattens me like a rolling pin pulverizing a blob of challah dough. I roll my shoulders and let out another beer-laced burp.

Squinting my eyes in the dim light, I pull out the crinkling paper from my apron pocket and read it for the millionth time. It is not a letter from Jim (those were all burned in the kitchen ovens the same day Danny discovered them in the back of my closet) but a letter on fancy hotel stationery from my best friend, Irena Plotkin. She is in London with the Haifa Conservatory. Her missive is written in typical Irena style—short, sweet, and to-the-point. "*She misses home, but what I wouldn't do to be in her slippers*," I whine out loud as I read her words. I've been a bundle of jumpy energy, and tonight I am even more restless than ever; excitement mixed with self-doubt zips through me. At times, the hands of the clock seem to stand still, and yet it is clear, as I glimpse down at Irena's letter, that the days and months and years have slipped away faster and faster, and with each blink of an eye, time is piling up behind me in unrecognizable, blurry heaps. I'm not what I used to be, and I'm not sure I am up for the physical and mental stress of this performance. My heart pounds with pent-up anticipation, my tense muscles are immobilized by my building impatience and fear for what's to be. Folding Irena's letter back into my pocket, I envy her freedom of travel and adventure, her easy rise to fulfillment.

It's now almost nine o'clock, and the sun still refuses to let go of the day. I am completely exhausted and ready to call it quits for the day. My mind races in a million directions, and my toes tap instinctively at the leg of the barstool in rhythm with the scratchy music pulsing from the other side of the partitioned rec center. My body is stiff and tired, and even though my figure remains in relatively good shape, my muscles twitch and burn—a crude reminder that I am not as young as I used to be. Still teeming with fury at Danny and his lack of compassion and understanding, I replay the fight we had earlier in the week. Danny still could not understand me. Or trust me. I wring my hands and twist my wedding band around my calloused finger.

My mother stumbles into the rec center, and I let out a small sigh. Coming straight from work in the dairy with brown streaks of dirt still covering her sweaty cheeks, she smells like fresh manure. I've grown to love this about her, not the odor but the fact that no matter how off-putting she appears on the outside, her humble dignity, compassion, and self-confidence could inspire even the most dejected of spirits. Filthy yet proud and strong, she walks slowly toward me. I drop my head sideways into my open palm, my elbow resting on the bar, and struggle to hold myself upright. She lovingly brushes back the veil of disheveled hair from my face.

"You're out late tonight."

"And so are you," I point out, a hint of pride behind my pout. "Did you just finish your work shift? Where's Abba?"

"Your father had some paperwork to finish in the office tonight. He's been trying to put together next year's budget. You know how it is. The board of directors has to go through a lot of red tape before anything can get done around here, and they are anticipating a huge windfall from your show. Anyway, I had to train a new volunteer at the dairy tonight, so I just stopped in for a lemonade before going home." With an affectionate smile, she adds, "The cherry on top is running into you."

My shoulders droop, and I roll my head from side to side over my stiff neck. A tight smile stretches over my face as she takes the seat next to me. "Danny said he would meet me, but I don't know what's taking him so long to get here," I lie. My mother has no idea that we have been sinking in quicksand lately. To tell her would truly break her heart, so I keep my issues with Danny to myself. I know exactly why he's late; in his own sad way, he's trying to let me know that he is in control and calling the shots. I secretly wish he won't show up at all.

"You look like you've had a hard day, Maya. Is everything okay? Have you eaten?" My mother reaches for my hand and gives it a loving squeeze, interrupting my thoughts about Danny. She can read my mind as if she lives in the crevices of my brain. Wise and kind as the day is long. That's my mother.

However, with my nerves stretched beyond their limits, not even my gentle mother can change the mood I'm in tonight. I just want to sit and sulk and indulge in a bit of self-pity for a while. I know I'll get over my nerves and the falling-out with Danny, like I always manage to do, and life will bounce back into its normal grind. I really do love him, even if I have to keep reminding myself these days. Pinching my lips into a tight line and keeping my gaze lowered so my mother won't notice my worry, I turn my head toward the enormous TV screen.

Temple of Doom, indeed. Harumph! I exhale another low burp.

I read the worry in my mother's twisted lips and tired red-rimmed eyes. I know she is concerned for me; I know she is aware that everything is really not okay. Things haven't been okay for some time. She waves her hand in my face, as if that would whisk away all the bad mojo. Reading my mind and clucking her tongue, she warns me, "Every marriage goes through trying times, but you two are going to make it through whatever it is that is upsetting you. It happens to the best of us, and there is no time to waste being disillusioned with the realities of life."

Patiently, she stares at me with her foggy blue eyes. She opens her mouth to say something more and then closes it abruptly, deciding instead to remain quiet and end the conversation. There is nothing left to say, so I sigh, bite my bottom lip, and remain silent as well.

Reaching into my apron pocket, I push aside Irena's letter and wrap my fingers around a small plastic bottle. Withdrawing two smooth pills, I pop them in my mouth and swallow them down. My mother pinches her lips together as if trying to dam up the rush of thoughts pounding in her head. She quickly wipes away a small tear that escapes from her lashes and momentarily turns away from me. Whistling through my nose, I swivel my head, searching for the bartender.

The young volunteer working behind the bar that night finally reappears, asks us what we want to drink, and nonchalantly bobs his head to the rhythm of the music playing in his head. A straggly piece of hair, wet with perspiration, dangles over his dark eyes as if he hasn't brushed it out for days. Why does every volunteer that comes to us think that living here is any different than living in the places they came from? We are not an escape from reality, as Jim thought. Before I could respond to the young volunteer, my mother answers him for the both of us in her clipped English. "We want two lemonades, please."

"No, I think I'll have another beer, please." I snap, a bit out of character, and point to the bar.

My mother stares at the three empty cans of Maccabi beer in front of me and winces. Sliding them sideways with her dirt-stained palm and arranging them neatly out of reach, she bends her head toward mine and whispers, "Maybe you've already had enough beer for one night, Maya."

Out of nowhere, a dizzying fog begins to creep over me, and my skin coats with a layer of slimy sweat that reeks of dishwater and boiled cabbage. A bubble of nausea clogs my throat, and I taste the bitter bile collecting there. I wish everyone would stop telling me what to do and what they think I need. I think I can manage to make my own decisions. I desperately want another beer, but I cluck my tongue and nod to the volunteer behind the bar. "Okay, two lemonades, thank you."

Looking up, I see Harrison Ford on the big screen thrashing through Indian markets. In the darkened space beyond the slatted partition, Madonna is crooning about being a virgin.

Blah, blah, blah…dizzying white noise.

My mother's voice is suddenly interrupted by the whine of Danny's weary call. I spin around on the barstool and watch my husband's approach. With a clumsy, heavy-footed march, he is coming back from a full day in the almond fields and an additional six-hour guard shift at the main gate. I wonder if he has eaten dinner yet. Still dressed in his uniform, his broad shoulders and burly chest move forward in alluring sync. His mop of unruly dark curls (I will have to remind him to get a haircut as soon as we start speaking to each other again) bounce wildly around his worn face; his leathery cheeks and sexy cleft chin are prominent behind a layer of thick black stubble. His jaw jumps and clenches like he is chewing on his tongue. Maintaining at a safe distance, he lightly kisses the top of my head and whispers, "Hi, Maya." For the first time in a long time, his lips soften into a tender smile. "Sorry I'm a bit late." My body melts with a tingling sensation, my heart skips a fast beat, and a low purr escapes my lips.

I love him.

And then my chest constricts, and I cannot fill my lungs with a full breath of air. I push myself away from the bar, jump down from my seat, and gesture for Danny to take my seat. The corners of Danny's mouth turn downward as he tentatively wraps his strong arms around my shoulders.

The last images I see flashing behind my heavy eyelids are a blur of color and movement: Aaron's dimpled and reddened cheeks, Danny's serious caramel-brown eyes, and a hazy field of yellow sunflowers where my mother is standing tall and proud. I slump against Danny's chest, and everything disappears.

24

Sofia

The papers would be unkind, but what did they know? It is true that the public never knows what really happens behind closed doors, and it couldn't be truer now. She had run out on them, on her one big chance, her shining moment. But Sofia couldn't think about any of that. Not now, anyway.

Boris had offered to stay and make a statement to the press. He insisted Sofia stay with Becca; he would handle the pack of reporters and correspondents at the theater. In all the chaos of the moment, Sofia didn't have to be told twice. She grabbed Becca's cold, bony hand and did not let go of it, even as the team of responders maneuvered her stiff body onto a gurney and rolled her into the back of the ambulance. Still in her feathered headdress and tutu, Sofia threw her puffer jacket around her shoulders and slipped her feet into her boots just before the medics slammed the ambulance door shut and blocked out the chaotic crush of reporters and fans and the chilling December air.

Now sitting alone in the emergency room, Sofia's entire body trembled. She wasn't sure if it was the frosty winter or the fear for her dearest friend that ran through her veins and rattled her every nerve. Either way, she was struck motionless with panic and horror, unable to control the tremors expanding from her core. Becca had remained unconscious, her face white and pasty, her lips blue and chapped, as the ambulance blared its siren and raced through the crowded streets. The paramedics sighed and whispered medical terms that Sofia didn't understand as they continuously checked Becca's pulse and arranged a plastic mask with an oxygen tank over her face.

With only her puffer jacket draped over her tutu and stockings, Sofia trembled in the cold, sterile seat under the muted TV hanging on the wall. The image of Becca's tiny, sick body filled her burning eyes, but the rumbling applause and cheers of the theater patrons still rang in her ears. Totally discombobulated and unable to get a grasp of all that was happening, Sofia shook her head from side to side and stared up at the tiled ceiling. *Where's Ben? Where's my phone?* It took her a moment to realize she left everything back in her dressing room at the theater.

"Miss Sofia Brenner?" A doctor in a white lab coat and thick glasses walked toward her. His name was embroidered on his left lapel: Dr. Leo Goldwhein. The man had to be in his sixties, although he had a full head of bushy white hair and a matching plummy mustache above his thin lips. His eyes, however, were two sapphires that shimmered with kindness as he spoke to Sofia.

"Yes, doctor. I'm Sofia Brenner. Are you the doctor who is seeing my Becca? I mean, Rebecca Kaplan? How is she? What happened to her? Is the baby okay?" Flustered and desperate with a head full of unanswered questions, Sofia reached out and grabbed Dr. Goldwhein's sleeve.

"Ms. Kaplan is still unconscious. The baby seems to be fine, but—"

"But what? Doctor, tell me. Is Becca okay?"

"Can you get in touch with Ms. Kaplan's family?"

This kind-looking doctor was beginning to annoy Sofia. She wanted answers, and she had no patience for his stalling tactics. Raising her voice and standing up out of her seat, she lied and said, "Ms. Kaplan…I mean Becca…has no family in New York. I am her only family here. Now, Doctor, are you going to tell me what's going on or not?"

Towering a foot above Sofia, Dr. Goldwhein stood back and replied calmly, "Becca has suffered a severe embolism. We can't really explain why these things happen. They just do." The tall white-haired doctor slumped in defeat, and Sofia could see pity welling up under his eyelids. "I need to speak to her immediate family, Ms. Brenner." He puckered his lips, and his mustache wiggled under his nose.

Sofia checked her temper and scanned the room. "Is there a phone around here I could use? Maybe I can reach her mother."

What in the world is an embolism? Sofia scratched her forehead as she dialed for an operator the pay phone on the wall next to the candy machine. She couldn't think straight, and the doctor's words left her more confused and lost than before. She wished Nathan was with her; he would know what to do, how to help. She drummed her fingers on the side of the phone as she waited for an operator to connect her collect call. Her knees were giving out under her weight, but she managed to balance herself against the side of the candy machine, banging into it with a loud thud. Listening to the white noise in the receiver pressed to her ear, Sofia coughed up a strangled bubble of air. She was supposed to be taking care of Becca, making sure she was healthy and strong. Making sure her baby was growing and developing. Making sure nothing bad would happen to her. But she had failed her. She couldn't protect Becca or keep her and the baby well. She couldn't…

Sofia's thoughts drifted, and her stomach churned with nausea. A sudden thought exploded in her mind and spun up a cloud of fuzzy emotions. Sofia felt her body become weightless, and the room began to whir like she was Dorothy in the tornado at the beginning of *The Wizard of Oz*. Her hip popped and zinged with an electric jolt. She fell against the candy machine, rubbed her lower back, and took deep breaths.

This was supposed to be her night. *Her* night. The troupe had danced flawlessly, and her performances had been nearly perfect. Only Boris and Nina from behind the curtains would have noticed her one off-sync moment when her hand flinched awkwardly in the final scene. The audience had been enraptured throughout the show, the continuous *oohs* and *aahs* getting louder and giddier as the show came to its climactic end. The media had attended and waited for her with cameras and notepads at the ready by the time she was taking her final bow. And now, in the blink of an eye, it was all gone. The moment lost forever.

The last place Sofia imagined herself to be on this night was the ER. All the planning, all the painstaking hours of practice, all her hopes and dreams simply smashed to pieces. She would have to abandon all her dreams. Give it all up. She had been beaten. She failed, and there would be no second chances. The only thing people would remember was that she disappeared after the show and couldn't even give a minute of time to the waiting press. They would remember her only as a self-absorbed, selfish prima donna. Her shoulders drooped, and her toes cramped. The realization that she would never become the shining star she was born to be—the brilliant superstar her mamoh had been expecting her to be—cut like a knife in her chest. All her lifelong hopes and dreams just vanished into thin air. *Becca, you have to be okay! I can't fail you also!*

It was nearly 2:00 a.m. when Sofia finally got ahold of Becca's parents. Mr. Kaplan had answered the phone with a start, obviously waking up from deep sleep, but when he had heard Sofia's voice on the other end of the line, he quickly aroused Mrs. Kaplan to take the phone call. Sofia's tongue stuck to the roof of her mouth, and she was not able to find the right words to put in plain words what had happened, so she simply explained that Becca had fallen ill during the show that night and that they had brought her to the hospital for some tests. Mrs. Kaplan sniffed back her tears and sputtered a string of Yiddish prayers. "Thanks to *Hashem* you are with her, Sofia." And with that, the phone went dead.

At 4:16 a.m., Dr. Goldwhein returned to the waiting room and walked straight toward Sofia. His shoulders were hunched, and his eyes behind his thick glasses were rimmed with swollen red circles. He looked much shorter than he did just hours ago. His voice was low and gravely. "Ms. Brenner, have you been able to reach Rebecca's family?"

Sofia uncurled from the uncomfortable seat and plopped her feet on the floor. She rubbed her tired eyes and stretched her burning muscles as she stood up and faced the doctor. "No, Dr. Goldwhein. I couldn't get through to her parents at this hour of the night," she lied again. "But can't I see her? Can't you tell me what the hell is going on? Please! I'm all she has!" Sofia could no longer conceal her impatience or her fear.

Dr. Goldwhein sighed and sat down. He waved his veiny hand at Sofia, suggesting she take her seat again. Sighing heavily, the doctor said, "It's her heart. It doesn't look good. Actually, Rebecca is conscious now, and she is asking for you."

"What? That's not possible, doctor. Her heart is young and healthy! Becca's barely twenty years old!"

"An embolism is an occlusion—a blockage, if you will—of a blood vessel by an air bubble. It can occur when amniotic fluid leaks into blood vessels, and it can last several days or even weeks. Her blood pressure was super high, so we checked her lungs. Sure enough, we found a clot there. This is what is causing her heart to fail now." Dr. Goldwhein stopped to let the news sink in. Then he continued, "The baby looks healthy and strong. We are going to perform a cesarian as soon as we get Rebecca prepped for surgery. For now, though, why don't you come with me so you can see her first."

Sofia jumped out of her seat and followed the doctor down a complicated maze of hallways. When they finally reached Becca's room, Sofia could only hear a symphony of mechanized bleeps and the rush of air being pushed through a ventilator. Becca's pallor had turned yellowish under the squeeze of the oxygen mask on her tiny face, and her hair was wet with sweat and matted to her forehead and neck. Sofia reached for her hand and held it tight in her own. Becca's eyes popped open, and a small tear ran down her cheek and around the oxygen mask to the corner of a weak smile forming on her lips.

Her heavy purple eyelids fluttered open and closed, as if keeping them open was too tiresome.

"My dear Sofia. You are here."

"Where else would I be, my beautiful Becca? How do you feel?"

"Like shit, Sofia. Are my parents here? Did they come?" Without opening her eyes, Becca coughed, fogging up the inside of the plastic mask.

"Take it easy, dear Becca. Your parents send their prayers for you, but they can't come until the morning. The doctor says they're going to do a C-section now. Are you ready to be a mommy?" Sofia felt the first tears that night tumble from her eyes and streak the thick stage makeup still plastered on her face. She would try to reach out to Mrs. Kaplan again tomorrow.

"Okay, I'm sure Mamoh and Tatoh will come, but now I need to talk to you, Sofia." Becca swallowed hard, wrinkled her nose under the oxygen mask, and waited a beat before continuing. "If I don't make it—"

"Shut up, Becca! Don't talk like that! Of course, you are going to make it! Hang in there, little mama. Your baby needs you!" The nurse looked up from the computer keyboard and shot Sofia a look. *Keep your voice down*, she said with her glare.

"Shh! Don't interrupt me. I have to ask you something important."

Lowering her voice, Sofia tightened her grip on Becca's hand and squinted her wet eyes. "Yes, Becca. I'm sorry. What is it? You know I'll do anything for you."

"Good, please promise me you'll take care of Natalie."

Before Becca said another word, Sofia wondered if the medications or anesthesia were making Becca delusional, making her speak a bunch of nonsense. Who was Natalie?

"Like you said before, my soul sister, my baby will need her *mamoh*. Please promise me you'll take good care of her and give her a good life." She turned her head and glanced at the clock on the wall. It read 4:44 a.m.

"Look at that. Triple fours. The matriarchs are talking to us." Streams of oxygen bubbled up through the plastic tubing and clouded the mask on Becca's face. Laboring for breath, her chest rose up and down, desperate for air. Sucking noises escaped from under the oxygen mask as Becca struggled to speak her mind. She sounded drunk, not sick. Sofia closed her eyes and prayed that when she opened them again, she would miraculously be back at the theater in front of a throng of reporters and adoring fans wishing her well and that the whole embolism-catastrophe was just a bad dream. Becca's wet, gurgling words interrupted her thoughts. "Remember, Sofia. Mothers have to make good choices, but sometimes they are the hardest ones for us to make. Promise me one last thing, sister. Promise me you'll call her Natalie, and you'll tell her how much I loved her." More gurgling from the air hose, more gasping as Becca tried to speak. More tears streaming down Sofia's burning cheeks. "Do it for me, and do it for her father. For Nathan." These were her last words as Sofia watched Becca smile and fight for her last chestful of air.

Maya

My head is spinning. There is a lump of phlegm in my throat, but I don't have the strength to cough it up. My eyelids are so heavy. I can hear voices, but I am too weak to open my eyes. I am lying in a bed that is not my own. Where am I?

"I think she's going to be fine, Shula. It might have been all the tension and excitement about the show. It might have been the pills. But there is good news here." A man is talking to my mother.

The last thing I remember now is Madonna singing in the background and the darkness of the bar. The air is stuffy and hot and hard to breathe. Then I see him. Danny. He is wearing his army uniform and smiling at me. The night comes back to me in grainy images. I try to open my eyes, and I see two figures standing next to me. One is a man in a white medical smock, the other is Imma in her dirty work clothes. As my eyelashes flutter, Imma turns to me and wraps my cold hand with her warm fingers.

"Darling, Maya. You're awake! How do you feel?"

I try to speak, but no sound comes out of my mouth. The lump of phlegm clogs my voice. I turn my head and cough gingerly into my pillow. Imma and the man in the white smock wait for me to catch my breath, and finally I am able to whisper, "Where am I? I feel like shit."

I recognize the man now. It is Dr. Nemrod, the kibbutz doctor. And I am in the kibbutz's infirmary. Dr. Nemrod looks taller than I remember as he stands over my bed, but his face is friendly and bright. He is good-looking for a man of fifty-two; his shoulders are broad, and his skin is tan and unlined. His aquiline nose and rummy-blue eyes give a wise and interested expression to his countenance. I always liked him.

"Excuse me, Doctor. What happened to me? Why am I here?" Suddenly, I hear another tune in my head. It's the music I had composed for *Le Cygne Solitaire*. My ballet! I nearly jump out of the bed, but I collapse back against the pillows with a weighty thud. The muscles in my lower stomach cramp and roll. One hand flops onto my belly, and the other still clasps Imma's protective grip.

"By the look of your current situation, Maya, you are not in a position to be rushing off anywhere. You are obviously not recovered from the blackout, and it will take time for you to regain your strength. The hormonal changes in your body are causing a lot of blood pressure fluctuations. If your blood pressure falls rapidly, like it did that night, it will continue to cause you to blackout. It can also make you nauseous for a while. And diabetes can also become a risk we cannot take! No, this time was only a warning, so we are keeping you in bed and in constant care. You are a very lucky girl, Maya. This could have been a lot worse!" Dr. Nemrod chuckled, and his blue eyes sparkled with optimism.

Questions began racing through my mind, and I let go of my mother's hand. This is more serious than I thought. Why is my blood pressure fluctuating all of a sudden? Why is Dr. Nemrod talking about hormonal changes and diabetes? How long have I been here?

"It all boils down to one thing, Maya. You have been here, unconscious, for five days. You must be more careful and watch yourself this time. Come in for regular checks and stay in bed! I'll inform Rivke that you won't be working for a while."

"What are you talking about, Dr. Nemrod? Is it what I think it is?" Imma's face lit up like a Shabbos candle on Friday night, and she ran her hand over my sweaty forehead.

"Yes, Shula. That is the good news I was talking about before. Maya and Danny are about to become parents again. You are pregnant, Maya!"

It takes more days to convince the doctor and my mother that I will be fine moving back to my own home. Reminding them that Danny will be with me for most of the day and all night is what finally clinches it, and I am now condemned to the restrictions of my husband and our bedroom.

Danny leaves for work at sunup and is home by lunchtime—those are hours I spend sleeping alone to catch up on my sleepless nights. We've been civil to each other, mindful of my sensitive physical condition and the realization that our family is about to include one more, but the news of the pregnancy sits silently between us and continues to aggravate the very delicate balance of our relationship. While Danny sleeps peacefully, I toss and turn with an unsettled disappointment. I've failed the show, I've failed the kibbutz, and I've failed to realize my one and only chance at my dreams. Only when Danny leaves do I relax enough to close my eyes and let go of my inner demons.

Thoughts of my show and my commitment to the kibbutz continue to weigh heavy on my conscience. Dr. Nemrod insists I stay in bed and away from the studio, my mother has arranged to bring me healthy meals (prepared especially for me by Rivke in the main kitchen), and Gali has vowed to visit at least every other day to wash and blow-dry my hair for me. She also brings me her old issues of *Dance Magazine* to keep me occupied and in bed. Danny constantly sings to me and brings me gifts of almonds and sunflowers to lighten my spirits. He comes home every day after his work shift and guard duty to eat meals with me. I know he is making sure that I am eating. We have not argued since the doctor informed us of the pregnancy, and I begin to look forward to spending time with my husband again. Just like the good ol' days.

Sure enough, though, the giddy "honeymoon" period begins to recede, and I grow restless to get back to my students and my dance lessons. I am frantically aware that any chance I might have had before to help Kibbutz Gan Notzah recover from its financial complications is now beginning to slip away. Still, so many people are counting on my show to buoy us through our economic slump and even raise our overall morale here at the kibbutz.

Now all our hopes and goals seem to have vanished into the cold, dark winter air. Our population is decreasing as more and more families are leaving the farm for the cities where they can make more money. Even our founding families are getting harder to convince that we need to stick together and see our problems through. Gali and David are staying put, and Danny doesn't think about anything these days except the baby. But Imma jumps between genuine elation about the birth of another grandchild and an unjustifiable guilt about encouraging the creation of our dance academy in the first place. Abba and the other board members are simply nervous wrecks, staying up late into the night trying to solve our current predicament. And all I can do is count the minutes on the ticking clock while my muscles atrophy in bed, and Maya's Dance Palace grows cold and empty. I hope the disgusting megabats haven't found their way into our rafters there!

Eager to get out of bed, I watch the rain pelt the window pane for a few minutes, and I finally manage to swing my legs over the side of the bed. My plan is to head over to Maya's Dance Palace for the first time in almost two weeks, before anyone stops by to check on me this morning. My head is groggy from lying around, and my back feels stiff. As I adjust the water temperature in the shower, I hear the front door slam and feet shuffle on the smooth Chattahoochee floor. "Who's there?" I yell from the bathroom.

"It's your favorite brother in the whole world. That's the only hint you get!" It is a man's chuckle that I know all too well. I quickly wrap my cotton robe around my body and shuffle out of the bathroom.

"Kobi! It is you! No way! How?… When?… Never mind, what a great surprise!" Sputtering a bunch of nonsense, I reach out to my younger brother, squeal with delight, and give him a tight hug. His gruffy cheeks scratch my neck as he picks me up off my feet and twirls me in the air. Hysterical with laughter, the two of us balance ourselves and crash onto the sofa. "You look like shit, little brother. And you definitely could use a shave."

"You don't look so hot yourself, big sister." I look down at my robe and twist my hair up in a knot behind my head. Kobi's arrival is a great surprise, even if it means I won't be getting to the studio this morning. Kobi roars with that infectious laugh of his, and the room vibrates.

"I was just about to take a shower, but first, some coffee."

He follows me out of the living room and sits in a chair under the kitchen window. It has stopped raining, and the sun's rays peek out from behind the wintery-white clouds still looming in the sky. Kobi drags a large hand over his buzz-cut hair and slumps over the table. "I am so tired…but I'm not here to talk about me. How the hell are you? Rumor has it you're expecting a little brother or sister for Aaron!" Kobi looks up at my belly, his smile lighting up his whole face.

"Yup, we can't keep a secret around here too long! We're due around July." A sincere smile spreads across my freckled face, up to my eyes.

"Great news! So I'm going to be an uncle again, and this time I will be here for the event!"

"What? Did I hear you right? I'm not due for months! What do you mean you'll be here?"

"It's such a *balagan*, Maya. That's why I came back. I know I can talk to you. Can we talk?" Now Kobi was rambling nonsense, so I nod my head and wait for him to continue. "I fucked everything up, Maya. I trusted all the wrong people and made all the wrong choices."

After hearing about his breakup with Devorah (he found his girlfriend of seven months in bed with one of his platoon recruits) and his almost-court-martial (for fighting with him), I have only one comment, "What do you mean you made the wrong choices, Kobi? You always follow your heart and your convictions. So maybe things didn't work out the way you wanted with Devorah, but you know you can't control other people. She isn't for you, and you had to find out the hard way. You'll move on and find someone who will love you forever. Until then, remember what you always say: our choices are not always easy, but they are not necessarily wrong."

Kobi looks up at me and smirks. "I'm so embarrassed, Maya. I failed. I lost Devorah, and I lost my control. I nearly got kicked out of the army because of her. No…because of me and my uncontrollable temper!" Kobi chokes up an uncharacteristic sob and rests his head on top of his forearms stretched out on the table. Then he continues in a muffled voice, "Everything I thought I wanted, everything I sacrificed, everything is just…" The electric coffee kettle whistles, and Kobi's words drift off. I turn back to the kitchen counter, prepare two cups of instant coffee, and sit beside my younger brother. My heart swells with a compassionate ache, and I reach over to rub Kobi's shoulder. I know how he feels.

He wipes his nose with the sleeve of his uniform, and as I watch his chest rise and fall with his heavy breaths, I realize for the first time how small he is. I remain silent, waiting for Kobi to finish unloading all of his pain and disappointment. After a silence that stretches over the better part of ten minutes, Kobi lifts his head and shakes it. "I don't want to fight anymore, Maya. I'm tired. All I want is to come home. No more love. No more fighting."

Kobi's confession strikes me like a bolt of lightning. He had always committed himself to defending our country, to fighting for love and humanity, to respect everyone's natural right for opportunity and free will, to choosing happiness…no matter what dangerous or troublesome consequences may come of the decisions he's made. His choices were always serious and sane, and I had always trusted Kobi to consider every detail and outcome. I open and close my mouth, but nothing comes out. Instead of talking, I lean over and hold him close to me. He rests his head against my chest, and I feel a shudder rise up through his shoulders. I imagine exactly what Kobi is feeling. How many times can a person fight for something, only to lose it all on the chance of making the wrong decision and still be expected to pick themselves up and keep moving forward? It's exhausting; that's for sure. But we each have a choice. We can make decisions—bad or good, easy or hard, disappointing or fulfilling—and move on. It looks like the time has come for both of us to forget about past choices and make some good, forward-looking decisions.

26

Sofia

One life ends. A new life begins.

The baby wailed, and the phone tweeted from between the sofa cushions where Sofia had abandoned it days ago. She didn't know which way to turn. Alone in the apartment, she wandered from room to room, ignoring the baby and the phone notifications and wrinkling her nose at the familiar odors of vomit, talcum powder, and baby formula that hung in the air. Today, there was an added aroma of day-old *kasha varnikas* that lingered from last night's leftovers that Tyotya Anika had brought over. Natalie, already seven months old, was having a hard time getting used to eating solid foods, and Sofia had a fussy appetite herself, so the home-cooked food remained mostly untouched in its plastic container, and Natalie was fed her powdered milk and tiny jars of pureed baby food. Huffing, Sofia shuffled into the kitchen and grabbed a jar of peas and another jar of what the label called "turkey sticks."

After feeding Natalie and laying her down in the crib for a nap, Sofia remembered her phone and checked her unanswered calls. There were nine voice messages and thirteen texts in her missed calls list. All these months later, friends from the Tantsor Academy, neighbors that had been worried that they hadn't seen her around, and her aunt and uncle had been calling regularly, but Sofia had no desire to keep up pretenses with them or explain how overwhelmed she was with the life that was thrust upon her with no warning or planning. Not to mention, the media had been hounding her since that last show at the Montefiori Theater with endless phone calls and vigilant posts outside her apartment and the dance academy, all waiting for the juicy story from Sofia Brenner herself—the washed-up, failed star of the ballet.

It turned out that Nina had filled in for her roles in the production of *Swan Lake*, but the additional presentation of *The Dying Swan* was not presented after that first night. Boris, thank goodness, had seen to that. No one else could fill Sofia's slippers in that performance. Sofia was grateful for that simple kindness from Boris, even though the press had already had a field day with the exploitation of Sofia's bad luck. It was all more than Sofia could handle and easier to ignore all the calls and attention than try to maintain her poise and dignity with the world that knew her as a rising ballerina in the prime of her career. Sofia's moment to shine had been stolen, and there would be no turning back. Sofia had danced her last dance.

On the other hand, Mr. and Mrs. Kaplan had not called since that bittersweet night of Natalie's birth; they had made it perfectly clear that they had completely disowned their oldest daughter and their first grandchild. The Kaplan family did not even come to the funeral or to the one-week shiva that was held at Sofia's apartment in Bay Ridge. Sofia spent days and weeks and months trying to understand how Becca's family could turn their backs on their own daughter and granddaughter, but there were no words to console her disappointment and sadness. Dyadya Sol tried to explain how their ancient belief in family, sin, and shame could sometimes make people act inappropriately, even if it meant their hearts were breaking inside. Both Dyadya Sol and Tyotya Anika tried to convince Sofia that the Kaplans were grieving in their own private way, but Sofia could not find consolation in her aunt and uncle's "devil's advocate" explanations. After all, she knew enough about rejection from her own parents and the choices they had chosen to make. Some choices might be difficult, but we have to do what's right.

And what's right is not always easy.

Staring down at the phone that weighed like a cement brick in her hand and reading the list of missed calls, Sofia's heart began to do somersaults in her chest. After months of waiting and wondering, the last voice message she had missed had been from Ben. She realized she had been missing the man more than she wanted to admit, but how had she missed his call? With shaky fingers, Sofia dialed for her messages and waited to hear Ben's scratchy, flustered voice, "Hi, Sofia. It's me, Ben. I'm sorry I haven't been able to return your calls, but I've been swamped with work on a new project. Not a great excuse, but I was hoping we could meet for dinner sometime soon. Let me know… You know where to find me." Sofia's hand, clenching tightly to the phone, collapsed next to her on the sofa.

Ben had gone missing ever since the show at the Montefiori Theater, and Sofia had tried several times to call him for an explanation of his disappearance and his apparent lack of concern for what had happened that night. With each passing day that turned into months of no response from him, Sofia had to come to the realization that her effort to find answers—or even attain closure—was going to go unresolved. Once again, she was feeling rejected and abandoned.

Sofia was jolted out of her unending miserable nightmare when the phone chimed in her hand. She looked at the screen and saw Ben's name. "No way," she muttered in disbelief and hit the green button to answer the call before it woke Natalie. In her state of shock, Sofia was not prepared for this now. She whispered "Hello?" and held her breath.

"Sofia, it's me, Ben. Can you talk?"

"Sure. What's up?" She knew she didn't sound as cool as she intended. Her voice cracked with each word that escaped her lips.

"What do you mean, 'what's up'? We haven't spoken for months… That's what's up." Now Ben's words sharpened, as if annoyed with Sofia's indifference to his call, and Sofia stiffened.

"Don't get annoyed with me, Ben! I've been trying to reach you, and you are the one who was too busy to get back to me."

"You're right. Sorry. I was hoping maybe we can meet for dinner. Say, Suki-Asia in one hour?"

Sofia wasn't sure she could handle meeting him at their former hangout. She rubbed the side of her head and sighed, "I can't do that, Ben. I have the baby and…"

"Oh, yeah. Well, maybe I can just come over with takeout?"

Sofia hadn't gotten dressed up to go anywhere but the supermarket and the laundromat for months, and those outings only required a minimum effort on her part—shorts, a T-shirt, and a pair of sandals, no makeup, hardly a brush through her hair. Neighbors were lucky to catch her out wearing a bra! She hadn't felt decent in, well, forever.

Between all she was facing these days—overnight motherhood, dealing with the uncertainty of the whereabouts of her own parents, Becca's death, and giving up on her dreams of fame in the ballet world (just as this last goal was close enough to taste)—the further prospect of losing Ben was putting the final nail in the coffin. How much more heartache and loss was Sofia meant to bear?

Ben would be there in an hour, and she had to look good. She had to look like her old self again. Standing in her closet, it took what seemed like hours to decide what to wear. A coat of clammy sweat settled over her skin, and her heart raced like it would explode right through her ribcage. In spite of the summer humidity, Sofia trembled with a chill. Finally choosing a pair of tight jeans and a red tank top that flattered her petite figure, she stuffed her feet into a pair of stiletto heels and stared at herself in the vanity mirror. She caked a layer of makeup over her pallid complexion, coated her eyelashes with glossy mascara, and brushed deep strokes of pink blush over her cheeks just as Natalie burst out screaming. *That will have to do*, Sofia quibbled between hushes and last looks in the mirror as she picked up Natalie and held her against her palpitating chest.

Ben was right on time. He stood in the threshold balancing a box of containers from Suki-Asia and a canvas bag filled with added treats. It was not lost on Sofia that he had gone out of his way to bring her some of her favorite things—books from the store where they had first met, chocolates from her favorite chocolate shop in Manhattan…what was he up to? His cheeks were unshaven, which made his fiery-blue eyes dazzle and his white teeth gleam behind a boyish grin.

"All for me?" Sofia teased with a flirty nonchalance, grabbing the books and the bag of take-out food from Ben.

"I guess I have a lot of catching up to do. Here, these are for you too. You mentioned these books a few times, and I hope you haven't read them yet."

New copies of two of her favorite books, *When Bad Things Happen to Good People* by Harold Kushner and *My Life* by Golda Meir peeked out of the tote bag, and a warm bubble rose up through Sofia's body. She had lent him copies of each of these years ago and never got around to replacing them on her bookshelf. The chocolates were simply an added perk; Ben obviously remembered how much she loves to snack on chocolate on her rare days off from dance lessons and recitals.

"Wow, Ben. You've really thought of everything. Thank you for the gifts." Sofia stepped backward, making space for Ben to step into the apartment. Just then, Natalie suddenly let out a screeching wail, and Sofia quickly shut the door behind them. She dropped all the food and packages on the kitchen table and scampered into the living room. Returning to Ben in the hallway, Sofia held Natalie out toward him and said, "This is Natalie. It's about time the two of you met."

"Is this Becca's baby? She actually looks a lot like you." Smiling, Ben tickled Natalie's chin and poked his finger into the dimple on the baby's cheek.

"Yes, this is the princess that's been keeping me busy all day and up all night." Sofia pushed Natalie into Ben's arms and turned to the kitchen. "You hold her while I prepare the food on some plates. You know where the living room is." Not looking at Ben, Sofia was overtaken by a comfortable, relaxed sensation, an ease she was not expecting. Suddenly, all the nervous energy that had been building up before Ben's visit began to melt away like the last snow before the spring.

They ate their dinner and drank an entire bottle of wine that Sofia had forgotten she had stashed away. But as the evening grew darker, so did their conversation, and the anxiety and uncertainty that had plagued Sofia earlier returned. Ben grew quieter and more reserved, while Sofia stayed away from any talk of dancing, of working at the academy, or of the baby. Natalie cooed and giggled in her swing in front of the TV, making Ben visibly edgy with the distraction.

Sofia cleared the table, and Ben set their glasses of unfinished wine on the coffee table in the living room. Sofia took her time washing up, knowing that the easiest part of the evening's performance had just ended, and the difficult finale was about to begin. *Let's get this over with,* she whistled to herself. *It's now or never, and this show has got to come to some kind of end.*

Walking into the living room, still drying her hands on a hand towel, Sofia instigated a complete change of subject from anything relating to the two of them or the baby. Still harboring a swell of resentment toward Nathan for his absence from Becca's funeral, she considered him an otherwise safe and neutral subject with Ben. "You know, Nathan's still studying in Chicago. He decided to stay out there for the summer session instead of coming home." Chuckling, she added, "He says the weather is nicer there in the summer than here in Brooklyn, but we know it's really his new girlfriend that's keeping him in Chicago."

"Oh? Nathan's finally settling down?" Ben took a large gulp of his wine.

"Maybe. Between what he tells me and what he tells his parents, we put two and two together and have assumed that the only thing that's keeping Nathan from proposing to Jacqueline—that's her name—or even from coming home at all…are his classes and his new job at the hospital. If the two of them can hold out until he finishes all his academic requirements, they'll probably marry right after he graduates. She's already a nurse practitioner in the hospital where he interns. They're both very determined to focus on their careers first." Sofia bobbed her head in acceptance of her cousin's decisions.

"Sounds great, I'm happy for him. But…" Ben hesitated, his thick Southern drawl drawing out his every word. It took some time before he continued, "Doesn't Nathan want to come home, here to New York and his family? And what will he do with both he and Jacqueline having such serious jobs? Doesn't he want to start a family of his own?"

Ben could hardly look at Sofia. He placed his wineglass on the table and walked over to Natalie. Rocking her gently in her swing and making inane goo-goo noises, Sofia did not expect the conversation to wind up here. She was finally seeing the answer that had been dangling in front of her all this time. There was no need to wait any longer to try to create sense of things or come up with the correct answer. Her head lightened from the foggy haze of the wine and the uncertainty that had consumed her for months. Although it seemed complicated, it really was quite simple; the choice was hers to make, and she was determined to make the right one. With as much dignity and composure that she could muster, Sofia twisted off the engagement ring she was still wearing and stuffed it halfheartedly into Ben's clenched fist. As her limbs throbbed and were about to give out on her, she walked him to the front door and whispered her final goodbye.

27

Maya

I never make it to Maya's Dance Palace that day Kobi returned to the kibbutz, and so I continue to rely on visits from family and friends to hear updates about what is going on at the school. Sadly, I'm told that classes have dwindled down to just two evening lessons each week and that overall attendance has dropped to only seven students from outside the kibbutz. A couple of nights each week, usually after dinner, Danny and I stroll the paths of the kibbutz and pass the neglected studio building and peek inside the windows to catch a glimpse of the classes taking place inside. Nadia has generously offered to come in from Haifa to cover our paying dancers' lessons. These twilight hours are a bittersweet time for me—it brings me both feelings of exhilaration to get out of the confines of my bed and home, and at the same time, it fuels a sad, strangling feeling of inadequacy and uselessness, of not being able to participate or to help support the financial needs of our community. The worsening decline of the academy just magnifies my inabilities and mirrors my feelings of failure and loss. But this is the only time Danny will consent to time out of the house for me, so I hesitantly look forward to those walks—to those glimpses into my past dreams.

Danny and I have come to a tacit understanding about our future together. We don't discuss it much, but the tension between us has shifted in a more positive direction. There was never a question of us remaining together as a couple—our love is the one thing we can both rely on—but with *Le Cygne Solitaire* buried and forgotten and the dance school heading toward total collapse, it is clear that the only sensible option for us is to stay together on the mutual path of family, children, community, and parenthood, just as we had always planned it. It has taken me a lot of time and consideration, but Kobi's return to the kibbutz has proven one very uplifting point: nothing is written in stone, and even when we think we are making wise decisions in the moment, we can always alter our future destinations and make new choices. The past does not have to define the rest of our lives. While I have come to the realization that my passion for ballet is merely a fantasy, it does not mean that I can't readjust my goals by finding new dreams and desires. Dancing might be a fun and enticing choice for a young girl, but it is not the wisest decision for a mother and wife. And that is what I have become. A proud mother and wife.

Having a family, being in a loving, mutual partnership with a man I love, supporting our community with dedication and hard work—these are my new choices. Ones that will no doubt bring me ultimate happiness and joy. Putting aside all my lifelong dreams of ballet will take some getting used to at first, but it will be good to be exactly what I am—a loving mother, a generous sister, a contributing community member, and a supportive and understanding wife.

Kobi has decided to move back on the kibbutz. He is staying with our parents until Abba can sort out a single cottage for him. In the meantime, Kobi has been appointed the head of security for our community—an extremely tense position that keeps him busy and linked with the state's military units in the surrounding Jezreel Valley. His years of experience in the army and his undying love of country make him the perfect candidate for this position. Some passions don't have to fizzle out, if you're lucky. I guess timing is everything. Kobi may have to make a few adjustments, but his focus and ideals remain the same.

This particular evening, the dinner served in the dining hall sits heavy in my gut. I hadn't been eating a lot in the last month of my pregnancy, but tonight, I just can't control the ravenous appetite that takes complete control over me. I eat a mound of *pelmeni,* dumplings filled with minced meat and wrapped in a thin, pasta-like dough. Rivke prepares them in the traditional Russian style—slathered in butter and topped with sour cream. Then I manage to finish two bowls of *solyanka,* a thick soup that is plentiful enough to be a meal in itself. To top it off, a serving of chopped pickles and lemon slices gives the meal an extra savory flavor. Danny stares at me and raises his eyebrows in disbelief as he watches me shovel down each serving. Something has gotten into me this night, and now I am wishing it would all get out of me—raging hormones, strange cravings, bulging baby...all of it. A sour gurgle releases from my throat, and I hold back the bile that rises from my stomach. I don't know if it is the summer heat or the intensity of the pregnancy, but I am suddenly racked with cramps. Just in time, Danny and I see Imma walking toward us on the path from the cowshed. Before I can utter another word, my mother reaches for her cell phone and begins speaking in loud puffs of incomplete sentences. Watching me double over and grab my belly, she is calling Dr. Nemrod. The spasms in my stomach are blinding my sight and squelching all sounds around us. All I know is that the pain in my belly is increasing with each passing second.

The next thing I remember is waking up out of a dark slumber in the kibbutz medical center. The smell of antiseptic seeps into my nostrils. Selena, a young nurse practitioner sent from Jerusalem's Hadassah Hospital to volunteer for the summer, is hovering around my head like a buzzing bee. My stomach muscles clench and burn as if a rope were being tied and tightened around my midsection, and my mouth feels dry and pasty. I raise an arm to rub my eyes with my fist, but a tangle of rubber tubes gets in the way and tugs at my skin. I lick my lips and listen to the muddle of voices floating around me. A quiet, concerned whisper rings in my ears.

"How is she, Doctor? How did the surgery go? Is the baby okay?"

"Calm down, Danny. Mommy and baby are both fine. Do you have a name picked out yet? Or are you going to keep us all in suspense until the official baby-naming ceremony?" Dr. Nemrod chuckles, picks up my arm by my wrist, and holds it gently between his warm fingertips. "Pulse is good. Now we wait until our tired mother wakes up."

"It's a girl." I chirp with a raspy, dry squeak, not able to hide the smile that stretches across my face. The doctor mentioned a baby-naming ceremony. Didn't he? He did not say *brit-milah* or circumcision. "It has to be a girl," I say a little louder. The nurse turns toward me and leans over the bed rail.

"She's awake, Doctor. I'll go and bring some water," she says, leaving abruptly from the room.

Danny is by my side in an instant, and Dr. Nemrod stands on the other side of the bed. Both men stand like a couple of Roman centurions guarding a small army, and I have to admit it feels good to be looked after and cared for with such intensity. My shoulders relax into my pillow, and my eyes flutter open and shut with excitement. I raise one hand again, careful not to pull at any of the tubes, and reach for Danny's hand. "We have a girl! I want to see her. Where is she? Please bring her here to me. Our little Ilana…"

Selena returns with a pitcher of water and a trail of visitors. As I slowly regain my bearings, I watch Imma, Abba, and Kobi shuffle into the room. Imma rushes to my bedside, while my father and brother offer loud shouts of *"mazal tov"* and slaps around Danny's shoulders. Dr. Nemrod tries to shush the men, but they are not paying much attention to him. My mother smiles at me and hands me a cup of water.

"How do you feel, my little Maya?"

"I can't wait to meet my new daughter," I say. I mean it, but something is squashing down on my chest, like a ten-pound dumbbell dropped from above my head. Giving up one for the other, I realize this was it, the definitive moment when I would let go of one dream and create a new one. I would never get the chance to present *Le Cygne Solitaire* to the world, but I was ready to introduce the newest member of the Sharret family.

Imma's eyes fill with tears, but the smile on her face assures me that they are tears of happiness. She turns to scold the men for the ruckus they are causing, and both Abba and Kobi scoot past her to offer me a round of gentler kisses and congratulations.

In the past five years since Aaron's birth, I never felt this gripping desire that is sustaining me now. As much as I wish I could have done more to make Maya's Dance Palace a thriving success, done more to help support Kibbutz Gan Notzah in its time of need, done more to be a better mother to Aaron and wife be a better to Danny, Ilana gives me new incentive. I had been missing it all along. My family is here right in front of me. My life is already filled with love and purpose…isn't it?

Silently noting the damp blots that are beginning to darken the bib of my gown, Dr. Nemrod jumps up and grabs ahold of the door. "I'm afraid everyone will have to leave the room now. It is time for mother and daughter to bond over their first meal together!" He slowly turns back to me, pinches the spot above his nose, and asks in a whisper, "Maya, do you need your pills?"

"No," I reply with a confidence I hadn't known in years.

"If you will it, it is no dream."
—Theodore Herzl

28

Sofia

For the millionth time, Sofia worried about the decision she was about to make. One more uncertain move, another world farther away from everything Sofia knew. Should she leave New York and everything she knew? Was it right to pick up with a young child and rearrange their entire world? After all, Nathan had done it, and it wouldn't be the first time Sofia had to pick up and start anew. She had a reckless feeling she knew what her mother would say; but now, after all those years, she wondered what Tyotya Anika would do. Her aunt had been right about Ben and so many other things. Sofia prayed for some of her aunt's wisdom now.

But it was too late to change her mind and turn back now. The flight was a never-ending trial of patience and restraint. Four-year-old Natalie could not be pacified, no matter what Sofia did. She tried reading to her from her favorite book, ironically called *Grumpy Monkey Are We There Yet?* She let her finish an entire share-size bag of

M&M's, most of the candy pieces carpeting the floor beneath their seats. She found movies on the plane's in-flight entertainment system, and when even that did not hold Natalie's short attention span, Sofia gave up her window seat to Natalie so that she could look out and play a game of naming each passing cloud. Four years at home as a single parent didn't hold a candle to the eleven-hour flight from New York's JFK Airport to Ben Gurion Airport in Tel Aviv. Was this truly the right choice? For now, she only had enough strength to hold herself together, take care of Natalie, and brace herself for whatever this new journey was going to offer them.

It took many months, morphing ever so slowly into years, of swimming in and out of the sadness that swallowed her after Becca's death, until Sofia finally managed to get her bearings and stand on her feet again. Needless to say, she found it difficult, and sometimes impossible, to make sense of the world or find the purpose in putting effort into anything at all. What was the point, it seemed to Sofia, if everyone you loved or needed wound up disappearing, especially when they were needed most? Sofia knew she was unfairly blaming Becca for imposing on her, for making her make choices she didn't want, and for dumping all her problems on her, but the last thing Sofia wanted—or needed—in her life was a child, especially if it meant having to give up her own life. Not that Natalie was a "problem," but after all, Sofia had been a rising ballet star and an independent woman with a very different life of her own. She had had plans and dreams and goals—until everything unraveled and came to a devastating crash in a single instant. Just like that, she was thrown off course and forced to create a new life for herself, one that suddenly included a baby. Becca ruined everything for her with her selfish decisions and wishes, and Sofia couldn't help but resent Becca for it.

But it wasn't Becca's fault, really. She had no other choice. Neither did Sofia.

There was a short period of time, right after Becca's funeral, when Ben had reached back out to Sofia. He came over at night after work and brought groceries and toys for the baby. He built a crib from a posh baby store in Manhattan and even changed a few hundred diapers during his visits with Sofia and the baby. His deeds were kind and gracious, but his hidden intentions spelled something much more threatening for Sofia. She saw where he was going with his constant pursuit and acts of generosity, and so, between her general mood swings and her nasty resentment that swung from Becca to Ben, she slowly pushed Ben away. Sofia had no idea where she was going or what she wanted.

Despite feeling trapped and bitter, Sofia consoled herself with her decision to respect her best friend's wishes and take care of Natalie. What choice was she really given? Sofia knew she could never abandon Becca's last wishes. Especially now! She knew she could not abandon Natalie either, a beautiful baby—guiltless and fragile and alone. Becca's own family had turned their backs on her; Sofia wasn't about to let that happen to Natalie.

She did the best she could to move forward. Boris had generously offered Sofia a teaching position at the Tantsor Ballet & Dance Academy, and Tyotya Anika offered to babysit with Natalie while Sofia was at the academy. It wasn't until Nathan called one night from Chicago that things began to look brighter for Sofia.

"When are you coming home, cousin?" Sofia begged, knowing that Nathan always had a way of making everything seem all right, even if this time it would have to be from long distance.

"Well, that's another story for another day, cousin. I'm done with the hardest part of my studies, but now I have to prove myself in a real practice. I have a few positions lined up here in Chicago, and Jacqueline just got offered a new big position at the hospital here."

"Does that mean you're not coming home? Nathan, please. We need you," Sofia whined like a baby. She knew he had no intentions at this point of leaving Chicago and Jacqueline, but she couldn't contain her desperate plea for her cousin's return home.

"I'd love to. Really. Maybe me and Jackie can make a short visit to New York for the holidays. It's almost Rosh Hashanah."

"That's nearly a month away! But I guess it's better than nothing. I know Tyotya Anika and Dyadya Sol will be so excited to see you again. Natalie will be head-over-heels delighted to see her favorite uncle again, and we're all dying to meet Jacqueline too." Sofia choked on the word *uncle* as it left her lips, remembering Becca's last words in the hospital.

"I'm Natalie's *only* uncle, Sofia." Nathan laughed. "In the meantime, I just had an idea."

"Can't wait to hear it. I miss you, you silly *shnuk*."

"Ha, well, I just pictured all of you sitting around and kibitzing and making up gossip about Jackie, and it suddenly hit me… Why don't you and Natalie move in with my parents? You and Natalie can take over my old room—*your* old room! And that way, you can save some money, be closer to the dance studio, and my parents won't feel like I've abandoned them while I'm here in Chicago. It's a win-win for all!"

That was almost four years earlier, and Sofia could not imagine back then that she'd be where she was now; just when she was getting a grip on the changes in her life—readjusting to living in

"Little Odessa"; abandoning Ben and the prospective chances for a future home and family of her own; answering to all the judgmental interrogations about Natalie's birth and Becca's death; giving up her chances of fame and recognition as a world-class ballerina only to teach younger dancers to replace her; learning to rely on her own strength and courage to make new choices and changes in her life, whether she wanted to or not. Four years sped by in a blur of transformation, and Sofia felt like she had gone from being twenty-five years young to eighty years old in four-point-zero seconds.

And then came the fire.

The skies over the whole neighborhood were filled with a smoky-gray film, and the air grew dense and hard to breathe. Flakes of white ash floated down around her and left specks on her T-shirt as Sofia hurried to pick up Natalie. It was a Friday morning at the end of July, and the sweltering heat of the blaze made her head dizzy with fever. Racing to the day care center, Sofia could never have guessed where the smoke and soot that clogged her throat and gagged her were actually coming from. It wasn't until Sofia reached the day care center and saw two babushkas and four young assistant teachers gathered around the reception desk, staring down at the sounds coming from a small radio. The women wore furrowed masks of confusion and concern on their faces.

Sofia stumbled into the day care center, sucked in the clean air, and coughed out a lungful of hot breath. "What's going on?" Sofia asked, annoyed that the women had barely taken notice of her arrival.

"Shh! We're trying to listen," spit the babushka with the big belly.

One of the young assistants from Natalie's class walked over to Sofia and touched her lightly on her shoulder. "It looks like there's a fire in town. I think I heard someone say it was the fish market. Do you know it?"

Did Sofia know it! It was Dyadya Sol's shop! She couldn't believe what she was hearing. Her skin rippled with a chill like someone poured a bucket of ice water over her. Her knees buckled, and her nails dug into her palms as she clenched her fists at her sides. Natalie's wail from the classroom down the hall reached her and pierced her eardrums. She didn't know what to do or where to turn at that moment, but she knew she had to get out of there. And fast.

As usual, Tyotya Anika had gone to the shop that dreadful morning with Dyadya Sol to help with the Shabbos rush of customers. The fire department claimed that the hopeless catastrophe was caused by an electrical short, an accidental case of poor wiring. Tyotya Anika and Dyadya Sol had died, obstructed by the flames where the firefighters could not get to them. By the time the fire trucks arrived, the deadly blaze had spread throughout the market and had trapped Sol and Anika in the back with no path to make an escape.

All was lost.

Sofia felt like she was drowning in the middle of the ocean with no lifeboat in sight. Sol and Anika had been the closest thing to family that Sofia could remember. They had taken her in, loved her and kept her safe, and had supported her since she was forced to leave her home in Ukraine. They were like parents to Sofia, and now she was left alone and lost in the world again. This time, there was nobody left to throw her a lifeline.

Nathan came in from Chicago for the funeral and took care of all the funeral arrangements. He settled the insurance claim for the market and managed to find a buyer for the apartment. In her intense grief, Sofia was grateful for that much as she had no idea what to do or who to call. Jaqueline did not come with him, which left Sofia asking more questions. If this was the woman Nathan was considering as a wife to settle with, wouldn't she be by his side now as he grieves the loss of his parents? *Shouldn't* she be here with him to support him? To comfort him? *How odd*, Sofia thought in the midst of it all. People were never what they seemed to be. By the time Nathan returned to his life in Chicago with Jacqueline and his work at the hospital, Sofia had sunk into the depths of complete loneliness and despair.

But Sofia had no plans to speak of. She had never given any thought to the possibility that Anika and Sol would not be around for her. Taken off guard so suddenly by the loss of her only remaining family, Sofia found herself drifting aimlessly, scared and helpless. Most days, she barely remembered to eat, and sometimes several days would go by before she realized she hadn't even showered. She stopped teaching her classes at the academy and didn't bring Natalie back to the day care center since that afternoon of the fire. She battled with Natalie over which of the two could cry longer, wetter tears. They were a pair of pitiful, lost souls with nowhere to run and nothing to hold on to.

Six months had come and gone since then, but it seemed like time was ticking away with a maddening slowness. Sofia had been stuck in a crippling limbo for what seemed like an eternity. She couldn't remember the last time she laughed. She should have known better, though. She should have learned from the twists and turns of her life that there would always be hard choices to make. Sofia was being tested again; she had to come up with her next move.

They say people have two natural choices when faced with a desperate decision. The fight or flight response is a survival mechanism that prepares people to either face or escape danger. People will either naturally fight whatever threat they are facing, or they will run from it. The unexpected fire at the shop and the deaths of Anika and Sol were the last straw for Sofia, and she had no more fight left in her. So after packing up all of Tyotya Anika and Dyadya Sol's *tchotchkes* and evidence of the years of living in the apartment, the next decision for Sofia was really a natural one, both figuratively and quite literally. She booked two one-way tickets on the first flight out of the city.

The plane began its descent, and over Natalie's bobbing head, Sofia looked out the window. Below them, she could see a far-reaching desert of sand, blue skies, and a line of date palms planted purposefully around the perimeter of the tarmac. A group of rowdy teenagers sitting in the last few rows of the plane began to sing *Ha'Tikvah* and startled Sofia. She glanced over at Natalie, who had finally fallen asleep and had not stirred from the sudden burst of the singing of the national anthem and the other passengers applauding the pilots on their successful flight. The wheels touched down gently and glided along the runway as the passengers began to unbuckle their seat belts and gather their belongings. This was it. Sofia's chance to make a new start. *It won't be bad*, Sofia whispered to herself. *Just different*. Again she looked down at the sleeping child next to her. She took a deep breath and peeked outside the window.

The palm trees that lined the runway were tall and green and conjured up recollections of the biblical stories her mother used to tell her. The tarmac was smooth and clear. The high-tech airport building was now coming into full view as the plane coasted toward the waiting gate and the glistening early morning sunshine. With the new day dawning in front of them, Sofia felt a rush of giddy excitement and anticipation. She was lighter, less burdened, more optimistic than she had felt in a long time. She brushed her fingers through Natalie's tussled red hair and sighed. *Even when life presents difficult choices, Natalie, we must always choose to be happy. It's never too late to choose happiness… We're gonna be okay, my sheine little one.*

Sofia began collecting their belongings, shoving everything into a sloppy heap in her backpack. Looking under the seats and doing a last-minute check to gather all of their belongings before disembarking, her fingers brushed the thin, leather-bound journal that had fallen between the armrests of their seats. She retrieved the notebook and flicked through Becca's scribbles, confirming that the loose leaves of Mamoh's letter, still trickling with a hint of Chanel perfume, were still tucked carefully within the pages. An old black-and-white photograph of her Dyadya Sol and Tyotya Anika on their honeymoon lay pressed behind the letter. In the photo, her aunt and uncle were splashing each other in the waves of the ocean with the Coney Island Ferris wheel hovering in the distance. It was her favorite picture of them, and it stung her now between her trembling fingers. Sofia carefully tucked the journal into her backpack just as her cell phone rang out a new notification. They had changed time zones.

Natalie sucked on her dry tongue and pursed her lips. "Are we there yet, Tyotya? By the way, happy birthday," a sleepy Natalie sang. They had both been anticipating the day; everything was falling slowly into place. Even if this year's birthday celebration was to take place in the air, flying over the world and into a brand-new existence, they were together, safe and happy. Sofia brushed the dimples on Natalie's face with her hand and let out a long, hot sigh of consolation.

29

Maya

Thirty-one years old. Aaron is already six years old, and baby Ilana is four. I don't know where the years have gone. Life is fleeting, and if we are not careful, everything can change in the blink of an eye. It's my birthday, and this is what is on my mind.

I convince myself that I'm not old enough to worry about regrets and lost opportunities, but for some odd reason, it is all I can think about. I blow out a long, exhausted breath of air, and squeeze my eyelids shut. Fading memories of Jim Turner—of all things—are planted in my mind. I can't stop thinking about the unfairness of life. For one uncomfortable, unthinkable second, I contemplate asking Dr. Nemrod for an updated prescription of pills.

Jim Turner, the movie-star volunteer fresh out of college and on the cusp of a promising career, was so young. So alive. He was younger than me, for goodness' sake, and he will never get the chance to make choices or realize his dreams. He had wanted a family, and he had such smart and innovative ideas for advancing the field of agriculture. He could have really been something. I wonder why I am granted a thirty-first birthday but Jim would never get the chance to see his thirtieth. I wonder, for the hundredth time today, how we are expected to make choices when life arbitrarily takes those choices away from us.

Sitting on my front porch, sweating and feeling waves of confusion rise from my gut, I wait for Gali. She is coming to style my hair and brighten the gray threads that poke through my flat lackluster strands. We are going to Tel Aviv tonight to celebrate my birthday. Danny, me, Gali, and David were invited to see a performance of *Sleeping Beauty* at the Tel Aviv Performing Arts Center. Irena is dancing the lead role tonight, the same role I had given up years ago.

For the first time in years, Irena will be in Israel for my birthday; she is usually traveling around the world, performing in shows with her internationally renowned ballet troupe. And even though we'll be watching her onstage from the audience, I'm positive we'll have a great time. The ballet academy in Haifa is sponsoring an after-party at the Hilton Hotel on the beach, where (as a birthday present for me) Irena has also booked us rooms for the night.

Gali arrives, and I jump out of my rocker. She is lugging a large canvas bag, no doubt filled with all her salon accoutrements for my special birthday makeover. Rambling with excited energy, she assures me that David has secured the Toyota Rav4 for us that evening and shoves me toward the cottage. I still can't seem to get Jim out of my head. He would have loved to go to the ballet with us. I see him as I did on the first day he arrived at the kibbutz—his bronzed complexion, his million-dollar smile, his flowing blond hair, and his healthy, muscular body. Clucking my tongue and wiping beads of sweat from my neck, I blink my eyelids to erase the image.

Gali stops midway to the bathroom and stares at me. "What's wrong, Maya? Aren't you excited for tonight? Hell, I wish I had friends like you who could treat me to a night at the ballet and a room at the Hilton. At least, we can tag along with you on your birthday!"

"No, I mean, yes! I'm totally psyched for this. Irena is so generous… I am very lucky! And the best part is I get to share it all with you. By the way, I can't believe Danny and my brother actually agreed to go to a ballet!"

"I'm sure it's the stay at the Hilton that convinced those two to tolerate a night at the ballet." Gali and I giggle for the next ten minutes before we can regain our composure and refocus our attention on my hair.

Three daunting hours later, I feel like a princess. Gali is an artist when it comes to hair color, but her true talent lies in her styling methods. She manages to curl, cut, and shape my thinning, dull locks into a flowing work of art. Just like that, thirty-one doesn't feel so bad. But I find myself still silently wishing that Jim could have been here with us.

So much for wallowing in the past. Or at least in what we cannot change. I look in the mirror one last time and thank Gali for the magic she has performed to make me feel so beautiful and young and vibrant. It is time to move on and be thankful for what I've got. Just then, the clanging of the kitchen bell fills the air, and it is lunchtime on the kibbutz. All the residents—in the fields, in their offices, in their stations—are about to converge in the communal dining hall. I'm so lucky that Rivke gave me the morning off today. Working in the sweaty, messy kitchen is the last place I want to spend my special day. Again I think about how grateful I am for my family and friends who show me such generous consideration and love. Gali aims an air-kiss at me, and we walk arm in arm toward the dining room.

When we get there, Romi is leading a rather large group of new volunteers up the steps in front of the dining hall. He has led several groups of volunteers into our community, but no more than twelve have officially joined Kibbutz Gan Notzah in the past four years. This new group of eight new volunteers is a pleasant surprise. Regardless of its decreasing popularity, the kibbutz movement in our country continues to recruit and welcome new residents. The only problem is that they do not stay for long. But Romi continues his efforts in ushering in new arrivals, training them for all kinds of agricultural work and preaching the ideals of patriotism.

We approach Romi and the newcomers, and one young woman in particular stands out among the rest. Her eyes are swollen and glazed, her hair is tied up in a messy bun on the top of her head, her sweatpants are splattered with stains, and her I♡NY T-shirt is wrinkled. But her stance is solid, and her back remains ramrod straight. Her shoulders are pushed back, and her chin points skyward as if it were being tugged upward by an invisible string. Despite the drained expression on her freckled face, the woman appears movie-star perfect, edgy, and sophisticated. Something about her keeps my attention fixated on her. Romi belts out a quick outline for their afternoon agenda in his broken English as the young woman in the I♡NY T-shirt stands on the perimeter of the crowd, gripping the hand of a small child.

"Hey, look at that, Gali." I point over to the group of new volunteers and whisper, "Our youngest volunteer yet! That little girl can't be any older than my little Ilana."

"Hmm, I wonder what her story is. We don't normally see children being brought onto the kibbutz."

"Come on, let's go in before it gets really busy in there. I bet Rivke will be able to give us the *spiel* about her."

"I didn't hear anything about the new arrivals," Rivke tells us without looking up from her mixing bowl when we join her in the kitchen. "All I know is that it is the largest group we've had in a while. Which is good news! So I'm very busy in here today." She clucks her tongue against her yellowing teeth and points her wooden spoon at me. "And since you have the day off for your birthday, Maya, my work will never get done if we stand around here *kibitzing* about *shtuyot*, nonsense!"

"Come on, Rivke. You must have heard something. What about the one with the little child?" Gali is determined this morning to get the whole story, and I have to admit, I am just as curious, not so much about the kid but about the woman with her. She looks so familiar to me, and she definitely looks like she doesn't belong on a kibbutz.

"David told me that he heard from your father that the woman with the child is a Ukrainian named Sofia, and she comes from New York City," Gali says, and she arranges a curl of my hair on my forehead. "The kid is hers, I think."

Rivke suddenly looks like she's seen a ghost. Her cheeks pale, and she wobbles back and forth like she's going to faint. "*Oy, mame maine!*" she croaks.

I take a step toward her and steady her just as her hip knocks against the counter. "Rivke, are you okay?"

Rivke doesn't answer me right away. Instead, she licks her lips and rushes to the kitchen door. Peering out into the dining hall, Rivke lets out another exasperated huff. Then slowly regaining her stamina, she turns back to me and Gali and shouts, "*Yalah, banot*. Get out of my kitchen, girls. I have a lot of work to do." She pushes us out, and we can hear the clatter of pots and plates on the other side of the door—a hurricane blowing through the kitchen.

Sofia. New York City. This woman could be anybody…and then it hits me. "I've gotta go, Gali. Grab me a plate of hummus and a few pieces of pita."

"Wait. Where are you going? We missed breakfast this morning, and I'm starving!" Gali yanks my arm and spins me around.

"I know, but I forgot something back at the house. I'll be right back and catch up to you in a few minutes." My curiosity piqued, I can't wait another minute. I have to find out if my hunch is right.

Back at my cottage, I scramble through the box I keep underneath the bed. Buried under stacks of old stockings, leotards, and CDs, I finally find what I am looking for. I grab the worn magazine and stuff it into my backpack. Rushing back to the dining hall, I hope I haven't missed her.

I stop at the door and see that Romi is beginning to round up the group of volunteers. I slow my breathing and wind my way through the noisy tables. "Hi, Gali. I told you I'd be right back."

"Here, sit down. I got you some food and an extra serving of Rivke's *babka*. She told me she made it in honor of your birthday."

"Sounds yummy, but wait a second. If I'm right, I've got exciting news for you." The smile on my face stretches from ear to ear, and I can feel the blood rush to my cheeks. Before Gali could argue with me, I spin and head straight for the table in the back of the hall where the volunteers are beginning to clear their plates.

But Sofia is not there. I scan the room quickly and find the little girl sitting by herself at the end of the table. She is too busy gobbling down a slice of babka—an untouched plate of salad pushed to the middle of the table—and smearing chunks of chocolate across her face with the back of her hand to notice my approach. I sit down in the empty seat next to her and say, "Hello, *motek*. What's your name?"

"I'm Natalie. But my tyotya told me not to talk to strangers!" *She's a feisty little one*, I think to myself. *So this is her niece!*

"A beautiful name, Natalie. But I'm not a stranger, dear. My name is Maya, and I live here. Are you and your aunt coming to live with us at Gan Notzah?"

"My Tyotya Anika and my Dyadya Sol died. We are looking for a new house to live in. Do you have a house here?" Natalie yawned, pushed away her cake plate, and rested her head on her forearm.

"*Baruch Dayan ha'emet*. May their memory be for a blessing, little one. I'm so sorry to hear that." Changing the conversation as quickly as I could, I replied, "Yes, I have a house here with my husband, and my two children stay in the gan for children."

"You mean children don't live with their parents?" Natalie bolted upright, and her eyes widened like two aqua lakes. As tired as she is, her inquisitiveness wins over her exhaustion. Just then, Sofia appears beside us and stands with her hands on her hips.

"Hi, Tyotya Sofia. This is my new friend... Uhm, what's your name again?"

"Maya. I'm Maya Sharret. Welcome! I was just getting to know your little Natalie. She's an angel, really. I have a daughter around her age too. Her name is Ilana." I'm babbling, but I take a breath and offer my hand. Then turning back to Natalie, I say, "I'll request that my Ilana be your special partner in the gan. Would you like that?"

"Yes! Does she like ballet also? Me and Tyotya Sofia *love* the ballet. But we don't dance anymore." Natalie rambles, exaggerating the word "love," poking her tongue out between her grinning lips. Sofia is quick to convey a severe glare at her niece. Natalie looks up and rolls her eyes.

"Well, it's very nice to meet you, Maya. I'm Sofia, and you have obviously been acquainted with my niece, Natalie," Sofia says with a note of weariness in her words. "I hope she wasn't bothering you. We both need some time to adjust to our new surroundings." Then without another word, she plops down in the seat next to me.

"Oh, of course not! Natalie has been a perfect little lady. And it is my pleasure to meet you both. I hope you and Natalie will feel welcome here. We could use a few more strong women around here," I say with a warm, inviting smile. "In fact, I think you and I can be good friends. If you need anything, you can ask anyone where you can find me. Everyone here knows everyone—and everything!" I wink at Sofia and then at Natalie.

Sofia chortles and nods her head. "I think I know exactly what you mean. Thanks, Maya."

Natalie pokes the piece of babka with her fork and frowns. "I'm too tired to finish this. Even though this cake is so good," she announces.

I spring up in my seat, and the words rattle like a freight train out of my mouth, "Well, if you don't mind me asking, Sofia, I'm a bit curious about something. Since you arrived, I thought you looked familiar… I think I know who you are, and if I'm right, I can't tell you how thrilled I am that you are here with us… I have to wonder if it is on purpose that you are here on our kibbutz or if it is a mere coincidence." Embarrassed by the insinuation that the infamous Sofia Brenner would actually be here at Gan Notzah because of Maya's Dance Palace, I clamp my mouth shut and twist my backpack onto my lap. Nervously, feeling like a star-struck teenager, I pull out the tattered old copy of *Dance Magazine* and place it on the table. I flip through the pages, hold my breath for a long second, and point to the half-page color photo above the article. "Isn't this you? Sofia Brenner from the Tantsor Academy in New York?"

Sofia raises a finger to her smiling lips and hisses, "Shh! Keep your voice down. Boy, it only took one day for me to be discovered here! I didn't think anyone would know me so far from home!"

I skim through some more pages and stop where the journalist praised her debut solo performance in *Le Roi Candaule* and highlighted her nomination for the *Prix Benois de la Danse* award. I point to a close-up photo of Sofia, smiling and waving to a crowd outside the theater. There is no doubt in my mind this is the one-and-only prima ballerina, Sofia Brenner. I watch the lines around her eyes crinkle as if she were going to burst into tears.

I snap the magazine shut and shove it back in my backpack. Natalie lets out a roaring yawn and tugs on Sofia's arm. Sofia swivels her head and stares at the child without saying another word. Finally, she whispers, "We've gotta go. We're tired, and there's still a lot to do to get settled." Sofia stands and grabs Natalie by the hand. "It was nice to meet you, Maya."

"But I didn't finish my cake, Tyotya Sofia." Natalie lets out another long and tired yawn.

"You didn't finish your salad either, my little hungry one."

I return to Gali, who is still waiting for me to join her. Gali is finished with her sandwich and salad and has begun to dig into a huge piece of babka when I take the seat across from her. Her eyes won't meet mine, and her lips are clenched tight around a bite of chocolatey cake. I can tell she is annoyed with me. "What the hell was that all about, Maya? You left me sitting here, like a shmuck, eating all by myself!"

"Oh, Gali, you have no idea. This birthday just keeps getting better and better!"

30

Sofia

Sofia tossed her dusty suitcase on the bed and screamed into the bare room. Counting to ten, she swiveled toward the cot in the corner, where Natalie was splayed across the threadbare coverlet, already dreaming her twelfth dream. The child stirred in her sleep but did not wake up. A tiny lady bug crawled up Sofia's bare arm and tickled her sticky skin. She found herself missing the excitement and pulse of the city. But what she immediately drank in here in just one day at Gan Notzah was the quiet tranquility that embraced her. It was all so serene and rustic, and Sofia was anxious to be able to absorb it all—until, she heard someone call out her name. Her peaceful new bubble burst.

Sofia had been hoping to make a clean start with this move. She was completely drained from living with ghosts and secrets and empty promises. She was looking for a way to be a good mother for Natalie, a way to provide a better future for the both of them.

And in less than twenty-four hours, she had been picked out of the crowd and labeled as before. She was still the famous ballerina, Sofia Brenner from New York City. She had wanted to be a part of something greater than herself, something more important than a performer on a stage. She had wanted to leave the old Sofia in the past and discover a new, better Sofia for the future. Two days into her new life, and she was faced with the same old haunts of the past.

She continued, however, to doubt everything—her motives, her strength, her faith. So far, nothing was turning out as she had planned. She even wondered if she should have changed her name altogether, breaking away once and for all from the old version of the independent prima ballerina she left behind once in Ukraine and then again on the shores of Brighton Beach. Boris was right when he warned her about her childish insecurities and self-absorbed tendencies, but she never expected to be recognized here in Israel. She wanted so badly to let go of the past, move forward, and create a new future. She thought this would be the perfect place to pick up the pieces and move on.

Had she been wrong?

Would her past always hold her and define her?

Wouldn't new choices allow her to have a new future?

Sofia began to unpack her bags, but the small chest of drawers and the paltry closet space in her new cottage would barely accommodate even half of her belongings. It only took a day of exploring around her new community to figure out that she had definitely overpacked. She would never need the assortment of outfits and fine clothes she had accumulated in Brooklyn and brought along with her now. In fact, she would probably be spending most of her time in a work uniform once her duties were assigned.

There was one outfit, however, she couldn't dream of leaving behind—the ballet costume she wore for her last performance in *The Dying Swan*. She carefully unfolded the crinoline of the skirt from its protective bag, held it up in front of her, and stood on her toes in front of the cracked mirror hanging inside the closet door. Pirouetting and bowing as if on stage, Sofia huffed a deep sigh and squeezed back the tears that were trying to escape from behind her heavy eyelids. She placed the costume back in its bag together with the feathery white headpiece and white satin ballet slippers and placed the bundle on the shelf inside the closet.

After unpacking her bathroom toiletries and placing the rest of her belongings (including Becca's journal, which she transferred carefully from her backpack) in her suitcase that she kicked under her bed, she began to unpack Natalie's things. Rummaging through all the junk that Natalie had collected and thrown in when she wasn't paying attention, Sofia found a set of Tyotya Anika's nesting dolls and the satin ballerina that her father had given her in Ukraine. *Where did Natalie find these things?*

Her face paled as the blood rushed from her cheeks down to her unsteady fingers. She cradled the dolls on her lap before burying them once again in the disarray of the suitcase. She shivered, despite the summer heat, with the notion that all her belongings—all that she owned—could fit so easily and inconsequentially into a couple of suitcases stashed under her bed. Natalie would be joining the rest of the children in the kibbutz's nursery in a few days, after they both had the opportunity to get adjusted to their new surroundings, so she zipped up Natalie's suitcase and put it out of her mind. Two suitcases shoved under a bed, filled with toys, storybooks, dolls, and a lifetime of memories.

Sofia plonked down on the thin mattress of her own single bed. A metal spring popped and stabbed her under her thigh, but she was too tired to care. A stack of clean sheets sat on the bathroom counter, along with fresh towels. The linens were frayed and graying, but they smelled of violets and sunshine. She decided, despite the slumber that was wiping her out, a quick shower was in order, and then she would get some sleep. The somber silence in the cottage made her a bit weary at first, but the song of the night creatures outside and the smell of sweet almond blossoms and sunflowers that streamed in through the open windows above her bed lulled her nerves and calmed her jittery stomach. She reassured herself that tomorrow would be another day. It wasn't too late to choose happiness.

Sofia woke the next morning with the soft, grumbling sounds of Natalie's whining. "I'm starving, Tyotya Sofia. What's for breakfast?"

She picked up her cell phone from the nightstand next to her bed and saw that it was already eleven o'clock. "*Damn, we missed breakfast,*" she swore out loud.

"What do you mean, 'we missed breakfast'? And watch your language, Tyotya. You're not allowed to say bad words!" Natalie warned with a wave of an accusing finger. "Are they not going to give us food?"

"Of course, we're gonna get food, my *sheinele*. We just have to wait a while for lunch to be announced." The home-cooked food in the dining hall the day before had reminded her of her days with her own family, fading memories in Ukraine and more recent memories of meals with Tyotya Anika and Dyadya Sol in Brighton Beach. *Home.* Sofia got Natalie showered and dressed before throwing on a pair of old jeans and a T-shirt. Her Converse sneakers matched the ones she had bought for Natalie just days before they left New York.

Sofia and Natalie made it to the dining hall just in time to beat the crush of the lunch crowd. The room was surprisingly cool, considering it was the middle of August, and all of the buildings on the kibbutz didn't have fully operational air conditioners, depending mostly on old ceiling fans to cool the communal spaces. She surveyed the room and silently took in the long tables that were filling up with hungry kibbutzniks. She noticed the noisy group of volunteers they had come in with the day before already sitting together in the back of the hall in front of the floor-to-ceiling windows. Despite the huge windows that exposed the dining hall to the surrounding gardens outside, the blistering afternoon sun was shining on the other side of the building, and Sofia felt a cool, unexpected breeze brush her cheek.

Sofia watched a young man dressed in khaki army fatigues and a rifle slung over his shoulder saunter over to a round table of young boys also dressed in army fatigues. One by one, his friends greeted the armed soldier with loud hellos and welcoming slaps on the back as if they were old friends seeing each other for the first time in years. Although she did not speak a word of Hebrew, many of the expressions spoken around her were familiar from her past in Ukraine and Brighton Beach. It almost felt like she never left New York. Like she was back home among her own family. More of her past that wouldn't let her go.

Some of the kibbutzniks had come into the dining hall straight from the fields—smelly and covered with grimy sweat—and some were dressed in clean blue cotton slacks and white button-down polo shirts. All wore heavy black work boots caked with the red sand that seemed to stick to everything. But it was the young soldier in full army uniform that captivated her the most. Farmers? Office workers? Military personnel? It was all too much for her to take in at once. Sofia clamped tightly to Natalie's hand and led her to the end of the food line.

But Natalie, being her precocious, chatterbox self, jerked hard on Sofia's arm. With a wide-eyed gawk, her eyes pinned on the armed soldier, Natalie asked, "Tyotya Sofia, why does that man have a gun? Is he a bad guy?"

"Starting over is not going to be easy." Sofia whistled. "No, *sheinele*. He's not a bad guy. He's a good guy! He's just here to protect us."

"Who is he protecting us from? Are there bad guys around here?"

"No, no bad guys." Sofia had to watch her every word. "We are totally safe here. He just wants to make sure everyone gets enough food to eat." Sofia knew her lame explanation would never satisfy Natalie's curiosity, but it was all she could think of in the moment. She wrinkled her nose, turned away from the guards, and joined the stream of kibbutzniks lining up with their food trays.

Sofia scanned the busy dining hall for the familiar face of her new friend. Maya was nowhere to be found. She led Natalie to the salad bar and helped her with her plate.

"You know I don't like salad," wailed Natalie. "Is that all they serve here? I don't like this place. I want the cake!"

"You can't have dessert before your meal, you know that, Natalie. Besides, this is our new home, and they eat lots of healthy salad here. So we'll have to adjust and eat the salad first." Sofia didn't mention to her niece how much she missed Anika's borscht and Mrs.

Kaplan's classic *medovik* honey cake and her delicious *pechenye yabloki* baked apples. The comfort and warmth she conjured from the memory of home-cooked foods (especially the treats that always made everything sweeter) made Sofia's skin tingle and her blood pump wild. She covered a coy smile with a subtle hand, thinking fondly of Becca and her insatiable sweet tooth, the same one that obviously ran through her daughter's veins. Straightening and looking sternly at Natalie, she said, "Now behave yourself, please…if you want cake after lunch."

Just then, the soldier with glimmering blue eyes and a smile that could melt the Arctic Circle was hovering next to them in front of the tray of olives. Despite the etched lines around his eyes, he looked younger than Sofia—maybe he was in his late twenties, if Sofia had to guess. He had cropped hair and a dimple in his chin. Sofia's heart lurched, and Natalie hugged her tightly around her hips.

"You are with the new volunteers that came in yesterday, no? How are you settling in? Can I help you with something?"

Swallowing hard and putting her hand up to her pounding chest, Sofia gaped at the man. "No, we're fine, but thank you. Should we know you?" Sofia couldn't help stare at the rifle hanging at his side.

"Forgive my manners. I'm Kobi. *Baruchim ha'baim*. Welcome to our kibbutz."

"Thanks. I am Sofia, and this is Natalie. We've just arrived from New York City." Sofia held out her hand and offered a friendly handshake, but Kobi just smiled at her and chucked Natalie under her chin with a gentle nudge.

"And now we know each other. Sofia and Natalie from New York City." Kobi had the sexiest, dreamiest, warmest smile Sofia had ever seen. "Hey," Kobi screeched, tearing Sofia from her private thoughts. He crouched down to look Natalie in the eye and asked her, "Did I hear you say you don't like salad? I don't like salad too much either, but I have an idea. Do you like chips? Oops, I mean, french-fries. That's what you Americans call them, no? Tell you what… Rivke makes the best french-fries you've ever eaten. I'm sure I can get her to make a big plate for us."

Natalie turned to Sofia, gloating with delight, and squealed, "I *love* french-fries! I mean chips! You were right, Tyotya Sofia. He is here to make sure we all eat!" Kobi crinkled the space above his nose and winked at Sofia. It amazed Sofia how easily the young child could be appeased. It was hard to resist french fries, and it was hard to resist the sweet, welcoming smile on Kobi's face. Flushing hot, Sofia bounced on the balls of her feet and began to feel hopeful that their big move to this kibbutz was not going to be too difficult for either herself or Natalie.

After grabbing plates of olives, pickles, and chopped tomatoes from the salad bar, Kobi pointed to the table where his friends had saved him a seat. "Come, join us for lunch. I'll introduce you to some of my friends. They are guards here on the kibbutz too." He pushed the butt of his rifle behind his back and indicated the table with his waiting friends with the plate in his other hand. Sofia glanced back at the table of volunteers but only took a second to swivel back in Kobi's direction. Natalie stayed glued to her side. Kobi's buddies—Dov, Eyal, and Gideon—remained seated as the trio approached them, but they brazenly stared at Sofia as Kobi introduced her around the table. "*Chevre,* meet one of our new volunteers, Sofia from New York City and her daughter, Natalie."

Daughter. The word whirled in the air and smacked Sofia right between the eyes. Yes, it was true that for the last four years, she had been like a mother to Natalie; and yes, they had come to Israel as a family unit. But Sofia would never—*could* never—pretend to be Natalie's real mother. Becca had given her own life so that Natalie could live, and Sofia could never substitute for that. Words spilled from her mouth before she could stop them. "Natalie is not my daughter. She's my niece," she explained. Sofia nodded and patted Natalie on her head. "My sister died, and Natalie and I have been together ever since." That explanation wasn't exactly accurate either, but it was as close to the truth as any other.

An awkward silence fell over the table until Kobi broke through the stillness and stuttered a quiet, *"Baruch Dayan ha'emet."*

"Hey, that's what Maya said to me last night when I told her about Tyotya Anika and Dyadya Sol. What does it mean?" Natalie stared at Kobi, waiting patiently for an explanation.

Kobi lifted his eyebrows in surprise and rubbed his hand over the top of his short hair. "It means that your loved ones should be blessed, and you should always remember them kindly."

Just in time to break the uncomfortable hush that had settled on the group, an older woman wearing a hair net, a stained apron, and a pair of worn-in green Crocs sandals burst through the swinging doors from the kitchen and strode right up to the table holding a plate stacked high with golden greasy french-fries.

"Wow!" whistled Eyal.

"Yeah, wow!" agreed Dov.

"None of that, *chevre*. Control yourselves because these chips are for our new friends." He winked at Natalie and grinned from ear to ear. "Hey, Rivke, have you met Sofia and Natalie from New York City?"

Rivke looked from Natalie to Sofia and swallowed a loud, strained gulp of air. She dropped the plate of chips on the table with a heavy C-L-A-N-K! Her face froze with panic, and her feet scrambled back into the kitchen.

"What happened, Tyotya? Did we upset that woman? Is she mad at us for asking for french-fries instead of eating salad?"

It was Kobi who answered, "No, Natalie. That's just Rivke. She is always a nervous wreck with children."

31

Maya and Sofia

Sofia couldn't believe her luck. The one thing she thought she was running away from, the one thing she thought she'd left behind for good. She had been assigned to work in the kibbutz's dance academy! For the past three and a half months, she had been taking turns with Maya teaching classes (not that there were so many students to teach, but Sofia had a feeling that Maya had something to do with her work assignment at the academy!) and taking advantage of her spare time to run through her old routines when no one was using the studios. She and Maya became close friends in no time, and they found they had a million-and-one shared interests; their love of ballet was just one common bond between them. Maya had explained the kibbutz's work schedule, their dining room schedule, the ins and outs of the children's nursery, and had even warned her about the megabats that hid in the rafters of the tailor's shed.

Maya was mopping down the floors of the large studio when Sofia began packing up her belongings for the day. Maya made sure to keep the wood floors polished to a shimmery shine and the mirrors wiped free of fingerprints and sweat-smudges. She smiled at herself in the mirror that covered the wall and then smiled at Sofia. Since the New York City ballerina arrived at their small academy on Gan Notzah, classes had begun to fill up again, and Maya's Dance Palace had reestablished some of its prior reputation. She shuddered at the recollection of how the academy had fallen into disrepair and how her small contribution to the kibbutz had nearly failed. But life had a strange way of fixing itself. "It only takes a bit of faith, patience, and luck," Maya mumbled appreciatively. Her friendship with Sofia was truly an added bonus these days, not to mention the hopefulness of the fresh, new romance that was budding between Sofia and her little brother.

They had celebrated the new year and the major Jewish holiday season at the kibbutz, but for Sofia, it was nothing like the joyous celebrations she recalled with her family back home. It wasn't the first holiday cycle in years she would be celebrating without her aunt and uncle, but their deaths in the store fire weighed on her this year as if a train had fallen from its platform and had collapsed right on her chest. She was thankful, at least, that Natalie seemed essentially unaffected by the burden of their losses, with little memory of time and familiarity with Becca, Anika, and Sol. Instead, Sofia would carry the pain and loss for both of them, even if she had to hide any sadness and teach by example—choosing to be happy and grateful in the moment. Taking care of Natalie, at least, gave Sofia little time to grieve. Becca would have wanted it that way.

So with the promise of the new year, Sofia was determined to make the best of their lives and their hopeful situation. When Kobi suggested that he and Sofia attend the volunteer-sponsored Sukkot party together, Sofia found herself…well, more than encouraged. She was remarkably ecstatic. She didn't hesitate in accepting Kobi's invitation, but she had been a nervous wreck ever since, realizing that she hadn't been out on a date with anyone since she broke up with Ben. The idea of going to the party with Kobi tonight both terrified her and made her skin crawl with excitement. She would have to talk with Maya and find out all she could about Kobi before he came to pick her up. She was beginning to trust her decision to move to Gan Notzah more and more each day. The move was proving to have been a good choice. A very good choice.

Maya noticed Sofia stuffing her backpack with her belongings and getting ready to leave for the day. She stopped dusting the stereo speakers and said, "Thanks for all your help today. You know, Sukkot is one of our favorite holidays here on the kibbutz. After all, it's a celebration of the harvest season. Sukkot celebrates the gathering of the harvest and commemorates the miraculous protection God provided for the children of Israel when they left Egypt. That's the part Kobi likes the best!" Maya winked at Sofia, clearly sending an intentional yet discreet message.

"In New York, and especially in Ukraine, we never had our own *sukkah*. In Brighton Beach, most people lived in blocky old apartment buildings, so we would build one big communal sukkah at the shul, and everyone would come with huge platters of food and sweets. By the way, I have a great new idea for *Le Cygne Solitaire*. I think I came up with a way to fix that tricky scene before the finale. And I have a great idea for an added surprise also!" Sofia beamed with the pride and deep-seated confidence she had always been known for. "But I'll show you tomorrow. Right now, I'm in a rush to meet Kobi on time. Will we see you at the party later tonight?"

"Oh, so you're leaving to ditch me for my brother, are you?" Maya joked with a knowing smirk.

Sofia blushed a deep crimson from the top of her head to the end of her long neck. "Well, technically…yes. But we'll definitely meet up here tomorrow." Just before she was about to turn and leave, Sofia added, "Hope I see you and Danny at the party later. And thanks for arranging for Natalie to stay with Ilana and your parents tonight. You know, Natalie loves Ilana like a sister!" She tossed an air-kiss at Maya, and Maya pretended to catch it above her head. Sofia suddenly felt the sting of Becca's absence and hid her weepy eyes as she left the studio.

Alone in Maya's Dance Palace, Maya took a deep breath, enjoying the musky smell of sweat and the worn leather of ballet slippers. She flicked off the lights and headed home to Danny.

Meanwhile, as she glided up the cobbled path to her cottage, Sofia looked up to the setting sun. The warmth baked her skin, and her face glistened in the soft pink light. A light layer of goose bumps covered her arms, and she filled her lungs with a deep breath of the cool autumn air. The almond trees were still getting ready to bloom, but she could smell the sweet, lingering fragrance of the sunflowers from the fields. Her cell phone began to ring in her backpack, so she reluctantly dug it out and answered, "*Shalom*." She loved practicing her conversational Hebrew lingo, even if it was one simple word at a time. The only local numbers she had saved in her contacts were Maya's cell phone, the main line at the security gate of the kibbutz (not because of Kobi but for safety purposes, of course), and the children's nursery. Not recognizing the number displayed on the screen, she wondered who else had her number and was calling her cell phone now.

"Hi, Sofia. It's Shula. Maya's mother."

Sofia's blood pounded in her ears with speculative fear. "Is everything okay? Is Natalie alright?"

"Everything's fine, Sofia. Sorry to have scared you. Natalie's great, but I got a phone call from Rivke in the kitchen. She's swamped with work for tonight's party, and she was wondering if you could go by the dining room and help her out for a while—before the party later tonight, that is."

Damn. What bad luck, Sofia grumbled, holding the phone away from her ear. She really didn't have time for this, but how could she refuse? "Of course, I can help, but I just left the studios, and I still have to go home first. I can meet Rivke in the kitchen in about twenty minutes, if that's okay with her."

She'd have to let Kobi know about the wrinkle in their plans. Still clutching her cell phone, she punched in the contact for the front security gate and waited for an answer. Moti, who was on duty and answered the phone there on the first ring, didn't know where Kobi was. She tried to reach Maya, but her phone went straight to voice mail. She left Maya a quick text. Sofia burst into a sprint and headed, discouraged and disappointed, toward her cottage. All the excitement and build-up for the evening rushed out of her like the air of a punctured tire. She just hoped she could get out of the kitchen quickly enough to meet Kobi in time for the party. She didn't want their first date to start off on the wrong foot.

She bolted through the back entrance of the kitchen and found Rivke fussing at the stove, a large pot bubbling and spitting with steam. "*Oy vey*, you scared me," Rivke squeaked. She dropped the plate in her hands, and dozens of schnitzel patties plummeted onto the floor. Clearly ruffled, Rivke got down on all fours and began scooping up the pieces of fried chicken cutlets. Her breathing grew deep, heavy, and ragged. Sofia bent down and picked up the broken shards of the serving plate. Rivke stood, rubbed the sides of her head, and heaved a loud, shaky lungful of air. In an inaudible whisper, she said, "I'm glad you came, Sofia. I think the time has come for us to talk."

Sofia brushed a strand of hair from her face and frowned at Rivke. "I'm really sorry. I didn't mean to startle you, but I'm in a big rush tonight. Kobi is coming to get me in an hour for the party."

"So leave this mess for now. We have more important things to discuss." Rivke counted to five and steadied herself on the edge of the sink. She looked green, like she was about to pass out right there in front of Sofia on the kitchen floor. Rivke squinted her eyes shut and murmured, "Okay, *mamaleh*. Sit down. First, let me start with a proper introduction. My name is Riva Brenner, head cook at Kibbutz Gan Notzah…and wife of Avrum Brenner, engineer from Ukraine."

Twenty-five long minutes later, Sofia found herself standing alone on the poorly lit porch of her cottage. Just twenty-five minutes ago, her whole life was flipped and turned upside down. Everything she thought she knew suddenly blew up in her face like a balloon exploding with too much air. She couldn't believe it. Any of it.

But…could it really be true?

Tears streamed down her cheeks as she tried to catch her breath. A numbing anger filled her lungs as she tried to fill them with humid, stinging air. Her mother was right here all this time!

In, out, in, out...

Electric needles stabbed her behind her eyes, and bile rose to the back of her throat. Sofia reached for the doorknob, fumbling with it for what seemed like an eternity. Entering the bare cottage, she collapsed onto her bed and drew her knees up to her chest. Large sobs exploded from deep in her gut and cut large rifts around her heart. She closed her eyes, and everything went black.

When Sofia finally opened her eyes again, she stared up at the cracks in the ceiling; she felt, any second, the walls around her would crumble and rain down on top of her, smothering her right there in her bed. She shuttered and kicked the tangled quilt from around her feet. She was suffocating, dripping with sweat, choking for air. Her cheeks stung with salty, dry streaks of dried-up tears, and her head felt like it would split in half with the slightest movement. How much time had passed since she left Rivke in the kitchen?

There was a pounding at the door and a sudden whoosh into her room. Grabbing the sides of her head, Sofia tried to drown out the noise and stop the pulsing ache at her temples. Blinking her eyes a few times, she dared to open them in the numbing light. A shadow stood over her at her bedside. Kobi. "Aren't you ready to go, Sofia? Or did you change your mind?"

32

Maya and Sofia

Sofia watched the volunteers, bundled in their army-green parkas, loading their duffle bags into the back of the van. The group hugged and shook hands and kicked around the muddy red dirt that coated the road. She could hear them shriek and giggle as they recalled their special shared memories of the past months. Not so long ago, Sofia had been part of that group—a group of foreigners looking for a peaceful purpose.

Sofia was no longer a transient visitor on Kibbutz Gan Notzah. For more reasons than one, she and Natalie had been accepted as full-time members and fell into the normal routines of kibbutz life. For the first time, Sofia understood the security and comfort that a community offered, and she often wished she had been able to appreciate this communal, familial life back in Brighton Beach. The *sochnut*, or immigrant absorption agency in Israel, had diligently followed through on the necessary paperwork to change both Sofia's and Natalie's visa statuses from "tourists" to "temporary residents." For a while, Sofia assumed that it was Maya's father and his position with the kibbutz's governing board that moved the bureaucracy along so smoothly for her. She also wondered if Rivke had had a role in the process from the very beginning.

No matter how hard she tried, Sofia could not think of Rivke-the-Cook as Riva-her-mother. Finding her mother, alive, after all those lost years, believing she had been discarded and forgotten, had hit Sofia hard and had left her beaten like an abandoned, cheap rag doll. For months, Sofia muddled about the kibbutz trying to put the pieces together. Rivke—or Mamoh (she had to keep reminding herself)—would come by the dance studio every evening after the dinner shift, wanting to meet and talk with Sofia.

Every night, Maya made excuses for Sofia, hating each lie she made up for Rivke, but she empathetically continued to show support for Sofia's pain and confusion. Her friend wasn't ready to face the facts.

But the reality was staring them right in the face. Rivke-the-Cook was indeed Sofia's mother. Riva had married Avrum Brenner, the love of her life, in Moscow in 1982. Just as the couple learned that Riva was pregnant with their first child, the engineering company where Avrum had been employed relocated him and his young bride to Ukraine, where he would continue his important work on an undisclosed project for the Soviet government. Avrum was proud of his wife and his prominence in the academic and civil circles they had been able to establish.

Sofia (their one-and-only child, as it turned out) was born just as the social and political atmosphere of Ukraine was becoming more and more volatile. Looking for independence from the Soviet Union, Ukrainians (especially those in the Jewish communities) kept their heads down and their mouths shut, lucky to remain unnoticed and out of trouble. They went about their business quietly and did not ask for unnecessary attention. While Tatoh traveled back and forth between Lutsk and Moscow for his work, Mamoh had secured the liberty to move about worry-free, working in theaters and introducing her gifted daughter to the ballet world.

Life for the Brenner family was relatively routine and unremarkable in those days, and the family of three was comfortable and happy. Sofia grew up with little to worry about. Her mother made sure her childhood was filled with friends, parties, and dazzling ballet recitals—until that one weekend when Tatoh did not return home from Moscow. Sofia could remember how jittery and distracted her mother had been, waiting for days for Tatoh to show up. All day long, she would sit like a statue at the kitchen table, and Sofia could still hear her muffled cries throughout the long, dark nights. And then, Sofia's jumbled recollections of those days flashed forward to the scene at the airport where Mamoh pushed her toward the plane with exactly one suitcase and zero explanations. She hadn't even been aware at the time that she had a valid passport! And there she was, being forced through the crowded airport by her bleary-eyed, pasty-faced, frightened mother. That was the last image Sofia had of her life before New York: Rivke-the-Cook looked nothing like the ghostly image of Riva-her-mother. The woman who had once been her everything.

Then, of course, came the letter. The one that Tyotya Anika shared with Sofia some seven years after-the-fact. The one letter she kept tucked inside Becca's journal and had been carrying around ever since her aunt gave it to her. She pulled it out now as she watched the group of departing volunteers from her window. The perfumed pages crinkling in her tightfisted grasp, Sofia reread her mother's fading words:

> *Our government has been very generous with us. Avrum's engineering education and training has been a stroke of luck for us. I am thankful for Avrum's work and the generous opportunities we have been given, especially as Jews here. But now, as Sofia's mother, this is the only choice I have to protect and love my child. Enough said.*

But was it really enough?

Sofia began to wonder again if her decision to stay at the kibbutz was the right one. Months ago, she was certain that the move was the sanest and safest one for both her and Natalie. Now she wasn't so sure of anything anymore. Things changed in the blink of an eye. She was only now beginning to see what Becca had meant about making motherly decisions and feeling the responsibility she had never before considered.

But what about her father? Rivke had revealed that Tatoh never returned to their home in Ukraine. She had made inquiries everywhere, for months calling on comrades from Tatoh's company and acquaintances in Moscow for any bit of information they could offer. However, everyone she asked was as tight-lipped as everyone had learned to be back then, and nobody could offer her any helpful information about his whereabouts. Countless days turned into weeks, and frightful weeks then turned into months without a single word of Avrum Brenner. Rivke recalled for Sofia the time after Avrum's disappearance and the fear she felt each time she saw a shadow on the sidewalk or heard footsteps in the stairwell of their apartment block. She confessed to having written several letters to Sofia after her husband's disappearance, but when all those letters went unanswered, she assumed her mail was being monitored, and it was too dangerous to keep writing. Even now, she avoided giving too many details about those days (some habits die hard), and Sofia knew not to press for more information about Tatoh than Rivke was willing to share. But Sofia did learn that it wasn't long after she had landed in New York to live with her aunt and uncle that Rivke made the quick decision to move to Kibbutz Gan Notzah.

If Avrum was alive and able to flee from wherever he was being held against his will, he would have known to look for Riva in Israel. From their time at university in the Soviet Union, Avrum and Riva were members of a secular labor Zionist youth movement called *Hashomer Hatzair*. The group had been established in the very same kibbutz where Golda Meir, the former prime minister of Israel herself, lived and worked as a poultry farmer in the 1920s. Moving to Israel, living on a kibbutz… It was their secret dream. As Sofia listened to the cook spin her story, she wondered how she never had a clue about any of this, of her parents love and support of Israel. A kibbutz is the very last place she would think she'd find her mother again. She never suspected her parents to be Zionists or laborers. They had never lived an openly religious life, and Sofia had taken it for granted that their religion was simply their tacit and unspoken way of life. Additionally, she had a hard time recalling a single time when her mother or her father showed any interest in any form of manual labor…

In the slow divulging of the details of her story, Rivke kept sputtering through unstoppable tears and a runny nose. Her lips quivered, and her rambling was randomly interrupted with hiccups and clicks of her tongue as she tried more to convince her conscience than to sway Sofia with the notion that she had done her best to secure the safety and survival of her family, a decision that, at the time, seemed plausible, if not necessary. That very same decision haunted her every day since. She explained how her heart had been shattered beyond repair with the scattering of her family, but it was the only way she could keep them all protected and out of danger. Her decision tore her to shreds, and she would forever question her choices and blame herself for ruining her family. She would not have Sofia living with the constant fear and uncertainty that lurked around each corner for her. No, it was better—*safer*—for Sofia to know as little as possible back then. And as silly and hopeless as it sounded to her now, Rivke admitted that she was still waiting for Avrum to find her. If Avrum was alive, he would have found her, and they would have reunited like the family they once were. She would have written to Sofia in New York straight away, hoping she would understand and come to forgive her. Her family would be reunited after all.

Sofia stared out the open window at the parting volunteers and fixed her hand on top of the journal and letter resting in her lap. Was it possible that Tatoh was also still alive somewhere out there? The high-pitched laughter from Diana, the boorish, lazy volunteer from Indiana, pierced through Sofia's thoughts of her father. For a second, she had fantasized about the next group of volunteers arriving with one highly educated engineer from Ukraine. She burst into a fit of bumbling sobs as the last volunteer boarded the van that would take them back to the airport.

Tel Aviv Center for the Performing Arts

One night only!
20.04.16 at 20:30

Le Cygne Solitaire

Maya Sharret, choreographer

Featuring
together for the first time

Israel's world-renowned ballerina
Irena Plotkin
and
New York's celebrated ballerina
Sofia Brenner

45 shekels in advance
55 shekels at the door

All proceeds to benefit
Maya's Dance Palace
Kibbutz Gan Notzah, Jezreel Valley

33

Maya and Sofia

Sofia glanced around the empty auditorium: the whir of the humming air-conditioning, the soft lights casting ghostly shadows over the auditorium, the daunting stage lying bare except for a single costume rack near the left wing. The theater manager said they were expecting a full house, and the media were already stirring up the crowd outside the theater doors. Video and audio recorders at the ready, Sofia barely made it past the pulsating flashes and taunting questions of the press as she made her way into the empty auditorium.

What am I doing here? I'll never be able to pull this off! She waved one hand in the air and made little circles with her twitching fingers. The uncertainty that shook her before her last show in Dumbo—that shook her every time before having to perform on stage—returned to her now, and she collapsed on the stage with a thump to her knees. She had not managed to outgrow that familiar stage fright that plagued her before every show. Out of nowhere, Sofia heard the clanking of metal and a familiar voice.

A soft singing whisper interrupted her trance. "There she is. Sofia Brenner. From New York City." It was Kobi, his military dog tags, a permanent fixture around his neck, announcing his approach. Sofia was surprised to see him there. Turning toward his advancing shadow, she sucked in a small hiccup. She spun on one knee and stood up, squinted through the dim light, and regained her balance in an awkward first-position pose. "Sorry. Didn't mean to sneak up and scare you." Kobi's beaming grin forced Sofia to relax her shoulders and release her balled fists by her side. "You ready for tonight?"

"Oh, Kobi. I was just remembering my last show in New York. It seems like a lifetime ago, but I'll never forget how nervous I was. And no matter how much I practiced, I couldn't get my hands to do what they were supposed to do!" She hung her arms slightly curved at the elbows in first position and stared blankly at her hands held in front of her.

"Isn't it your *feet* that you dancers are supposed to worry about?" Kobi's joke was dry, but his attempt to ease her tension made Sofia smile.

"I just couldn't get it. I needed my hands to follow my lead, but they had minds of their own. I needed to perform the perfect show, to be the perfect swan…" Sofia shook out her hands and circled her fingers again in the space next to her head. Reaching, grabbing, the intricate hand movements came back to her now.

"I'm sure you managed it, though. No? To me, you are the perfect swan, and I am sure you will be the perfect star tonight." His sapphire-blue eyes twinkled with pride and fascination. Sofia's legs buckled.

Trying to contain her anxiety, Sofia teased, "Are you kidding? I have to dance with the one-and-only Irena Plotkin. There's no way I can do this. I don't know how your sister convinced me to do this."

"Well, I can tell you this. After Irena, Maya thinks you are the greatest dancer on today's stage. She told me so just last night." Kobi winked at Sofia and continued, "Seriously, she's been waiting for this moment to showcase her ballet for decades, and she wouldn't want just anybody to dance the lead roles! If she can't do it herself, there is no one better for this show than Irena and you."

"But I haven't performed in years. I don't know if I still have what it takes, Kobi. And to top it all off, I've gotta share the same stage with the world-famous Irena Plotkin!" It wasn't lost on Sofia, in addition to her usual opening-night jitters, that she would be giving up the sole spotlight in this performance. She wasn't sure if she was more ruffled by having to give up the number-one spot in the show or the idea of having to perform behind one of the world's most recognizable names in ballet. Either way, her stomach pitched with dread, and her head spun. And in that one moment, the realization that she would have to be playing second-string to Irena suddenly brought back a flood of memories.

Of all things, it was images of Nina Cassel that began to flood her mind. Sofia swallowed down a lump of guilt for the years she had tormented Nina with derision and had made her feel unwanted back in Brooklyn. Suddenly, a loud burst of nervous laughter exploded from her lips, and she felt her cheeks blush with candid shame; she almost forgot Kobi was still standing next to her.

"Once you have it, though, you don't lose it, Sofia. I imagine it's much like learning to drive a car. Once you get it, you get it. Oh, I'm sure it has been challenging for you to practice and prepare for tonight, but there's no doubt in anyone's mind that you can do this. There's a lot of people counting on the success of this show, Sofia. You are one of us now, and we've been waiting a long time for this. We need you to find your strength again and give it your all."

"Just because a person wants something doesn't make it a reality, Kobi. I want to help the kibbutz, and I want to support Maya's ballet. But wanting these things and being able to achieve them are two completely different things!" Now it was Becca's smiling face she saw looking down at her and filling her mind with soft, comforting words. *I'm proud of you, Sofia. You made the right choice.* Sofia quivered and shook the ghostly fog from her head.

"You have a point," Kobi conceded before he turned his back and settled on the edge of the stage. He sat cross-legged and patted the space next to him. His eyes shimmered with a familiarity, and Sofia sensed that he knew what she was actually feeling without saying another word—her insecurity, her need for purpose and passion, her need to confront things head-on instead of from the sidelines… Sofia hesitated, then shuffled over to him and sank down onto the heels of her feet.

Kobi gently grabbed Sofia's hand and held it between his two palms. "Dancers speak with their movements. Your movements say you can do this, Sofia. We're all very proud of you." He looked up, and his steely gaze melted through layers of Sofia's fears and tension. He continued, "Think of all the choices you've had to make in your life, all the difficult yet necessary decisions you've had to face. Now imagine all your dreams and desires. We can't always make the easy choices, but we learn to make necessary and right choices. Your dreams, Sofia, are necessary and right for you and for those you love. Make the choice and make your dreams come true. You can do it."

A flash of care crossed his tender smile as he squeezed Sofia's hand still resting in his.

Maya suddenly appeared on the stage and stomped over to stand over Kobi and Sofia. She had a clipboard in one hand and her other hand pinned to her hip. Sofia recalled how Boris used to run around backstage before a show, bleating commands and reminders to the troupe. Maya was so flustered with panic and anxiety; Sofia knew the feeling well. Maya's sudden tornado-like presence made her and Kobi both jump up at the same time.

"What are you two doing here? We have a show to get ready!" Maya screeched. Sofia never saw Maya so jumpy as she was at that moment. "Kobi, can you please go and make sure Imma and Abba are okay and that Aaron is with them? They are all still waiting in the lobby, but they can come in and take their seats in the auditorium. The theater manager told me they have reserved seats in the front row for them. And you and David and Gali too." As an afterthought, she quickly added, "And also, can you get Ilana and Natalie out here to rehearse their marks? They're waiting with Danny in dressing room number three."

Sofia and Kobi were still clasping hands. Sofia made an exaggerated turn and began inspecting the tape marks placed earlier around the floor, while Kobi tumbled off the stage into the sea of royal-blue velvet theater seats. With his back to both Maya and Sofia, he waved an arm above his head and murmured, "Yes, sir, boss. Right away."

Maya huffed and dropped the clipboard. It clamored with a loud bang on the wood stage, and Sofia jumped backward. "I'm a nervous wreck," she said. "And Danny was just telling me that Natalie got attacked by the bats this morning! In broad daylight! Wouldn't you know it, of all days for something to go wrong…"

Sofia gasped. "Oh, my god. Is Natalie okay? Did something happen to her?"

"No, she's fine now. Sorry, I didn't mean to frighten you." Sofia couldn't ignore the fact that Maya was the second person in less than ten minutes to say those words to her. Meanwhile, she was never more scared in all her life.

Maya noticed the scrunch of Sofia's eyebrows and the panic that filled her stare. She clutched the clipboard to her chest and took Sofia by the hand. "Listen, I really hope you know how grateful I am to you for doing this show with us tonight. With everything going on between you and Rivke and having to take care of Natalie… Well, I know you have a lot on your plate now—"

Sofia cut her off. Breathing out a long, nervous burst of air, she tried to sound as strong and committed as she could. In reality, Sofia needed to prove to herself—more than she needed to convince Maya—that she was going to get through this evening and live to actually tell about it tomorrow. She inhaled deeply, trying to calm herself, and said, "The girls will be great tonight. I have no doubts about that. And Nadia really did a miraculous job with their last-minute costumes!" And remembering Kobi's pep talk from just minutes before, she added, "And besides, it's a pleasure to help, Maya. I know it's not just for you and me. The whole kibbutz is counting on us tonight. We have a purpose to fulfill, for ourselves and our families. Besides, I didn't realize how much I missed performing for an audience, and this ballet is really going to be a big hit. I can just feel it."

Maya tingled with a sudden swoosh of air from the air conditioner vent above them. A strange, washed-out image began to take shape on her clipboard as she stared at her scratchy stage notes. She heard a muffled whisper in her ear; it was the voice of her old friend,

Jim Turner. *Good job, Maya. You didn't let go of your dreams...you should be proud of yourself.*

Maya shook her head as if that would shake out the haunting voice of her long-lost friend, but she kept her eyes on the clipboard in her hands. It was finally hitting her. She did not need to know exactly how things would turn out in the end, she just needed to have enough courage to step up and follow her heart—wherever it would lead her. And, her main role may not necessarily put her on center stage after all, but she had an equally important supporting role from the wings. "I don't know if I ever told you this, Sofia, but you've really been a true inspiration. You've really helped me in ways you'll never know."

Sofia snorted and shoved Maya's shoulder. "What are you talking about, Maya? Are you going to get all sentimental on me now? Don't. We don't have time for that."

Maya forced a chuckle as she straigtened up and huffed, "What I really want to say is"—Maya's smile was warm and wide—"thank you."

Sofia couldn't remember the last time anyone had thanked her. She felt a heat rush to her cheeks, and she stared long and lovingly into Maya's eyes. Lifting her chest as if a thread was yanking it upward, Sofia's toes began to tap against the wood floor, and she let out a soft murmur, "It is me who needs to thank you, Maya. You and your ballet have given me something to dance for again!"

The curtain climbed for the last time, and the packed theater vibrated with ongoing eruptions of excited applause. Sofia's added surprise for the final act of the performance had not even begun. She quivered with anxious delight, wondering how the four-year-old angels were going to fare in putting the special "final touch" on the performance. Waiting offstage in the wing for the finale to unfold, Sofia stood in the darkness looking on with her own mother, Irena, Ilan, Nadia, Maya, and Danny surrounding her like a cozy blanket on a chilly winter's day. She was certain she saw a spark in Danny's eyes as he grabbed Maya's hand and held it stiffly at his side. Sofia was amazed when Maya agreed (albeit reluctantly at first) to add the last scene for Ilana and Natalie to the recital. The girls were about the same age as Sofia and Maya were when they started dancing, and it seemed only natural that they should be part of the cast that night in *Le Cygne Solitaire*. If Sofia and Maya could do it, so could the girls.

It was Rivke in the dressing room with the girls who had helped to put the finishing touches on the girls' makeup and costumes, much like she used to do with Sofia in Ukraine. And it was Sofia now, taking a huge gulp of air into her lungs and squinting into the glaring stage lights, who jumped from one foot to the other with heart-wrenching anxiety and stress. Sofia told herself that she was not alone. She never had been abandoned either. She was simply moved. Changed. Her choices were still her own, and her dreams were still alive. She could feel them when she thought of Becca's courage, Ben's passion, Anika and Sol's unconditional support, or her mother's protection, encouragement, and love.

Things just simply changed.

While Irena seemed as calm as if she had just finished a random rehearsal, Maya conveyed the same nervous energy as Sofia behind a gentle smile of maternal anticipation. Sofia blew out a rush of air from her heaving chest and repeated over and over, *The girls can do this. We can do this!* Sofia wasn't sure if this was a prayer or a command.

Staring out at the young girls under the bright stage lights, Sofia sucked in a loud lungful of air. Natalie's strawberry-blond hair had been pulled back in a tight bun behind her head, accenting her narrow nose and the set of her determined, upturned chin. Sofia was stunned by her likeness to Nathan. She was truly the vision of a little angel in her white leotards, white crinoline skirts dotted with diamond rhinestones, and a halo of white feathers crowning her head. The orchestra started playing—pianissimo at first and slowly gaining more momentum—as the two angels twirled and pirouetted on the stage. Maya and Irena each grabbed one of Sofia's hands and squeezed tightly. Swiveling her head from one to the other and grinning from ear to ear, the trio let out a collective sigh of satisfaction. Sofia's eyes began to sting with wet tears that threatened to fall—not tears of sadness but tears of happiness and pride—and the muscles in her neck began to unwind. A mix of love, gratitude, and satisfaction filled her entire body, from her satin pointe slippers to the crown resting on her head. They did it! Kibbutz Gan Notzah—and Maya's Dance Palace—were saved. Rivke pushed her way past Maya and Irena and stood right behind Sofia, her eyes glued to the young ballerinas on the stage. The older woman smoothed a loose strand of hair behind her daughter's ear and thanked her for the dozens of roses she had delivered earlier that day for the girls.

"The dressing room looks like it is filled with every flower in Israel. You really let the girls have it! But, of course, you remember that every prima ballerina deserves flowers for their debut performance!" She paused and let out a tired sigh before whispering, "I wish your Tatoh could be here with us now. I can still remember your first show, my *sheine meidel*. Me and your Tatoh were so proud of you! You were perfect then, and you are perfect now. A shining star." The tender lilt of her mother's old-world tongue and the vivid memory of her parents waiting for her backstage after her first ballet recital pierced Sofia in the pit of her stomach.

The stream of tears that had been building and were now uncontainable tumbled from Sofia's eyes, and through the haze of her drenched eyelashes, she saw a teardrop fall down her Mamoh's cheek.

"And now you are here, right where you should be. With your Mamoh and our new family. Some of our dear friends and family are missing, but they will always be our family. We can remember them, hold them close in our hearts, and choose to be happy."

Sofia could hear the earnestness in her mother's words, and they embraced her with a warm, comforting relief. Her heartbeat slowed, and her feet took root in the worn planks of the floor. She leaned over and rested her head on Rivke's shoulder just as the orchestra struck their last chords, the cue for the final curtain call. "You're right, Mamoh. I know life throws us all into difficult situations, but it is up to us to move forward, make the right decisions, and choose to be happy." Sofia choked back her tears and reflected, *After fleeing from homes, countries, and even loved ones, here they were—in the oddest of all places—together again.* From both sides, Irena and Maya nudged Sofia's shoulders forward and led her onto the stage, the three of them taking their places behind Natalie and Ilana for their final curtain call.

A Note from the Author

Save the Last Dance is a work of literary fiction. Characters portrayed herein are products of my imagination and do not refer to any actual person, living or dead. Nevertheless, the rich and complex cultures of the locales mentioned play a substantial role in the development of the characters and the story. I have drawn upon reality as authentically as I could in order to support the fictional story. I have, however, taken certain liberties with dates and names that seasoned travelers and natives of Israel, New York, Russia, and/or Ukraine might catch; deviations from reality and arbitrary details are deliberate on my part to fit the narrative.

For example, if you are ever in the Dumbo district of Brooklyn, you will not find a theater called the Montefiori Tobacco Factory. Nor will you find a ballet academy in Brighton Beach called the Russian Ballet & Dance Academy or a restaurant called Galina's.

And while there were close to three hundred kibbutzim in Israel in 2010, you would not have chanced upon one called Gan Notzah. Additionally, one of Israel's largest public bus companies is, indeed, called Egged, and in Tel Aviv, there is a theater for ballets and performing arts shows, but again, I have changed the name of the venue for Maya's story. And the Russian Ballet Conservatory of Haifa does not exist but in my imagination.

I mention the Kryvyi Rih State University of Economics and Technology, which does exist today in Ukraine.

All references to cuisine, geography, national customs, holidays, dialects, magazine, awards, and celebrated dancers and ballets are depicted as accurately as possible as I try to create an authentic picture of the cultural shades of the characters and story. All other businesses, locales, or studios are purely creations of my imagination.

I would like to give a shout-out to my wonderful publication team at Newman Springs and a special thank you to Lyndie Smith who made the whole publishing process so much easier for me.

Nata Levi, you helped me provide an accurate description of Russian and Ukrainian modern culture. Thank you for your time and input in sharing some of the cultural vernacular, observances, and wonderful conventions portrayed throughout this story. Also, Dora Lichtenstein, thank you for your selfless time in reviewing this manuscript. I could not have completed this project without your support.

Also, I could not have put this novel together without the continued care and support of my dear friend, Karen Newfield. Who would believe that after thirty-nine years, we would still be reading and writing together. We've come a long way since those scribbles on the bathroom walls! You are a genuine talent and an invaluable friend. (And thank you for your patience and helping with the cover!)

And, of course, there is all of you—my devoted readers. A huge thank you to all who have read my stories and continue to enthusiastically support my passion for writing.

About the Author

MANDI has been an educator for approximately thirty years and a writer ever since she could hold a crayon. She studied at the University of Miami, where she received degrees in English literature, Judaic studies, and business law. Later, she earned her master's degree in English education. Additionally, Mandi has also written academic curriculum for UNESCO and books for children and teens. When she was just six years old, her first story (about making a chocolate birthday cake for her father) was published in her elementary school's newspaper.

Mandi's passion for adventure and her personal family history has helped her build multicultural layers into her stories. She often draws from her many travels around the world and her Jewish-American-Cuban-Eastern European background to combine interest and depth in her tales.

When Mandi is not traveling, writing, or teaching, she enjoys going to baseball games, listening to music, dancing, shopping, and reading. She currently lives in South Florida where she teaches English and reading, and provides academic support for English to speakers of other languages. Mandi's current published titles include *Just Call Me Miri* and *Outnumbered*. Please visit her at www.mandieizenbaum.com.

Printed in the USA
CPSIA information can be obtained
at www.ICGtesting.com
LVHW090046100524
779688LV00001B/105